second CHANCES

OTHER BOOKS AND AUDIO BOOKS
BY MELANIE JACOBSON

The List

Not My Type

Twitterpated

Smart Move

second CHANCES

What if Mr. Wrong is really Mr. Right?

a novel

MELANIE JACOBSON

Covenant Communications, Inc.

For Jimmy Bennett, who always loved me

Cover image: *Bike by Fence at Beach* © iofoto

Published by Covenant Communications, Inc.
American Fork, Utah

Printed in the United States of America
First Printing: March 2013

19 18 17 16 15 14 13 10 9 8 7 6 5 4 3 2 1

ISBN-13: 978-1-62108-344-3

Acknowledgments

My family is amazing. They are patient with the time I spend writing and are proud of what I produce. I couldn't do it without their support.

I'm grateful for patient and honest critique partners and beta readers like Brittany, Kristine, Rachel, Susan, Krista, Amy, and the many others who care enough to be honest and spend the time to help me improve.

Thank you to the writing friends I've met along the way who have patiently answered questions or been generous in their teaching. I owe my editor, Samantha Millburn, a thank you for strengthening my stories. Thanks also go to my publisher, Covenant, for supporting me in my career.

A special thanks goes to Erin Elton Schurtz, producer of *The Mormon Bachelor*, for answering so many questions and Ashley Chapman for sharing her experiences as a bachelorette.

I'm so appreciative for all of you who make it possible for me to do what I love every day, but most especially, I'm thankful to and for Kenny, the best gift my Heavenly Father has ever given me.

Chapter 1

I TORE TRENTYN BACH'S LARGE square head in half and dropped him in the garbage.

My roommate Molly winced at the sound of the photo paper ripping. "Sorry," she said.

"This is officially irony," I said. "We develop a whole web series to reform the Huntington Beach dating scene, and the star gets himself into a relationship."

"Raina is a cool girl. We should probably be happy for him."

"I know. I'm trying." It would be easier to cheer them on if they hadn't become official two days before I needed Trentyn to do things like save my business and revolutionize love and romance in HB.

"What are you going to do?"

"I have no idea. I don't know who I could convince to step in."

Molly ducked behind her Mac until only the blue streaks in her black bob showed over the monitor. She turned her Pandora station up and left me to stew until I wanted to talk it out. Greatest best friend/employee ever. I snatched up my phone from the dining room table/office desk and texted my future sister-in-law, Ashley. *Can you dump my brother for three weeks?*

Her reply was instant. *Sure. Wait. I mean, HECK NO. Bachelor problems?*

I snorted. *Are there any other kind?*

She sent back a picture of Ryan Gosling with the message, *Hey, girl. Smile.*

So I did. Unfair trap.

The soulful ballad playing on Pandora gave way to a party rock anthem the USC marching band used to play after every touchdown during my senior year there. Molly reached over to switch the station, but I waved her off.

"Leave it. Maybe it'll motivate me to come up with a good idea." I drummed my fingers to the beat, but by the second chorus, I still had no answers. I switched to picking at the lime-green polish Molly had lacquered onto them.

"You really don't think Derek would work?" she asked. Derek was my brother, Matt's, roommate.

I shook my head. "Too mellow."

She grinned. "You're very kind."

Derek fit the surf bum profile. He worked in Matt's surf shop, the Board Shack, if the waves weren't great. If they were, he didn't work at all. He surfed until they were mushy again and sometimes remembered to show back up at work to finish his shift. Reasonably cute but not quite husband material.

That kind of summed up the whole elders quorum of the Beachside singles ward. It brimmed with hot guys, but most of them wanted to play, not settle down. It had been a subject of massive complaint at girls' nights out for the last couple of years, but it wasn't until I flamed out of my job at the Dane-Cooper Group that I decided to tackle HB dating reform. Here's the recipe for either genius or disaster: a newly jobless junior advertising exec with something to prove, a late-night viewing of *The Bachelor* finale, and a dozen twenty-something-year-old girls pining for a cleaner Mormon version—and suddenly, I'd cooked up a Mormon bachelor web series.

"This seemed like such a good idea at Jen's house," I grumbled.

"It still is," Molly said. "There has to be some other guy out there who would do this."

"Name him."

She opened her mouth, but nothing came out.

"That's the problem." I went back to drumming my fingers. When I'd blurted my idea at the *Bachelor* viewing party and excited squeals had nearly burst my eardrums, I knew it had viral potential I could mine to impress future clients, so I hustled to set everything up. I found restaurants to sponsor free dates, friends to man cameras, girls to apply to date the bachelor, but . . .

No bachelor.

It wasn't even a surprise. Our bishop blamed "casual dating" for the falling marriage rate in our ward. In Beachside, the second a couple publicly paired off, it was a good bet an engagement announcement would hit your mailbox soon. So we moved herdlike from group activities to dinner parties to movie nights to volleyball games to barbecues. Everyone hung out. Flirts flew.

But the girls were all kinds of sick of it.

Enter *The Mormon Bachelor*, practically a tutorial on how single dating could be fun and not mean the death of your options. How hard could it be to talk a guy into going out with twenty-one different girls when he didn't have to plan anything or pay for any of it?

Almost impossible, it turned out.

I called Ashley. "Give me my brother back. Seriously."

"No. What happened to Trentyn?"

"Turns out Raina was harboring mad, deep love for him, and now they're *together*." I sang *together* with a Disney princess lilt.

"So postpone filming."

"You realize I have a small business loan from the Bank of Your Fiancé riding on making this work? And on *not* making the sponsors I've lined up think I'm a flake?"

"Then find a new guy," she said, sounding halfhearted.

Ashley, with her front-row seat to the bachelor search, knew exactly how many guys had turned down the show before Trentyn. We'd started with a long list of potentials, but some guys couldn't commit the time, some guys thought they'd lose their man card when their friends got word of it, and a few guys didn't want to be on camera. One thought doing the show would earn him a player reputation. The excuses went on and on. I banked on Trentyn Bach's try-anything-once motto and talked him into it. But that spooked Raina Taylor, our friend from the ward, into asking him out after secretly crushing on him for three months.

So, yeah, glad for her. Completely freaked out for my project.

"Find a new guy, hmm?" I repeated. "Great idea! I bet if I walk outside right now, I'll trip over a Mormon dude who knows what he wants to be when he grows up and holds down a real job, hasn't been blacklisted by half the girls in the ward, and whose winning personality and amazing good looks will slay all the ladies. *That I haven't thought of already*."

"It's Huntington Beach." Ashley's effort to sound cheerful came off more like a determined telemarketer. "He may not be on your doorstep, but he's probably somewhere in a two-block radius."

"Did I mention he has to clear his schedule for three weeks? No problem. I'll walk a block or two and trip over *that* guy."

"No, you won't," she said, her tone resigned.

"No, I won't."

"This is so unlike you to be so down about everything."

I groaned. "I know! But I've banked *everything* on this working out, and it's falling apart before I start. I'm kinda, sorta freaking out."

"Sorry," she said, and sounded it. "I can't give you Matt, but I can lend you an ear anytime you need to vent."

"Thanks, Ash." We talked wedding-flower details for a couple of minutes before hanging up.

Molly turned down the music on her computer. "Try one of the LDS dating sites. The guys on there are obviously looking for a relationship. Maybe you could turn someone up outside of HB."

"Even if the right guy were on there, I don't have—"

"Time. I know. I don't even know what to tell you. But since I finished the graphic layout for the Board Shack summer sale, I'm going to reward myself with *Brides Behaving Badly* until you can look at it." She hopped over the back of the sofa behind me in the living room and stretched out her petite frame, kicking off her red Converse and fishing the remote from the cushions.

I messed around on the LDS Lookup site, but it was hopeless. After another ten minutes, I quit and dropped my head to the table with a thunk.

"Ouch," Molly said. "How about rescheduling the first weeks' sponsors and moving them to last to create some wiggle room?"

"We'll look unprofessional." I shoved my fingers through my hair and pulled it into a blonde curtain over my face to hide me from reality. "Besides, I put some of the best dates in the first week so we could get big buzz right off, and I know a couple of the businesses will bail in a heartbeat. I can't give them that chance."

Molly's expression told me she knew all of this. She wrinkled her forehead like she did when she puzzled over two fonts for a layout.

We stared at each other through my hair for a moment, her forehead furrows deepening. A commercial for a butter spread playing on the TV behind her filled in the silence. When it ended, the first notes of a melancholy sea shanty rang out, and her thoughtful expression collapsed into panic. She dove for the remote.

"Don't," I said, glaring at the TV. The hottest, jerkiest pirate in the history of ever leaped to the prow of a giant galleon and smirked into the camera. "What are the chances?" In a truly cruddy coincidence, the ad campaign that had led to my angry exit from Dane-Cooper now starred my ex-boyfriend

Nick in its flagship television commercial. I'm sure he had no idea who had crafted the campaign that led to him brooding on a ship's deck and making all the Southern California ladies between twelve and a hundred-and-twelve swoon, but I could take the credit. Or the blame.

Instead of looking all costumey and ridiculous, he looked windblown and delicious and way more Dread Pirate Roberts than Captain Hook. I mouthed his first line of dialogue with him. "They say I'm the scourge of the Seven Seas." His eyebrows arched, and a slow smile spread only to one side of his mouth. "Ye should come see for yerselves at the Venice Pirate Experience," he purred. He played down the pirate accent so he sounded mysterious instead of cartoonish. I imagined the fainting started here.

Another smile with a careless shrug. I'd seen that gesture a thousand times in real life; this commercial wouldn't bother me so much if even that small shoulder movement weren't so hot. "I've had my fill of wenches. I be looking for a good lass. Bring your rogue if ye must." He lifted his cutlass and ran his finger along the edge. "I can handle him." The camera pulled back to a wide-angle shot of Nick standing in the prow as the galleon sailed toward the sunset.

"Louisa . . ." Molly pressed pause on the remote.

Something in her tone didn't sit right with me. I glanced over to catch a nervous but determined expression flicker across her face. I shot up. "No," I said, certain I knew what she was about to suggest.

"Maybe you should consider—"

"No!"

"But the girls will go nuts for him." Molly jabbed a sparkly purple-painted fingernail at the television. The sunset in the frozen image outlined Nick's broad shoulders, shoulders I knew glowed with a golden tan from hours spent playing beach volleyball every week. "You know they would," she said.

The spot had aired for the first time nearly two months ago in the LA/Orange County cable markets, and it blew up. It was insanely difficult to break out a local commercial in Southern California. Thirteen million people lived here, and huge national ads filled our airwaves, squeezing out smaller local businesses that couldn't afford the airtime.

I think the pirate ad worked because, instead of trying to run an advertising blitz that competed directly with the other massive Southern California family attractions, I'd gambled on an appeal to women's sense of romance and fantasy. The spot not only worked, but it had also gone viral; women shared it like crazy, attracting millions of Internet hits. He'd become the pirate version of the Old Spice guy.

One afternoon, my boss, who had hated my idea until the client had expressed their enthusiasm for it, explained how *he* had come up with my concept—not the first time he'd taken credit for my work—to Dane and Cooper themselves in the boardroom. I'd stormed straight to my desk, where I typed up my resignation letter and walked out of the biggest marketing firm in Orange County.

Sometimes my temper was . . . not so good.

But I got two consolation prizes out of it. Although they cast the commercial after I left, Nick would be furious if he knew my idea indirectly led to him prancing around publicly in a pirate costume. More importantly, my grand exit forced me to take a risk and open my own marketing firm. Now I even had an employee, the loyal and longsuffering Molly. We called our company Hot Iron Media Services, as in "strike while it's hot."

I also had my brother, Matt's, start-up loan and his account for the Board Shack, which helped, but I'd scrambled to pull in anything else besides a few mom-and-pop businesses. Higher-profile clients wanted firms with more experience and bigger accounts, but having the right project in my portfolio could change all of that. Enter *The Mormon Bachelor* aneurysm.

I mean, idea.

If we could make it viral and prove we could handle something so large scale, we could attract slightly bigger accounts and begin building our clientele that way. I had no doubt that if I could land the accounts, I could deliver marketing campaigns they would love—and even better, campaigns that would build their businesses.

But it would take something borderline crazy to get the momentum going, so after weeks of aggravation, we'd secured bachelorettes, dates, and a star. And now I had two days to redo a four-week process—and Molly's sparkly purple fingertip pointed to a solution.

"Don't be stubborn," Molly said.

"I'm not. Even if I ask him to do it, he's going to say no."

She dropped her hand. "Why would he say no?"

"Because I dumped him, duh."

"But he's an actor, and you're going to offer him great exposure. Hours of TMZ have taught me only one thing: actors will do nearly anything for attention."

"I can't even guarantee him exposure," I said. "We're only guessing this is going to blow up."

She sighed. "Remember when you used to be good at arguments because you gave real reasons for stuff?" She turned the TV off and rose to her knees, leaning forward to make her point. "You know this will be huge. You're too good for it not to be."

"He's not the right guy for the job. He's about as deep as a puddle."

"You don't know that," Molly said.

"Of course I know that." It'd been three years ago, but I'd dated him for six months, and he had proved it pretty conclusively.

"We're young. People figure out stuff about themselves in their twenties all the time. Maybe he's changed."

"He's still acting, still being anyone but himself. This won't work if the girls don't think he can fall in love."

She growled, a funny sound coming from her tiny frame. I think she meant to sound threatening, but it came out sort of kittenish. I tried to look intimidated.

"I'm tempted to jump over this sofa and beat some sense into you with your laptop," she said. "I'll spell it out: We. Need. Cash. The two-job thing is getting old, and I'm running through my savings. If this web series will let you get the clients that pay the bills, you need to make it work. I'm worried about being homeless and hungry."

Guilt gnawed at my guts. Molly had signed on to work with me because she loved the idea of a girl-powered company shaking it up in the stagnant local ad market. She had a stellar portfolio; her eye for layout and design would make the art team at Dane-Cooper sick with envy. She'd told me she had faith in me, but she still had to wait tables at night, and at this rate, she might have to pick up even more shifts.

I couldn't do that to her. It was one thing to fall flat on *my* face; I wouldn't risk taking her down with me.

I mustered a smile. "I'll ask him. Assuming he'll talk to me at all." I waved my hands in the air, clenching and opening my fists. "Look at me! I'm grasping at straws."

"He'll talk to you," she said, rolling her eyes. "Every boy talks to you. In fact, if you'd pitch it to some of the guys in the ward with you as one of the dates, you'd have no problem at all finding a new bachelor. Is it hard to be so beautiful?"

I grinned at her gross overstatement. "Beautiful" was stretching it. I was a textbook California blonde, I guess. I liked that my hair shone more honey-toned than platinum, and thank goodness for summer so I could get it sun-bleached for free. Matt and I had the same dark brown eyes. Ashley called them Hersheylicious, but not when I was around because I pinched her the last time she did it. Most importantly, I'm five-eight, which is tall compared only to Molly's five feet flat but still enough to make me a threat when I played a pickup game of beach volleyball. "Pity me and my trophy status. I'm going to do something awful to my hair, wear baggy clothes, and shuffle when I walk. Then we'll see who wants to be the bachelor when I offer myself up purely as a sweet spirit."

"Quit being so judgey. It's not like you date ugly guys."

I shrugged. "I'm not saying physical attraction doesn't matter. But I've dated some plain-looking guys because they had cool personalities."

"That's true," she said, annoyed at losing the point to me. "But you've also dated super-hot guys with lame personalities. For six months at a time." She jerked her thumb toward the TV to make her point.

"So why are you making me ask him?" I demanded.

"I only have your word for it that he's lame. Maybe you only think that because you broke up."

"No, it's *why* we broke up. He's a fame chaser. All his 'personality' is a thin candy-coating of charm."

"So get him to charm the viewers. Go call him."

"I can't call him." When Molly looked like she would erupt, I held up my hand to stall the explosion. "I don't have his number. I'll have to find him some other way."

"Too bad there's no search engine set up to easily do that. If only someone would invent Google." She pushed herself off the sofa and headed back to her Mac. She tapped a few keys and scowled at me. "I hate waiting tables, Lou. Make this happen."

I didn't want to admit that I'd Googled Nick Westman more than once in the last three years. And that I knew how to find his fan page. Easily. "All right. I'm going to fix some dinner, and then I'll get on it. Someone from the Santa Monica ward probably has an e-mail address for him."

"No need. I got the info," Molly said. "And I already e-mailed him."

"What?"

"Yep. I put your name as the subject line, and then I put, 'Hi. I'm Louisa Gibson's roommate and business partner. She's got a cool idea to run by you. You should call her.' And I gave him your cell number."

"Very funny."

"I'm not kidding." She rose, which didn't change her height over her laptop screen that much, and leaned forward to stab the table with her finger. "I. Hate. Waiting. Tables."

"I am going to kill you slowly." I jumped up and rummaged through my kitchen cabinet then slammed the microwave door shut on my Cup O'Noodles and punched in the numbers so hard my index finger throbbed.

"I get that you're mad," Molly said, edging toward the hallway leading to our bedrooms. "But if you kill me, you won't have time to hide the evidence before Autumn and Lily get home. Am I worth the prison time?"

Before I could answer, my cell phone shrilled from the table.

"Answer it! Maybe it's destiny!" Molly said, trying not to laugh at my expression. If I had to guess, I was sure I looked scared.

I checked the caller ID display. "It's a three-one-oh area code."

"That's Santa Monica. Do you think it's him already?"

"No thanks to you, I guess I'm about to find out."

"Go ahead. And while you do that, I'll be packing a bag so I can run away from home if this doesn't go well."

"Good idea," I snapped, annoyed that traces of her grin reappeared before she darted back to her shared room with Lily.

I snatched the phone up and stole a calming breath. "Hello?"

Chapter 2

"Hi. Louisa? Is that you?"

I recognized his voice right away.

"Nick. Hey." Molly was deader than disco as soon as I hung up.

"Long time no talk," he said. "I got a message from your roommate to call you." He hesitated. "Do you, um, do you know anything about that?"

I cleared my throat with a nervous laugh. "I do, but maybe you could tell me what she said, just in case?"

"Someone named Molly said you had a cool business idea to run by me, and I should call you. I guess I could have e-mailed her back with questions, but . . ." Another pause. "I'm on my phone. Calling is easier than typing on the screen."

"I hear you." *I hear you?* Facepalm. *I hear you* was what old golf dudes said to each other when they complained about their sciatica. Or at least my dad's golf buddies talked that way. I tried again. "So Molly had this idea that you might be interested in a . . ." I trailed off this time, not sure how to pitch this since Molly hadn't given me any time to think.

"Is this a business opportunity where I need to come to your house and bring some friends?" He sounded wary.

I choked out another nervous laugh. "No, it's nothing like that. I mean, yes, it's a business thing, but not like one where you sign your friends up." Except it kind of was, because several of mine had signed right up to date the bachelor. Who I needed to find. I pulled myself together with a reminder of the clock ticking down toward the first date in two days. "Let me start over." I drew a deep breath. "Have you heard of *The Bachelor*?"

"Who hasn't?" he said. "It's all my sisters and mom talk about when we do Sunday dinner."

I pictured them all sitting around his parents' beautiful dinner table in the airy dining room of their Bel Air mansion, a gorgeous home paid for by the phenomenal success of his father's special effects studio. His family had been the best part of dating Nick. Well, after his kisses.

"My girlfriends too," I said. "It gave me an idea, and I'm running with it." I needed to present this as the *best* opportunity ever, so I focused. "I don't know how hot the YSA scene in LA looks right now, but I'm back in Huntington, and it could use some work."

"Really?" He sounded surprised. "I thought HB was the dating hotspot. Isn't that where they do that huge young single adult conference?"

"Have you been to it?" I doubted it. I helped organize it every year, and there's no way I would have missed him, even in the crowd of over a thousand.

"No. I heard about it last year, but it conflicted with my shooting schedule, and I couldn't make it."

"It's fun," I said. "But you'd see what the girls here complain about: tons of flirting that doesn't go anywhere." I warmed to the topic. "In fact, that's pretty much all I heard every week through the whole last season of *The Bachelor*. I have all these amazing, beautiful friends who sit home too much on the weekends because guys are afraid to ask them out."

"You mean intimidated-by-their-beauty afraid?" He sounded confused. "Isn't that a thing movies and TV shows make up?"

"No. Guys around here worry about getting tied down before they check out all their options. And if a girl says that hanging out with a guy and watching movies with his friends isn't a real date, she gets called possessive. Or high maintenance."

"And this happens every single time?" The disbelief was clear in his voice.

"Of course not," I said. "But sometimes it feels that way."

"So you've mentioned *The Bachelor*, a business idea, and the messed-up dating scene in the OC Mormon Mecca. I'm putting it all together . . ."

"I'll connect the dots," I said. "I'm producing a web series called *The Mormon Bachelor*. I need a guy who can step up and show how to treat a girl right, who represents the best parts of young, hip, LDS culture, who would love to go out with twenty-one beautiful girls—"

"You think *I'm* that guy?" He sounded like he was trying not to laugh. "The guy you dumped for being—how did you put it?—'One-dimensional and committed to all the wrong things'?"

I winced. I hadn't been especially diplomatic when I ended things. Or even decent. I had been in a place of massive frustration, and if he could quote my exact words back to me three years later, they had obviously done some damage. "Sorry. I was a jerk."

"You were . . . blunt." He fell quiet, and I didn't know what to say. When the silence stretched to nearly uncomfortable, he cleared his throat. "So you were trying to talk me into going out with twenty-one beautiful women like it would take a lot of arm-twisting?"

"It wouldn't?" I asked. "I mean, for all I know, you could be involved with someone. Or crazy busy with work for the next three weeks."

"Three weeks? Starting when?"

"In two days."

That met with another silence.

"Are you shooting anything right now?" I asked. "I know that can make your schedule hard to work around."

"No," he said. "Not right now."

"Yes!"

"Hold on," he said. "I still don't have any idea what you're expecting from me. Being in between roles doesn't mean I'm ready to do this."

"Right, I know. Except I think when I explain how huge this could be for you, you might be way more into the idea."

"Huge for me?" A long pause. "I'm willing to listen, but I can't right this second. Do you still surf?"

"Yeah."

"What are the chances your bosses would notice if you met me to catch a set in the morning?"

"I'm my own boss now, so chances are pretty high that I'd notice but even higher that I probably won't care."

"Why don't I come your way in the morning, then? I haven't surfed the pier in a long time. I'll check the surf report and text you with a time, if that's cool."

"That's cool," I said. "I'll see you in the morning."

I hit end and set the phone on the table. Molly's head popped around the corner from the hallway. "How will you reward me?" she demanded. I glared. "For what? Total humiliation?"

"It sounds to me like you have a business meeting in the morning with the hottest pirate on the seven seas."

"No. I'm going surfing with my ex-boyfriend, no thanks to you. And I've got between now and way-too-early-o'clock to figure out how to sell him on this bachelor idea."

"You'll figure it out. And *then* you'll reward me."

I sighed. "You're right. You deserve more than me griping at you. Grab a seat at the table." I headed toward the cabinets and rummaged through one of them.

"Whoohoo!" she said, bouncing over to her chair. "Your snack cabinet is way better than mine. What do I get?"

I prowled toward her with my hands behind my back and my brightest smile on. "What do you get?" I stepped behind her and rested my empty hands on her shoulders, pressing her into her chair. "You get to go through the LDS Lookup site and send e-mails to potential bachelors so that when this thing with Nick flames out tomorrow morning, we still have a teeny, tiny prayer of making the show happen on time."

I dropped into my seat across from her and pulled my laptop toward me.

She stared. "Can't I just have chocolate?"

"Sure. Need me to remind you where you keep your own stash? Otherwise, work," I said, pointing at her computer. "I have my own research to do." I didn't bother explaining that I would be browsing the Board Shack website to see if Matt had stocked any new girls' wet suits in the last couple of weeks. If I was going to be in neck-to-knee neoprene in front of an ex, it was going to be the cutest neoprene my steep family discount at the Board Shack would get me.

I'd let Molly sweat over the backup options from Lookup, and I'd focus on finding the magic words to talk Nick into taking the gig. I had to face facts: I needed him, but I had to find a way to make him feel like he needed me more. Or needed *The Mormon Bachelor*, anyway.

And somehow, in all of that, I had to make sure the only deep water we waded into was the Pacific. We'd spent hours together surfing during our relationship; it had been a big part of "us." In one brief phone conversation, he'd already referenced our past. I didn't want to think about it, and I'd have to find a polite way to dance around it while still talking him into being the bachelor.

The next two months' rent depended on it.

Chapter 3

Seven thirty.

I hadn't been up that early since I quit Dane-Cooper, but here I stood on the cool sand by the Main Street pier, wondering why Nick would get up even earlier to drive all the way down here just to surf this spot. If he wanted a good ride, he would have hit way less traffic heading a bit farther north of his place to Malibu. But whatever. It gave me a chance, and I would take it with a smile that suggested I wanted to be there and not hiding under my covers.

I glanced down at my wet suit, the pink panels on the side brightening the stark black. I'd brought my short board, knowing that's what Nick would choose for surfing the pier, but I didn't know what else I could do to prepare to see him again after three years. Well, besides having watched every single acting part he'd had since then. Even his reruns. In my defense, it was interesting to see someone you used to make out with play assorted villains and murder suspects on all of the crime shows and courtroom dramas. I made my roommate Lily's jaw drop once when I pointed him out in a trial scene. "See that serial killer? I used to go out with him."

"Lou?" the serial killer's voice behind me said.

I whirled to see Nick walking up and cursed myself for not being smooth and turning around slowly.

"Hi, Nick." I'd guessed right about him bringing his short board. His wet suit fit him as well as I remembered, and his bronze skin pretty much glowed even in the weak light of a June gloom morning. He smiled and flashed his pretty teeth. His perfectly highlighted salon hair flopped just so over one eye.

I forced my eyes to meet his, offering a return smile I hoped projected confidence and surfer-chick cool. "You want to talk or ride first?" I asked.

"I've been good. How about you?"

Oops. Social niceties. I blushed and hoped he would chalk it up to the sun. The weak, weak sun. "Great," I said. "How are you? I see your work sometimes."

"Probably on accident," he said. "I don't do much big stuff anymore."

"I don't know about that," I drawled, fighting a grin.

He colored this time. "I guess you've seen the pirate commercial?"

"Aye, matey."

He snorted. "That's it. Let's ride."

He jogged into the water and hopped on his board to paddle out. I stayed right behind him. He sliced through the water easily. The waves were okay today, maybe waist high. About a third of the way down the length of the pier, we both pulled up and straddled our boards where we could see each new set of waves forming. One swelled toward us, but it didn't look right, and neither of us took it. The water smoothed out again, leaving us to bob while we waited for a better set to form.

After a minute, Nick dragged his eyes from the horizon and glanced over at me. "I was surprised to get your roommate's e-mail."

That makes two of us, I almost said. "Molly . . . likes to take initiative. Thanks for humoring us."

He cocked his head for a moment before nodding. "Sure. No problem." He scanned the water again. "Might as well tell me about it. The next set is no good either."

It wasn't the most interested tone I could have hoped for, but at least I had an opening. "*The Bachelor* is an obsession for a lot of Mormon girls, but all of them complain about the exact same thing: they want a Mormon version where they can watch two people with high standards fall in love without a champagne-and-hot-tub overload."

"Fall in love?" he said, staring at me full in the face for the first time since paddling out. "In three weeks? Seriously?"

I shrugged. "It's not like the bachelors on the actual TV show fall in love in such a short time either. But you'll be dating enough girls during that time that if you're really open to the idea, I bet you'll find someone you could consider exploring a relationship with."

He considered that for a moment. "Why does this have to get done in three weeks? That's a super tight schedule."

"Momentum," I said. "I need to get this project off the ground pretty quickly, and once we start airing the episodes, I want them to show back-to-back so viewers stay engaged."

"No pun intended?" he said, a slight smile playing around his lips.

I splashed water at him. "Wow. Still not punny."

His full grin appeared. Yeah, girls would definitely tune in for this guy—if I could sell him on the idea. I hated that I had been so easy to sucker with his good looks too. The raging crush on his Dex Hall character that I'd had as a teenager had made me easy pickings when he flashed that practiced smile at me three years ago. I knew now that he'd studied his smile on film hundreds of times to get it exactly right. Lame.

"I think this is good," he said, intense concentration replacing his smile as he watched the next wave surge toward us. He angled his board at a slight diagonal to the shore and paddled. I gave him a few seconds' lead time and then followed suit. His wet suit. His super-fitted wet suit that made his blue eyes look even bluer . . . man, they popped on camera. *Oh, please, please let this work.*

I missed the drop-in. I settled back down on my board to wait for another chance and watched him take the wave in. He stayed light and loose on his board, adjusting easily to carve down the face. I'm not sure anyone ever thought surfing looked easy, but only people who surfed could understand the skill in what he'd just done. I'd been riding since I turned six, and I'd caught my fair share of waves, but Nick shared my brother's uncanny ability to sense what the ocean would do. They made it an art.

The next swell coming felt right, and I took it until it closed out. I knew Nick would already have started the paddle back out so he wouldn't have to fight the impact zone. Sure enough, when I dropped down and swung back over the wave to do the same thing, I spotted him back down the pier, waiting near a massive pylon.

This time as we waited for a good set, I tested my progress with him. "Last night you seemed kind of stoked about having ready-made dates set up for you. How does it sound now?"

"Twenty-one hot chicks sounds like a good time." He shaded his eyes for a moment as he scanned farther out on the water and then dropped his hand. "But I'd also be dumb to jump into that kind of a scheduling commitment starting . . . tomorrow, you said?"

I nodded.

His eyebrows shot up. "Did you really think I'd have a wide-open calendar for the next three weeks? Or that anybody would?"

"Up until yesterday, somebody did," I said. "And technically, we're talking closer to four weeks because you'll pick four girls for second dates, two of those will go on to family dates, and then the finale." His eyebrows crept higher with each of these additions. "I know this sounds like I'm making this whole thing up as I go along, but I've done hours of research and prep for this. Everything is lined up and ready to go."

"Except your bachelor."

"Except our *star*," I said, wondering if the emphasis would appeal to his healthy ego.

His lips twitched. I couldn't tell what it meant. Was that an almost smile? A suppressed frown? He swung his board around and took off. "Party wave," he called over his shoulder, a signal to share the ride.

This time when the wave closed out, he let his board glide into the whitewater and bounced to use up the last of the wave's energy. I smiled at his Huntington Hop as I dropped to my stomach and took the whitewater in.

"Star, huh?" he said when I collapsed beside him on the sand.

"Star. With twenty-one premium girls to date. It's a hard gig, but I think you're the man for the job."

"Or the understudy for the original star." He leaned back and tilted his face toward the emerging sun, his eyes closed as he soaked up the warmth.

"I wouldn't look at it that way. It's more like the stars aligned to get us the best guy for the job after all."

He cracked an eye for a second to smirk at me. "That's bull."

I sighed. "You don't owe me any favors. I know that. And I'm not asking for one. I'm offering you a chance to become an Internet sensation."

He snorted, but he didn't open his eyes. "I'm kinda one already."

"I know the pirate commercial is viral, but this is your chance to go viral as you, not Jack Sparrow-lite."

He winced and met my eyes. "Jack Sparrow-lite? Still not pulling punches, huh?"

I flushed. "I didn't mean that you're a knockoff." I collapsed back on the sand and threw an arm up to block the sun. "I know it's hard to believe, but I'm usually better at pitching my ideas."

"Yeah . . . I'm going to have to take your word for it."

Almost on instinct, I shot my hand out and poked him in the side, where I knew it would tickle him. He jumped, and I snatched my hand back.

"Maybe I don't need to pitch you," I said. "If I show you pictures of the bachelorettes, that'll pretty much seal the deal."

"Nah," he said.

My stomach sank. He wasn't going to bite. I hoped Molly had found somebody amazing and impulsive almost to the point of insane on Lookup last night, or my plan was toast. Stinky, burnt toast.

"I'll do it," he said.

I sat up and stared. "You'll do it?"

"Got water in your ears?" he asked, his tone mild.

I snapped my dropped jaw closed. "Nope. I heard you say you'll do it, which is fantastic for both of us."

A small but definite smile flashed at me. "I'm taking that on faith. What do I need to do?"

"We need to get you ready for the first few dates," I said. "And I'll take you through the profiles of the girls you'll be meeting so you can prep."

"I'd rather not." He twisted to look at me. "I'm doing this on a whim. I'd rather be surprised every day. I'm not sure you can even prep for twenty-one dates in a row."

"All right," I said, relieved and fighting not to show how much. "Any other stipulations you want to put on this?"

"Why don't you walk me through the process, and I'll go ahead and have my diva moments when something comes up that won't work for me."

Self-deprecation? Huh.

"Do you want me to draw diagrams in the sand? Because I can if that works for you, but there's also the crazy option of sitting down and looking at everything in an organized way. You know, to prove I'm a legit professional."

He cocked his head. "I'm pretty sure legit professionals don't use the word *legit*."

I smiled. "You mean like how classy people never actually use the word *classy*? Fair point. How about this: I want you to feel comfortable with this decision, so why don't we meet up somewhere in a bit in our grown-up clothes, and I'll tell you everything you need to know about this once-in-a-lifetime opportunity."

"You know what's funny about once-in-a-lifetime stuff? Everyone thinks that phrase means something great, but maybe it means a once-in-a-lifetime super cruddy event. Like probably a planet-sized meteor crashing into the earth would be a once-in-a-lifetime thing, but I don't think we'd be all stoked about it."

"You're into semantics this morning."

"I kind of am," he agreed. "I've been thinking about words a lot lately. How they fit together." He colored and laughed.

"For a part?"

He shrugged.

"Okay. Forget once-in-a-lifetime. Think jackpot. A giant girl jackpot."

"Does it make me sound superficial if I say I'm more into regular-sized girls?" he asked.

I fought to keep a straight face. "I can't laugh and encourage this kind of behavior. How will it affect our business relationship if I kick sand at you instead?"

"I'll have my first diva moment and storm off."

"Noted. Save sand kicking for later."

"Cool. Let's put it on a to-do list for when we have artistic differences."

I smiled. "Is that code for 'when you have a tantrum'?"

"Meltdown. It sounds marginally more manly."

"Semantics again," I said.

"Yes," he said. "And now I'll quit teasing you. What were you saying about meeting up?"

"I'm thinking we should shoot for somewhere with tables and cool drinks and a Wi-Fi connection."

He sighed. "And here I thought that one of the perks of doing business with you would be production meetings on the beach."

"I'd be down for that except sand and my iPad don't get along. Let's do the Waffle Box. Do you have somewhere you can change? If not, I know Matt won't care if you duck into the Board Shack and make yourself comfortable."

"That'll work," he said, shrugging. "I was going to drop in on Kade, but the Shack is closer."

"Kade Townsend? I didn't know you guys were friends."

"Yeah. He comes to our ward sometimes when he has tournaments."

Kade had won a silver medal in beach volleyball during the last Olympics. It shouldn't surprise me that Nick would know someone newsworthy. Even though Kade was in my ward, we hadn't exchanged two words. And Nick lived an hour away and still felt comfortable showing up at Kade's place unannounced. Like it was no big deal to show up at an Olympic medalist's house just because.

Between his dad's studio and his own acting career, Nick was one of those überconnected people who knew everyone. That clearly hadn't changed. When we were going out, we couldn't walk through Whole Foods on a cheese run for his mom without bumping into at least two people who stopped him to talk. After a few months, it didn't shock me anymore when we dropped in on a burger joint and had some A-list star come over to chat with him about the Malibu surf report. Or when we'd go to a wrap party for a music video and the starring pop tart would wander over and hang on his other arm, cooing and ignoring me. Stuff like that happened all the time. Especially that last thing. Which got tiring. And sped us toward our inevitable breakup . . .

I realized I'd zoned out again. "I'll text Matt and let him know you're coming. Let me run home and change, and then I'll meet you at the Waffle Box. Shouldn't be too bad since it's a weekday. Half hour sound good?"

"That'll work. You must be living close by here, huh?"

"Beach Walk," I said, naming the neighborhood popular with many of the professional Huntington Beach singles.

He whistled, soft and low. "Beach Walk? Good for you. Going independent is definitely paying some bills."

Roommates are paying the bills, I silently corrected him. *Or at least making the rent manageable.* But following the time-honored business strategy of "fake it till you make it," I smiled and nodded. "It's nice over there," I said. "Mellow. And close by, but I better jet if I'm going to meet you in thirty minutes."

In a movement as fluid as the waves behind him, he rose to his feet and held out his hand to pull me up. I accepted it, noticing right away the light calluses on his palms, as if he'd actually spent time sailing and hauling rope instead of just playacting his pirate part. He hadn't had those rough patches before. As soon as I found my balance, I slid my hand back out again under the guise of scooping up my surfboard.

We walked to the Strand, the concrete boardwalk running along Pacific Coast Highway.

"Catch you in a few," he said as he headed to the Main Street crosswalk.

I waved and then jogged to my beach cruiser, a gorgeous cherry red Electra my parents had given me for Christmas. I strapped my board into the side rack of the bike and then pedaled in the direction of home, making it in less than ten minutes. I wheeled my bike into the garage and darted into the house, beelining for the bedroom. A fast rummage through the closet produced a denim skirt and a vintage blouse I loved. I snatched my red Toms from the closet floor and frowned at the thinning canvas over my big toe. *Note to self: make money soon or learn to love holey shoes.* My Toms were not long for this world.

I scurried back down the hall, nearly ramming into Molly when she stepped out of her room.

"Yikes, girl." She grabbed at the doorframe to steady herself.

"Sorry. It went great with Nick this morning. We're good to go."

"He's going to do it?"

When I nodded, she squealed and did a happy dance, the bold green stripes of her shirt transforming her into a bright blur for a moment. "Yes!" She stopped and stared at me. "Are you good with this?"

"Sure. I'm glad we found a fix. Thanks for thinking of it."

"Uh-huh." Her eyes narrowed, and her expression grew thoughtful. "How did it go this morning?"

"I told you. Great."

"But how did you feel? Was it weird seeing him again?"

"Not really. I see him all the time on TV."

She shuffled closer. "That's what I mean. You watch everything he's in. Don't deny it," she said, holding up a hand when I opened my mouth. "I've seen it all saved on the DVR. And don't tell me it's normal curiosity about an ex either. Tell me the truth: do you still have a thing for him?"

"No!"

"I'd understand," she said. "But we better not even start this if you've got lingering feelings or whatever."

"Nothing is lingering," I said. "I'll cancel my recordings of him. I didn't know you were reading so much into it."

"I wasn't before. But that's when it didn't matter. Now that you guys are going to be hanging out all the time, I'm trying to figure out if it matters now."

"It totally doesn't," I said. "Don't stress. And be happy, because you can quit the LDS Lookup search. I can't believe Nick Westman is going to save our bacon, but he is."

"Um, I think I'm going to keep my Lookup account open," she said, looking somewhere near the ceiling.

"Good golly, Miss Molly," I said, jumping out of the way even as the words came out of my mouth because she *hated* that. I barely missed her pinch. She snagged a bit of my shirt, but I escaped. "Have you been making eyes at the boys on there?"

"No," she muttered, red-faced. "But a couple made eyes at me. They sent me winks or whatever they're called. And one guy was kind of cute."

"Go, Molly," I called over my shoulder as I dug through my cabinet for a granola bar. I always needed to refuel after surfing. It would hold me over until we ate at the Waffle Box. It would also allow me to order something small and keep the size of the bill down. Even though I could write it off as a business expense, I'd let Nick run the tab up and cut corners on my side. I could always plead a ladylike appetite. Maybe he wouldn't remember how hungry surfing made me.

I hustled out to the street, where my Audi sat waiting, a conceit from my overconfident days at Dane-Cooper when I'd had a few big bonuses in a row and thought I had a lock on the partnership track. I'd probably give up my apartment and sleep in the backseat before I gave the car up, but maybe with Nick on board for *The Mormon Bachelor*, I could make my car payment *and* rent. It felt like far longer than two months had passed since the days when paying both was a no-brainer.

More determined than ever to turn Nick into an LDS viral sensation, I shifted the car into gear and drove to the Waffle Box, parking behind it on Fifth Street. When I rounded the corner, I spotted Nick leaning against the low iron fence that marked the restaurant's outdoor dining section. He'd switched into plaid shorts and a tight check-out-my-muscles T-shirt. He looked hot, yes, but in such an attention-grabby way that I wanted to roll my eyes.

"Been here long?" I asked when I reached him.

"Just got here," he said. "There's no wait. We can grab a table now."

The hostess behind him nodded her agreement without taking her eyes off of him, something else that hadn't changed. I smothered a smile. Nick could wear all the tight T-shirts he wanted if it helped *TMB* blow up.

"Are you . . ." she asked.

"Yes, he is," I cut her off. "Table, please." Nothing says, "I can handle this massive Internet project I just tricked you into doing" like choosing a table decisively. I picked the table farthest away from the other diners and the passing sidewalk traffic. "Step into my office."

"Ladies first." He held out one of the seats for me before sitting down himself. Oh, the girls would eat him up. Yes, yes, yes.

The hostess handed us our menus and then slipped her hand into her pocket. She had one corner of her cell phone out before I stopped her with a hard glare, and she shoved the phone back and hurried off. It wasn't my job to put up with fan photo ops anymore. I smiled at Nick and adopted my professional tone. "I'd like to start with the ground rules."

"No champagne and excessive hot tubbing," he said. "Got it."

I smiled. "I meant on the business side of things." A waiter in shorts and flip-flops walked over. He set two glasses of ice water down in front of us and pulled out an order pad. He didn't say anything, just nodded. Definitely a passive-aggressive surfer who wanted to be on his board instead of bored at work. "Go ahead," I said to Nick. "Order what you want. I get to write this all off."

"All right. I'll take the Belgian waffle with extra strawberries and a side of bacon."

I scanned the menu and added as he ordered. His total would come to around ten dollars. With tax and tip, I could afford to order something five dollars or less. I drowned a sigh in a long sip of water and then gave Mr. Passive-Aggro my order. "Oatmeal, please."

The surprised look on Nick's face said he remembered the massive platters of sausage and eggs I used to down after surfing. "I'm trying to cut my cholesterol," I said to answer his unspoken question. I tried to picture the old Wilford Brimley oatmeal commercials, but all I got was a mental snapshot of him scowling.

I shook my head to clear it.

"Something wrong?" Nick asked.

"Got an unwelcome visit from Wilford Brimley. You know how that goes." He nodded as if he totally did. "Yeah, whenever he comes around my daydreams, I stare at him until it creeps him out and he leaves."

I choked on my water, and it took me nearly half a minute to clear my windpipe and breathe properly. I'd forgotten his sense of humor was so quick. This would film well. Like refresh-the-video-a-million-times well. Up to now, I'd pictured all the women sighing over their laptops when his face flashed on their screens. For the first time, I pictured how his dates might play out if he deployed his sense of humor as the dangerous weapon it was. Oh man.

"Just so I don't die laughing, maybe we should get back to the ground rules."

He inclined his head with a small smile on his face as if to grant me permission.

"I mentioned that a big goal of this project is to change the attitudes and maybe even the dating habits of the Beachside Ward," I said. "But this is also my chance to build my portfolio and reputation in the marketing field. Losing Trentyn means that I may need to put dating reform on the backburner for this first go-round and tackle that in a second season."

His forehead furrowed. "Why do you have to backburner it?"

"It's not your fight," I said. "Trentyn and I spent hours talking about how broken dating is around here and how to fix it. We had all these ideas for how to make it fun and cool again to go on real dates instead of hanging out all the time."

"Tell me again why this dude isn't the bachelor right now?"

I grinned. "I guess we figured out the solution so well that he went and got himself a girlfriend."

"Good for him." Nick fell quiet for a minute. "I could get behind dating reform."

I shifted in my seat and realized I'd been tapping my glass. I wiped my fingers on my napkin. "It went beyond that. We both wanted to show something positive and real about the LDS singles experience and prove that there is such a thing as a young, hip Mormon."

"Past tense, huh? It sounds like now that you've got me, none of that is the point anymore." His tone held no judgment, but his cocked eyebrow showed that he wanted a response.

"Kind of," I admitted. "But don't take that in a bad way. Of course you're hip. We're going to make *that* point beyond my wildest what-if scenarios. But Trentyn truly wanted a relationship out of this at the end. I don't expect you to go in with the same goal."

I trailed off with a shrug. He looked at me like I should have more to add, so I did. "It's not fair to spring this three-week commitment on you *and* expect you to take on all of these super-high ideals or whatever. I'm recalibrating my expectations a little—"

"Nice business-speak."

"I'm a businesswoman," I said, smiling. But I couldn't tell if he meant it as a compliment. "Anyway, recalibration. You'll be a great hook to build an audience. I'll tackle reform next time. This might be one of those blessings in disguise."

Nick leaned back on a long, slow sigh. He opened his mouth but shut it again instead of saying anything. The waiter dropped off our breakfasts, and I busied myself with settling my paper napkin in my lap and pushing the oatmeal around my bowl like I was trying to study the effects of centrifugal force on breakfast mush. The conversation had gone off the rails somewhere, but even as I played it back in my head, I couldn't find the exact point of breakage.

Whatever had bothered him, Nick inflicted it on his waffle. He sawed at it like he wanted to teach it a lesson. I spooned the oatmeal into my mouth in rhythmic scoops, not tasting it as I swallowed. I didn't want to say anything and deepen Nick's funk; I remembered his moods. He didn't have them often, but he could be impulsive when upset, and I didn't want a dramatic "Never mind, I quit!" moment to erupt.

"I forget that you don't always realize how you sound to other people," he said after a couple of bites.

Oh, *really*? Condescending much? I dredged up another smile. "I think I'm going to let that sit for a while. Sounds like maybe there's something I need to learn from that statement."

"How were you going to tackle these 'higher ideals'?"

"The main thing is being positive without being fake, I guess. After every date, Trentyn was going to write up a blog post about it, but we were going to moderate the comments." I sighed. "You ever read the comment trails on any news article? They're full of trolls and nastiness. People get mean. We expect some people to be jerks about the series, but I don't see any reason to spread the hate, so we'll only let the positive comments through."

"But is that real? To weed out the criticism and only put up the opinions you like?"

"Sure. I'm only going to weed out the garbage people say just to get a reaction. It's not fair to you, for one. But it's definitely not fair to these girls you'll be dating. What about the lame people who go off on anti-Mormon rants in the comments? We're not the forum for that."

He nodded. "I understand what you're saying, but I wonder about transparency. Won't that help everything feel more authentic?"

I stared at him, trying to figure out how to answer him without being offensive. I wanted to ask why transparency and authenticity hadn't mattered to him three years ago; if they had, I wouldn't have walked. But three years ago didn't matter; twenty-four hours from now mattered big time. "You're asking good questions, but you shouldn't stress about stuff like that. As the producer, that's my headache. From a marketing standpoint, this is the right call. *TMB* isn't about controversy."

He pushed his plate back, although over half of his waffle still remained. "So my job is to sit around and look pretty? I'm good at that."

Again, he had that suspiciously neutral tone.

"That's not what I meant."

He shook his head. "No take backs. Don't worry about it. I've built a whole a career on this face. How do you want me to act?"

"Actually, *not* acting would be the most perfect thing. I know you're doing this as a favor—"

"I'm not."

That stopped me. "Okay. You're doing this for the exposure . . ."

He shrugged and didn't contradict me.

"The thing is, if you could keep your mind open to the possibility of finding someone, that would be the most perfect thing. And if you aren't open to the idea of finding someone, then I guess, yeah, act like you are."

"What does tomorrow night look like?" he asked. "That's the first date, right?"

"Yeah. And the girl is awesome. You're going to Dana Point Harbor for a sailing lesson and then to dinner at Le Petit Bateau Sur-la-Mer. It's a new seafood restaurant right on the sand."

"Not to be crass, but who's paying for all this?"

It was a reasonable question, but it surprised me. He used to whip out his AmEx Black Card for everything back in the day. "Most of these episodes are sponsored by the businesses where we film. Your meals and sailing lesson will be comped. On the few dates that aren't comped, we're showing some cheap but creative options to give people ideas of the fun things you can do even on a budget. We don't want anyone to have excuses not to go on 'real' dates."

"Who's we?" he asked.

"What?"

"You keep saying we, but I only see you. I'm wondering who the rest of we is."

"Molly, I guess. My business partner and graphic designer. And 'we' used to be Trentyn."

"Are you sure you're only bummed about his new girlfriend because of this series?" he asked.

I couldn't help it. I laughed. "Are you hinting that maybe I'm hung up on Trentyn?"

"You obviously thought twenty-one other girls would think he was a catch. Why not you too?" He smiled as he asked, looking entertained by my giggles.

I pulled myself together so I could answer him. "Trentyn is pretty awesome, but in a Golden Retriever kind of way. I'm more . . . Rottweiler, maybe? At least in this analogy. I'd chew poor Trentyn up."

He laughed. "Rottweiler? I don't think so." He pulled his waffle back toward him. Good thing too. I'd have hated wasting the ten dollars it was costing me. "What kind of dog am I? And yes, I realize I'm totally setting myself up," he said before forking up a healthy bite.

"I don't think I can answer that and win."

"Ah, Lou." He shook his head, but he still wore a smile. "It doesn't have to be about winning. That was a question about learning. Seriously, take a stab at it. What kind of dog would I be?"

"You're a husky."

It was his turn to choke, but I couldn't tell if it was on a laugh or a piece of waffle. "I have never, ever been described as husky. Maybe I should skip the bacon."

My cheeks heated. I'd blurted out husky because they looked like calm and collected dogs and always had those arresting eyes. "Sorry. I don't know dogs."

"It's okay," he said. "I pushed you to answer. Can't complain about what I get."

"I meant the Siberian kind, if it helps."

"Because I'm so cool? I'll take it," he said, slapping his hand on the table.

I rolled my eyes. "Yeah, that's what I meant."

"All right, I'll quit teasing. But you make it so easy."

"You should be nicer to the person lining you up with almost two dozen hot women. Maybe I'll substitute a couple of them with actual dogs to keep it interesting."

He shrugged. "Not every one of these dates will be stellar. There will probably be some nights where watching me hang out with a dog *would* be more interesting."

I had a hard time imagining any conversation with Nick falling flat; every time I'd ever been around him, conversation flowed with the ease of flipping on a faucet. He was gifted that way with people. I'd never met anyone with a better command of small talk. "If I roll over, shake hands, fetch and beg, will you promise not to give me three hours of nearly dead air no matter how bad the date is?"

"Okay, but only because you begged. But can you do this thing?" He held up his hands like paws in canine-begging style.

"*Now* can I kick sand?"

"Tell me more about tomorrow night. Time, dress code, blah, blah, blah."

I did, typing as I spoke, putting it all into a bullet-pointed e-mail for him. When I finished, I set my iPad aside. "How much of a challenge will it be for you to get down here every day for these dates? I think at least two-thirds of them are going to be around Orange County."

"The good old OC," he said. "There are worse places to be. I filmed an indie a couple of years ago in North Dakota in the middle of January. That wasn't my favorite."

I'd seen that film, of course. He had looked pretty miserable in the bleak winter-dead landscape. Guess that wasn't acting.

"I know being in the OC isn't exactly a hardship. It's more the driving here that I'm worried about. As a commute, it stinks."

"Kade will let me crash at his place. He'll think this whole thing is funny. Not that there's anything wrong with your idea," he rushed to add. "He'll just think it's funny that I'm the bachelor."

"It is kind of funny, isn't it?"

"Yeah."

I suspected our reasons for finding it funny differed. I had broken up with Nick because he represented all the things that exhausted me about dating in the Hollywood LDS scene. The constant networking, the rare dips below the fake social surface, the never-ending demands on his time by people who "needed" him for something, like his connections. The girls. The girls that never, ever went away. He'd never cheated on me, but he'd always insisted that he couldn't ignore any of them no matter how brazenly they hung on him because they might represent a future career opportunity.

And now I was throwing twenty-one girls at him. To prove that dating wasn't dead and good guys are out there. The irony nearly choked me. Or maybe it was the oatmeal.

"What else do you need to know?"

"Who's filming? How many people are coming on this date with me?"

I picked up my napkin and blotted at my mouth. I hated having to give answers that made me sound weird. "I'll be filming," I said.

"You're kidding."

"No. This is a start-up, basically. I don't have the funds for a lot of staff, but I promise you I know what I'm doing. And Molly has solid editing skills, so you're going to come off looking great."

Hesitancy crossed his face again.

Noooo!

"You won't even know I'm there," I said. "I promise. Think of me like the random camera guys on one of your sets. I won't be doing any directing. Only documenting." Uncertainty lingered in his eyes. "If you have any concerns about how you're coming off, we can revisit the terms of our agreement, but my whole focus will be to make you look good. Not that you need help, of course." I was babbling. I should have stopped right there, but it was such an awkward statement to leave hanging. So I kept trucking. "I mean, you already look good, hotness-wise, and—"

"Thank you," he said. This time he couldn't hold back a smile, but it looked like he was barely winning the fight against out-and-out laughing.

"You know what? I know I keep saying this, but I'm usually way more smooth than this. In marketing terms, you are a hot commodity, and you'll sell yourself."

"Much smoother," he said with a nod.

I laughed. "I give up. My mouth is broken today. Meet me at the harbor tomorrow at six thirty, okay? Your first date is Alicia. She's beautiful. You'll thank me, I promise." Surly McServer lurked near the doorway, trying to duck eye contact, but I waved him over. "Check, please."

"Dana Point, six thirty, beautiful woman, got it. I guess I'll run home to grab some clothes and get a haircut."

"Don't cut your hair," I said, digging through my wallet for my last twenty. That left me four dollar bills. Period.

"Why not?"

"It's not a bad thing to keep the slightly piratical look going."

He groaned. "I didn't even think about that. Sailing on the first date. Are you sure you didn't secretly set this all up to trap me from the very beginning?"

"No," I said, grinning. "If I had, it wouldn't have worked out nearly this well." I stood and tucked my iPad and wallet back into my straw tote. "See you tomorrow night."

"Yeah, yeah," he said, standing too. "This better lead to the part of a lifetime, or you're going to owe me a favor so big you can never, ever repay it."

I smiled. "You haven't seen these girls, Nick. I won't owe you anything."

I waved and headed down the sidewalk, waiting until I rounded the corner before dropping my smile. *Please let him fall dead from love for Alicia at first sight*, I silently pleaded to whomever listened to frivolous prayers. *Because I'm about a month away from living on oatmeal and sleeping in my Audi. And I don't think I love it that much after all.*

Chapter 4

Know what frivolous prayers get you?

Definitely not serious answers.

Three minutes into filming, and there was some love at first sight, all right. But it was all on Alicia's side. I'd contacted the bachelorettes to let them know we had changed the bachelor, and every one of them had said they were still in. Except I hadn't told them who the new guy was. And that might have been an error in judgment; the shock of seeing the hottie from the pirate show TV ad standing in front of a sailboat waiting for her robbed Alicia of speech. Not sound though. She did this weird squeal—a high, faint noise that sounded like it escaped against her will before her jaw clamped shut. She took a step toward him and tripped over a huge—unmissably huge—coil of rope.

Nick's hand shot out to steady her, but that made it worse. She jerked back, and he ended up having to take an odd leap-step to her side to catch her weight as she overbalanced, semicollapsing against him. I liked the potential that implied for the ratings—it looked like he'd made a girl swoon on sight, for pity's sake.

I kept my eye on the camera screen, watching the action unfold. Nick braced himself and slipped a hand under Alicia's elbow. She grabbed his arm for support and took a step back. Even from ten feet away, I could see the red flooding over her cheeks.

"Hi, I'm Alicia, and I swear I have never done that before." She let go of his arm, and her hands drifted up to pat her hair, although every pretty blonde strand lay perfectly straight.

Nick flashed an easy smile. I don't know how it didn't buckle her knees again since he'd dialed up his highest charm setting. "Hi. I'm Nick, and I've never done any of this before either," he said, sweeping his arm to include the camera, the harbor, and the sailboat, where a crusty-looking dude named

Randall stood waiting for them to board. I'd have to edit Nick's gesture to the camera out. We didn't want to remind anyone of the fact that this whole date wasn't so organic it was practically farmer's market certified.

"You could have fooled me," Alicia said. "I saw you standing in front of a sailboat, and I thought for sure I'd stepped right into the Venice Pirate and Dinner Show. Space-time continuum confusion. Sorry."

Nick's expression didn't change at the mention of the commercial, but he'd probably prepped himself for it to come up.

"I've had a little space-time fuzziness before. I understand."

He totally had when he played a cadet in *Star Brigade: Return to Earth* about eight years ago in his first feature-film role. It was still one of my favorite things he'd done.

"You think you're steady enough to get some sea legs?" he asked, and Alicia nodded, her hair bouncing in her enthusiasm.

Molly and I followed them to the sailboat, and Nick went through the introductions with Randall. We climbed aboard, and I kept rolling as Randall pointed to different things and made Nick and Alicia repeat the names back to him. Multiple times.

I mentally marked the moments that would work to tell the story of this date without words. Most of it would play out against a music soundtrack, but I had no idea what song I would use until I knew where the vibe of the date landed.

Nearly an hour after stepping aboard, Crusty Randall finally decided they had done enough practice moves to graduate to the harbor. He jumped to the dock and loosened the boat's moorings before hopping back in and guiding the vessel out. For the next hour, wind filled the sails, and Alicia did a great deal of shrieking as she batted her hair out of her face and proved she hadn't internalized a thing Randall had made her repeat.

Nick, on the other hand, moved far more comfortably around the deck, tugging and releasing lines with little coaching. Often, he stepped over to help Alicia, and while she looked delighted to have him near her, Nick shot me a flat-eyed stare every time her back was turned. Those definitely wouldn't make the air.

Molly caught my eye and leaned over. "We need to put the wind to our backs. The mic is picking up the sound too much," she murmured. We repositioned ourselves as quietly as possible, not wanting to distract our stars. Alicia giggled as a rope slipped right through her fingers and Nick, his face the picture of patience, leaned down to secure it.

Molly sighed. "*I* could do this after listening to Randall for fifteen minutes." She said it too quietly for anyone else to hear, and I swallowed a laugh as Alicia shrieked and tugged a piece of hair from her mouth again. She had an elastic around her wrist but must have thought the windblown look worked better for her.

When Randall directed the sailboat back to the harbor and docked again, I breathed a sigh of relief. By the end of the excursion, even Nick's ability to act patient had worn thin, and it made it harder not to laugh when Alicia squealed.

What a weird turn of events. I liked Alicia. A lot, actually. She'd dropped in on our girls' nights plenty of times. She came off as levelheaded and fun. It made me wonder who had body-snatched her tonight. If Nick had this effect on all of his dates, it would be a looooong four weeks for all of us.

We disembarked, Randall and Nick both scrambling to help us with our film equipment, probably to create distance between themselves and Alicia, who stood on the dock looking bewildered. Maybe she needed to get her land legs? I stepped from the sailboat and decided that must be it as I reoriented myself to the fact that the ground beneath me was staying still.

Alicia threaded her arm through Nick's and smiled up at him when he reached her, saying something he leaned down to hear. The moment would have to go unfilmed so I could touch base with Randall. "We'll air this tomorrow by noon. Don't worry," I said when he scowled. "Pacific Breeze will come off looking like the date of a lifetime."

"Only if you don't put in any shots of her." He jerked his head in Alicia's direction. She didn't notice, too riveted to Nick's face to pay attention to anything else.

"I'll make it work, I promise. Thanks, Randall. I'll e-mail you the link tomorrow as soon as it's live." He shook my hand and then his head as he climbed back onto his sailboat to do whatever it was salty old sea dogs did when they were rid of their novice students.

I strode over to Nick and Alicia. "Hope you guys are hungry. Le Petit Bateau is holding a table for you."

"Another little boat?" Alicia asked as she translated the name to English. She'd returned from her mission to France only six months before, which was why I'd picked her for the French restaurant date. "I don't know if I can handle that!"

"You'll be fine," I said. "Unless you find using a fork challenging." I smiled as I said it, hopeful that the grounded and fun Alicia I knew would turn up in time to catch the joke and save the rest of the date.

She giggled. "If not, Nick can help me. You were so great on the boat."

One of his eyebrows crept up and then smoothed out. "Thanks. Let's eat, yeah?"

"Yeah," she said. We trailed them to his car, a different one from the Range Rover he used to drive. Now he had an Xterra, new-looking but not fancy. He opened it with his key fob remote, and I filmed him earning bonus points with girls everywhere as he walked to the passenger side and opened Alicia's door.

"Boys, take note," Molly said. "This is what real men do."

Molly and I climbed into the backseat and tried to disappear as we trained the camera on them.

"What did you mean by another little boat?" Nick asked Alicia, and she explained about her mission, sounding normal for the first time. He responded with a story about playing soccer in the streets of a slum where he'd served in Guatemala.

One thing that had always struck me from our conversations about his mission when we dated was how seldom he talked about it. He'd mentioned once that his favorite thing about serving there was never being recognized. That was it. No conversion stories or testimony stories or even funny companion stories. It bothered me to hear him tell Alicia more about his mission in the ten-minute drive to the restaurant than I had learned from dating him for six months. Still, even with that dissonance, I made another mental note: this needed to make the date's highlight reel. It would show him as a humble guy, good with kids.

Inside the restaurant, the hostess led us to a patio table. "You can't turn your camera on until Mr. Assad talks to you."

I nodded at the mention of the owner, the most persnickety sponsor I'd dealt with. I hoped he hurried while Nick and Alicia situated themselves. "Don't say anything good until I can roll tape," I said.

Nick glanced at me and seemed to be puzzling out whether I was joking or not. I only kind of was, so my blood pressure climbed a bit as he and Alicia discussed the menu. I didn't want to disrupt the flow of their date, but their conversation would be perfect for advertising the café. I edged closer to the table. "Seriously, guys. I don't want to interrupt, but I need to get footage of you talking over the menu choices. If you keep going, I'll just have to make you do it again for the tape. Can you talk about anything *not* related to the restaurant for a few minutes?"

Nick shot me another look, clearly annoyed. It had always bugged him when he didn't get his way. "So tell me about growing up in the OC," he said to Alicia. I nodded, and she told him all about Anaheim and living in the shadow of Disneyland. Finally, Mr. Assad emerged from the kitchen.

"Hello, hello, Miss Gibson," he said with a courteous bow. He'd not shaken my hand once in any of our business dealings, I think because of a cultural thing about women. His Syrian accent was still strong; maybe the habits of his native country stuck with him too.

"Hello, Mr. Assad. Do we still have your permission to film?" I asked, smiling.

"Yes, yes. That is why I have you come on Wednesday night. Not too busy. But if you will please stay in this section so it doesn't distract other customers, yes?"

"Yes," I said. "I already filmed the exterior shots and ocean views last week, so when dinner is over, we'll get out of your hair."

"I am not concerned, Miss Gibson. Our food is excellent, and no one has a better view," he said, sweeping his arm to include the entire Pacific outside of the widow. "We are past the dinner rush, but please, stay only here, nowhere else in the restaurant."

I nodded. "Definitely, Mr. Assad."

He beamed, and I waved as he scurried up front to the hostess stand.

"Wow. Worry much?" Molly asked as I pressed record on the camera.

"Talk about the food all you want now. And say really good stuff about your choices," I directed Nick and Alicia. They picked up their menus.

"It's normal for small-business owners to hover like that," I whispered to Molly. "I can't really get a foot in the door with the big corporations, but the price for working with the local types is that they micromanage." By now, Nick and Alicia were nearly slobbering over the French/Mediterranean fusion options in front of them, and I wanted to capture them raving over the food. I zoomed in and finished my point. "It's okay. I do the exact same thing with Hot Iron."

Normal Alicia stayed through dinner, laughing at normal pitch and volume and making her fair share of jokes. Maybe she had only needed time to let her nerves settle. By noon tomorrow, any of his future dates who cared to look would know who they'd be meeting when their turn came up, so maybe we wouldn't run into this problem again. It would be funny once but then get old fast.

Halfway through her baba ganoush, Alicia excused herself for a restroom break. I leaned over and snatched a roll from the table then hurried after her, hoping this didn't breach the perimeter Mr. Assad had established. It was a good time for a check-in with her, something I couldn't believe I hadn't done right after the sailing lesson. The trial-and-error part of the learning curve never went away in marketing. I smothered a sigh and nearly caused a pile-up when Alicia stopped short and whirled to face me, causing me to jerk to a halt and Molly to nearly plow into my back. She caught herself on my shoulder and then peered around me to investigate the hold up.

"Having a nice time?" Molly asked Alicia, and I flicked the record button to capture her answer.

For the first time, she stared straight into the camera. "Are you going to follow me into the bathroom? Because that's weird."

I grinned. "No, we're going to do a check-in. We'll do another one when Nick drops you off." I looked past her to the hallway leading to the restroom. "That lighting is pretty good. Do you care if we shoot you there?"

She held up her hands in mock surrender. "I'll go peacefully. Don't shoot, don't shoot."

Yep, that's the Alicia I knew. Too bad for her that more of that hadn't come out in the first two hours. Or more to the point, too bad for Nick. She stopped halfway down, and we positioned her so that one of the plantation-style wall sconces cast even more light onto her face.

"All right, I'm going to ask you some questions about the night so far, but we only want to hear your answers, so if you respond in complete sentences, I can cut out all the stuff I ask, and we'll just hear you talking. Cool?"

She nodded.

"What did you think when you first saw Nick?"

A dreamy look rippled over her face. Seriously. I couldn't even create that with a special effect if I tried.

"He's so hot," she said, a sigh escaping her. "Just like in the commercial. I can't believe I got to go sailing with my own fantasy pirate."

Her cheeks flamed, and she straightened. "Um, could you take the fantasy part out?"

No chance. "You'll feel way better about your answers if you don't worry about each one you give. Just relax and talk to me about the date. Did you enjoy sailing?"

"Sailing was super fun. I talk too much when I'm nervous, but Nick is patient."

Yeah, right. Obviously she hadn't caught any of his snarky looks at me.

"I like that," she continued. "And, of course, he looked totally at home on the sailboat." The dreamy look resurfaced.

"How about the conversation between you? How's that going?"

She smiled. "Did I mention I talk too much? But he asks lots of questions. He's an enabler! He's a conversation enabler! And that's a good thing, I guess. I should probably ask him more about himself when I go back to the table."

"Do you sense any chemistry?"

She blushed again, and it felt like prying to ask it, but the audience would want to know. "I don't know. I mean, he's very cute. But I don't know what he thinks of me. He's probably used to dating way hotter girls. Didn't he date that one model girl?"

I shrugged. He'd dated a few model girls. And actresses. And everything in between.

"Um, I have to *go*," she said, jerking her head toward the restroom door.

"Right," I said, lowering the camera. "We're going to do a check-in with him outside."

"Okay." The nervous giggle from the beginning of the date popped out, and she pressed her lips together before swallowing and asking a question. "So, basically, he's going to tell everyone who wants to know exactly what he thought of me?"

"Yeah, but I'm sure he'll only have nice things to say."

"I guess I didn't think of the details like that before I agreed to this, huh?"

"Don't sweat this. Do you really think I'd go out of my way to make you or anyone else look bad?" I used my most reassuring tone.

"No. But you can't save me from myself if I screw up all on my own." She slipped into the bathroom before I could come up with another half-convincing response.

Molly exhaled. "She hasn't been the coolest Alicia ever. It must be hard for Nick to connect with girls if he's always making them nervous."

"I don't think so," I said. "He dates a ton."

"Have you been tracking him that closely?"

"No, I'm guessing based on what I saw in the singles ward before I moved out. But the bigger point is that he's good at making people relax around him, so maybe Alicia's reaction is a fluke. We need to go do his confessional interview now anyway, so I'm sure we'll find out how he's taking all of this."

At the table, Nick sat making a circle on the linen tablecloth with the condensation from his glass of water. He smiled as we walked up. "I refuse to let you guys come to the bathroom with me."

"How about outside for a check-in?"

"Sure," he said, placing his napkin on the table and pushing back.

Outside, we put him in front of one of the lit restaurant windows for ambiance, and I gave him the speak-in-full-sentences prompt and asked the exact same questions I asked Alicia.

"I think Alicia is a put-together-looking girl. I was impressed with her . . ." He trailed off as he struggled for the right word. "With her enthusiasm," he finished.

Molly snorted, and he grinned.

He described the sailing as "relaxing, like slightly more active yoga." If it were anyone except for a Santa Monican, I'd have laughed, but I think the people of Santa Monica have to agree to do yoga and eat only free-range food before they're allowed to sign a lease anywhere in the city. When I hit the chemistry question, an odd look crossed his face, like I had asked him to strip naked or something. "You want to know if I feel any chemistry with her?"

"Yes. Or not really, but the audience will want to know."

He paused so long that I formulated a substitute question. Before I could ask it, he spoke. "Alicia is a cool girl. I think we both had blind-date nerves, but those are settled down now, and she has some great stories to tell. I think any guy would be stoked to be out with her."

I pressed stop. "Well done." He'd neatly sidestepped explaining that they had no chemistry—or at least it didn't look that way on my side of the camera—without criticizing his date in the process. She came off looking great. And in turn, so did he. I knew his former network had done a ton of media coaching with their child stars; the lessons had stuck. "We have enough footage of dinner. We'll let you eat in peace. I'm going to set the camera up on a tripod, and Molly and I will go eat while you guys get to know each other more."

"You're going to cut out all the faces I made during sailing, right? I just have a hard time with the shrieking thing."

"Don't we all," Molly said. "And yes, we'll cut the face-pulling out. But you shouldn't do it anymore. It's not nice."

"Ha," I said. "Don't take advice from her about being nice. Also, don't make faces." I reached up and squished his face as I said it. Molly's eyebrow went up, and I dropped my hand. It had been way too easy to fall back into our old rhythms. I'd think through my impulses like that from now on.

"I'm blowing off steam," he said, grinning.

"Is that what actors do on real sets?" Molly asked.

"No, they go for smoke breaks. I can take that up if you'd prefer it to me pulling faces."

"Can I vote for neither?" I asked. "How about you keep a straight face and gripe all you want in your check-ins? We'll keep the camera off for those parts."

He nodded, and I followed him to find Alicia back at the table. She looked relieved to see us, and I wondered if she thought he'd bailed on her during her bathroom break. After I set up the tripod, I pressed record and schlepped my camera bag outside, where Molly and I followed the rocky steps down to the beach.

"No offense," she said once we settled down on the sand with the sack lunches we'd stowed in the camera bag, "but this isn't my favorite way to do a moonlit meal at the beach. You need to be taller. And more muscly. And a lot more male."

"I'm crying on the inside." I flicked sand at her, deliberately missing her ham sandwich.

"What was with that face squeezing thing, by the way?"

"Oh, my gosh, you're paranoid. Nothing. Trying to lighten the atmosphere, keep the talent comfortable. That's all. Can we talk about stuff that matters? Like what should go on the date video tomorrow?"

We ate and brainstormed how to put the clips together for the next half hour until my phone went off with a text from Nick letting me know they had finished eating. "They're done," I said. "Let's go butt back in."

When we reached the top of the stairs a few minutes later, Nick and Alicia stood waiting for us.

"Cool!" Alicia said. "I'm jealous you guys got to take a walk on the beach."

It might have been a hint, but it didn't matter because Nick gave a tiny head shake behind her. Interpreting it, I smiled. "That would be awesome on video, but unfortunately, I have a deadline to meet for your date's sponsors, and that means getting home and starting the editing pretty much right now. And since Nick's our ride . . ."

"Oh, right. I'm way tired, so I couldn't even go for a walk if I wanted to," she said faking a yawn, but it made the rest of us yawn for real.

"Better get everyone on the road," Nick said, producing his keys.

He drove us back to the nearby marina, and when he parked, I leaned over the seat to explain the last part of the evening.

"You'll have to imagine that walking Alicia to her car is the good night-on-the-doorstep moment. Once you guys have said your good-byes, I'll interview Alicia, and Molly will interview you separately, Nick."

"You mean you can't just interview us together so we can get our stories straight?" Nick asked, which made everyone laugh, and the weirdness of having their good night scene filmed faded.

Nick walked Alicia over, and after a couple of nice-to-meet-yous and a short hug, he left with Molly trailing him.

"How do you feel the date went?" I asked Alicia when they disappeared. "Will you go out with him if he asks you back for a second date?"

She sighed. "He won't ask me out again. We hit our stride too late. Or maybe we didn't hit our stride at all. I couldn't relax, and if I can't do that, then this won't work."

"So you wouldn't want to go out with Nick again?"

"I'd definitely be interested, but you know how you know when something isn't clicking? I know. We didn't click. Or he didn't click with me."

I knew. I remembered clicking with Nick the first night we met, and I didn't see the same connection between them, but I admired her for being level-headed about it. I could walk away from filming this date with my good opinion of her restored.

She gave me a hug exactly like the one Nick had given her, and then she climbed into her car and drove away. I headed back over to Molly and our victim/star.

"Are you happy with the way the evening went?" he asked. "Do you need me to do anything differently?"

"You were great," I said. "Thank you for being so patient with all of this."

"No problem. What do I need to know for tomorrow?"

"You're going parasailing. Dress to get wet. Eat beforehand. They booked you guys right at dinnertime when they're slow. You'll be checking out a new gelato place downtown for dessert afterward."

"Sounds good," he said.

"Tonight's date goes on the blog at noon tomorrow."

"I don't think I'll watch," he said.

"Are you one of those actors who can't see themselves on the big screen?" I asked. I couldn't remember a time I'd seen him watch his own work, now that I thought about it.

He laughed. "No. I'm one of those dudes who can't stand to watch himself be awkward on a blind date. It'll mess with my head if I watch the playback."

"Fair enough. But I don't think you were awkward at all. You did great, Nick." I said it to encourage him because it was the smart thing to say while wearing my "producer" hat. But I found I meant it. Not many guys would have handled themselves so well.

"Let's go!" Molly called from her car. "We have a long night ahead of us."

Nick's forehead wrinkled. "You're really going to get this out by noon tomorrow?"

"No problem," I said. "We've already talked about what footage to use and how to set up the narrative." I took a deep breath before asking my next question. "So you're good with writing the blogs like Trentyn was going to do, right? It just needs to be your thoughts and experiences."

He leaned against his car and folded his arms across his chest. I would need to capture that gesture for the camera because his pecs looked great.

"You're joking," he said, but not like he found it very funny. "What was that big speech you gave me about me not trying to fill Trentyn's shoes? You know, because there's no shot of me finding a relationship like he would have? That's what you said, right? But now you want me to go on and on about my feelings on a blog to a bunch of people I don't know?" he asked.

"I think I did a very, very bad job of making my case yesterday." I took a deep breath, trying to figure how to get what I needed from him. "It's not that I don't think you're capable of finding a relationship."

"Yes, it is."

"No, it's that I figured you wouldn't want one."

His eyes narrowed for a split second. "I'm not even going to ask why you assumed that."

"Good. That way I can't screw up my answer." He smiled, and I relaxed a bit. "A blog post would add a really cool insight to the whole experience for the audience. It doesn't have to be some big, deep thing." His lips thinned, and I hurried to clarify. "Not that you aren't capable of that"—although I'd never seen it—"but there's no reason to make you put your innermost thoughts out there for everyone. I'm thinking more like a quick write-up about your general impressions of Alicia and any standout moments, good or bad. Just jot." I smiled my best please-I'm-begging-you smile.

He scowled. "Jot? That's not how I write."

"What can I do to sweeten the pot?"

"How about you don't ask me to blog? It's not my thing," he said, frowning. "I think we've reached my first diva fit."

I shot him a pleading look, but he only shook his head. My shoulders slumped. "I understand. Thanks for doing the rest of it. See you tomorrow night?"

"At six?"

"Yep." It gave me twenty-four hours to craft an argument that would convince him to do the blog posts, but I didn't have much hope. I'd dealt with his stubborn streak before. It hadn't changed.

"Bye," he said, reaching out and pulling me into a hug. I returned it and stole a quick sniff near his neck to see if he still smelled the same. Tide, soap, and Nick. The scent cocktail unleashed a flashback of the countless times he'd held me this same way, and I took a quick step back.

"Bye," I echoed, hurrying away before the word even left my mouth. If only Smellovision were real, my new Mormon Bachelor would be irresistible. I'd make a point of not breathing too deeply around him in the future unless he wore some "Eau de here-are-the-bad-memories-too." Sheesh.

Chapter 5

Seven in the morning. Hated it yesterday because that's when I had to get up; hated it even more today because that's when I finally got to sleep.

I hadn't pulled an all-nighter like that since I had to study for my physics final. That was the last time I ever took a science class because it "sounded interesting," the two stupidest words I might ever have said out loud.

We finished putting everything together some time after the sun came up, and I glared at the vicious 7:07 shining on my digital clock face. I didn't care if we got so many hits it crashed the Internet or if Mr. Assad, Randall, and everyone they'd ever known or been related to called to complain about their portrayal in the clip. If I didn't get some sleep, I'd lose all brain function. I was shutting out the world until lunch time.

As if he read my mind, at about five minutes past noon, my brother called.

"It looks great," Matt said. "What did Nick think of the night?"

I sat straight up. "You liked it?"

"Yeah. You did good."

"Thanks. I don't think Alicia will make the second-date cut, but Nick had an all right time. I'm going to see if we got any comments yet. I'll call you back."

I snatched my laptop from my nightstand. Fourteen messages, including one from Nick midmorning.

I was up anyway, so I "jotted."

I opened his attachment and read through it. A blog post!

In clean, tight prose, he managed to describe the thrill of sailing without sounding cheesy, the delicious food without sounding gushy, and Alicia without . . . well, without saying much at all. But the much he didn't say was flat out masterful.

Nothing makes good food taste better than enjoying it with good company. Alicia helped me navigate the unfamiliar French terms on the menu, and I could not have asked for a better ambiance. Can guys say romantic *and not sound like a lame Hallmark commercial? Because that's how this place felt: romantic. There. I said it. I'll punch anyone who disagrees. (Now I sound manly again, right?) I don't know how anyone could eat at Le Petit Bateau with someone like Alicia and not think of himself as the luckiest guy in the room.*

Yep, brilliant. He never said Alicia was good company; he just said that food tasted better in good company. He said the place was romantic without mentioning the date itself and implied that any guy should feel lucky to dine out with Alicia without suggesting that he felt that way. And he was funny. And his personality totally came across in the writing. And I couldn't find a single typo.

I pushed my hair out of my face and pulled up the website, copying and pasting his post in before too many more people saw the video without it. Once I pressed publish, I sat back and wondered why I'd panicked to do it so quickly. It's not like a thousand people had been waiting by their computers, obsessively refreshing our website until the first date came up.

In fact, maybe no one would look. Maybe I had lost weeks of my life trying to make something impossible happen, and in a few short days, I'd have to accept defeat and give myself a pep talk about all the things I'd learned from the experience.

Oh, heck no. No way.

I scrambled off my bed so fast my legs tangled, and I hit the floor with a thump. I untwisted and flew down the hall to Molly's room. "Get up!" I said, pounding once before throwing it open. "Get up!" I took two steps and flopped onto the bed beside her, bouncing up and down to wake her. She groaned.

"Get up, get up, get up! We're live! Go tell the whole world! Any electronic device you have that talks to people, use it! Tell them! Make them come see!"

One of her arms emerged from the covers and flailed, but I jumped off the bed. "Gotta go set the world on fire. I'll be back in five minutes if you don't get up on your own."

I snatched my laptop from my room, curled up in the corner of the sectional sofa, and called Matt back. "Check it now. He did a blog post. Read it and tell me what you think, and then tell everyone you know to read it, and tell them to comment. Gotta go!" I hung up before he could answer and pulled up my Facebook and Twitter feeds. I pasted in the link for the blog and tagged Alicia, then realized I should probably friend Nick and do the same thing for him. I pulled him up and sent the friend request, but I hoped he didn't answer it too soon. I wouldn't have the willpower to resist stalking his page, one of those prerogatives of ex-girlfriends everywhere.

Lastly, I sent out an e-mail to a bunch of friends with blogs and big Facebook and Twitter followings. They'd all promised to give *TMB* a shout-out. Once I burned through that burst of energy, I realized Molly still hadn't appeared. "Molly!" I hollered, and about a second before I would have hopped up to dive-bomb her again, she came shuffling down the hall wrapped in her electric purple plaid comforter, her hair matted on one side and big raccoon circles under her eyes.

"You have never looked hotter," I said. "Also, I'm getting you waterproof mascara for Christmas."

"I hate you," she said, her shuffle unbroken until she reached the fridge. She fished out her carton of orange juice and chugged it down, her throat pulsing as she swigged. It reminded me of a pelican eating a fish.

"It's mesmerizing and kind of freaky to watch you do that," I said.

She ignored me until she finished drinking and returned the carton with a satisfied sigh. "Okay, I can deal with you now."

"Actually, don't even talk to me. Go social network your face off."

"Awkward verb."

"I'm not a writer. Let's start paying some bills!"

"We're not getting any money for this."

"Yet," I said. "*Yet.* Very important three letter word. We'll get ads. But we have to put a show up for them to advertise on first."

"When you put it that way . . ."

She plopped down in front of her Mac, and soon I heard the sweet sound of mouse clicks.

A few minutes later, my e-mail pinged with an alert that I had a comment pending approval on the blog. "Ohmygosh!!!!!!" it read. "It's the HOT PIRATE!!!! I'm SO going to watch this! SQUEEEEEE!"

All righty then. I approved the comment to let it post. Two minutes later another message popped up. "HAHAHAHA! I love that pirate guy!" Then the commenter used a pirate phrase that sounded very, very wrong in that context, and I decided it would *not* make it onto ye olde blogge. No sooner had I rejected it than another comment came in. "Alicia is the best! That guy probably thinks he's too good for her, but he's an idiot if he doesn't pick her."

"Molly? What do you think of this one?" I asked and then read it aloud to her.

"Uh, I think that's a friend of Alicia's who doesn't see her clearly."

I rolled my eyes. "Stop Alicia-bashing. She was nervous. A lot of these girls are going to be nervous. You can't hate every girl who doesn't act like you think she should."

"I won't. Just the ones who act like airheads," she said. "They're a disgrace to the double-X chromosome."

"Settle down, Gloria Steinem. Do you think the comment is too negative against Nick to let it through?"

"Yes," she said.

"And you're not just saying that because it's pro-Alicia?"

She shrugged. "It's not the *only* reason I'm saying it. It's a slam on him for no reason, so I say don't post it."

A few more comments trickled in over the next hour, and then they stopped. People must be finishing up lunch breaks and getting back to work. It'd be interesting to see what happened to the traffic after the regular workday and dinner ended.

Most of the comments focused on Nick, "the hot pirate." I hoped it meant that lots of people were clicking "share" and pinning and doing anything else that would get the word out. His commercial's four million views on YouTube suggested a pretty solid fan base. A tenth of a tenth of those for our blog would be fantastic.

Molly stood up. "I've now exploited all of my social networks. If you wake me up before three, I'll kill you."

"Thank you and sorry, but mostly thank you," I said. "Remember my wake-up call fondly when you're counting your piles of cash because this all worked out."

She snorted and shuffled back to her room. "Good night, crazy."

Matt called me back. "It's a good blog post," he said. "He sounds super polite. It's hard to tell if he's being nice or if he's into Alicia."

"True. But I can't make him spill his guts. I'll let him get a few of these under his belt before I get all demanding."

"You're the boss," he said. Which was exactly the kind of thing that made him the coolest brother on the planet. He'd fronted me a hefty chunk of change to start Hot Iron and then had sat back and tried not to meddle. Yep. The coolest.

"Okay, so parasailing today, and tomorrow is rock climbing," I said. "We're going to exhaust him in the first three dates."

"If you keep throwing pretty girls at him, he probably won't care." He paused for a minute. "Do *you*?"

"Do I what?"

"Care about him dating all these girls? Does it bother you?"

His question surprised me. "It wasn't that bad of a break up," I said. "I mean, I was ruder than I needed to be, probably, but it's not like he broke my heart or anything. I definitely didn't break his. Why would this be hard?"

"I don't know. You were with him longer than anyone you've dated. I didn't know if that meant extra baggage or deep scars or whatever."

I laughed. "No baggage, no scars. We're cool. I'm not as confident that he'll find the girl of his dreams in this mix as I was with Trentyn. But if he does find Mrs. Right, then . . ." I trailed off.

"Then?"

"I'll offer to use my new camera skills to shoot his wedding. And it will help the ratings of the series a ton. And I'll pay back your money even faster."

"I'm not worried about it," he said, his tone one of long-suffering.

"But I am. I mean, not about paying you back. But about owing you."

"Worry about your groceries or something. Speaking of, I think if you shop in Mom's Famous Overstocked Pantry this week, you might find a bunch of your favorite food stuffed in there."

I smiled. "Tell her to stop worrying too. I'm not starving." Yet.

"You need to drop by and let her see for herself."

"I will." Two more alerts popped up in my inbox. "Oops. This business that is totally going to pay back your investment needs doing. I better go take care of it."

"Later."

I hung up the phone and read the messages. The first, more squealing about the pirate, went on the blog. But the second one caused a small tempest in my belly. "The whole HB dating scene is a joke. It's a bunch of fake plastics, and you guys are the worst of the fakers because you're perpetuating the myth. You should be ashamed of yourselves. You all need to reexamine your commitment to the gospel and its principles because it has nothing to do with looking the hottest or going out with the most people." The commenter signed him or herself only as "Disgusted."

I sat back, annoyed that someone could get so worked up about a dating show. My fingers flew over the keys, stringing together retorts like "bottom-dwelling troll" and "rageaholic" and "pathological joy zombie" before I sat back, satisfied.

I read through my response, congratulated myself for my exceptional skills in snark, and then deleted the whole thing. It felt good to get it all out but not good to return the rudeness. I'd popped off at the mouth too often in my life to think I wouldn't regret letting my temper get the best of me. As much as I'd love to give Disgusted an ear—or eye—full, I needed to let it drop.

I'd rather think about how well everything had come together so far. I set the computer aside and headed to the front door. Since I already had on a T-shirt and yoga pants, I slipped on my pink suede flip-flops, one pair in a row of four that reflected their owners in the apartment as clearly as if they sported name tags, and rounded the corner to the garage. Just touching my bike made me happy, and by the time I'd rolled it out and ridden the half mile to the beach, the cool breeze off of the water had already blown out the cobwebs of sleep deprivation from my brain.

I breathed in the scent of sea salt and warm sand, soothed by it the way I had been ever since I was a kid and realized that everywhere else in the world didn't smell like my hometown. I rode northwest, away from the touristy city beach near the Main Street pier and up toward the Bolsa Chica wetlands. I had plenty of company from other bikers for the first mile, but it thinned as I neared the turnoff for the bridge that crossed the bog nearest the highway.

I locked my bike up, chose a bench, and took a seat. The mean-spirited e-mail had only bothered me because I was exhausted from the all-night editing rush, but I had a month of long nights ahead of me. I'd need my head in a better place or my emotions would seesaw so much that I'd earn myself a one-way ticket to Crazy Town. I'd cope better if I came up with a plan. If my brother knew how little pillow time I expected to get now, he'd throw his first fit of our business partnership. He knew better than anyone how strung out I could get without consistent sleep.

I inhaled the crisp salt air. This. This was how I would cope. Time near the water or, even better, in it whenever possible. That's all I needed to face the looming hours of filming and editing. I sat watching egrets land and fish, letting the sun renew me. When I hopped on my bike an hour later, I hummed all the way home. My head was in a good place, and this was all going to work out exactly like it should.

Two hours later, I was even more convinced of that after whipping through another two dozen comments, all of them unequivocally nice. Lots of girls raved about the pirate again, but several commenters expressed everything from curiosity to excitement about where the show would go. I decided to count those as official season-long viewers and called it good.

Several friends e-mailed me to tell me they were going to kill me for not signing them up to date Nick and then to congratulate me on the site. The best e-mail came from Mr. Assad, who said simply, "I'm very happy with this outcome. I will call you to discuss your help with my future advertising." *Yes!* I wanted to tell Molly, but I eyed the clock and decided I'd better not test her threat by waking her too soon. I reread his e-mail a few times. It was my first tangible proof that this whole plan would work out the way I had hoped when I started it. After discovering several retweets with our site link and almost forty new likes on our Facebook page, I drew a deep breath and tried not to let it out as a squeal. My instincts had steered me right. That light at the end of the tunnel was definitely *not* an oncoming train.

A call to Crusty Randall confirmed it. "You did all right," he said. "How much to buy one of them small ads on the side of your page?"

Ever the optimist, I'd already worked up a few sidebar ads, and I promised to put one up right away that would link to the Pacific Breeze website. It was only fifty bucks, but between Molly and me, it represented a tiny life raft where before we had nothing. This time I couldn't resist telling her, but my roommate Lily saved me from myself by opening the front door.

She took one look at the huge grin on my face and dropped her backpack to rush over and give me a hug. "You know I think you're crazy for staying up so late." She stepped back, smiling. "But it must have paid off."

"Literally," I said. "I got an advertiser for the blog, and both of our sponsors last night are happy with their coverage. Did you watch it?"

"Not yet," she said. "Let me change, and I'll do that."

"Careful. Molly's still sleeping."

She slipped into their room and traded her fingerpaint-smudged khakis—a hazard of teaching first grade—for pink running shorts. She topped them with a clashing Dodgers shirt. And she still looked cute. "Let me at it," she said, settling in front of my laptop. She pressed play, and the date soundtrack blared out. I tried not to stare, but every time I sneaked a glance to watch her reaction, her eyes were riveted to the screen.

Four minutes and thirty-six seconds later, she clapped her hands. "Killer job, Lou! Having Nick fill in is going to be the happiest accident of your life. What's the response so far?"

I described some of the positive e-mails I'd received, skipping the contribution from Disgusted since contention tended to upset her. "You're right about Nick," I concluded. "I think more and more of his YouTube fan base will be appearing soon."

"That's great," she said. "I bet a lot of them aren't Mormons, so it'll be fun for them to see what we're about."

"Do you think I should have him holding a Book of Mormon in every frame from now on?"

Her tinkling laugh rang out, and she stood to head for the door. "Goofball. I'm going for a run. I'm making roasted root veggie casserole, and I always have too much left over, so save room for dinner." She slipped out before I could refuse. She seemed to have the same radar my mother did for whether or not I was eating properly. I pulled down my box of instant oatmeal packets. Properly? No. Definitely not. But enough. If I chased it with ramen, maybe.

With a sigh, I added water and stuck my bowl in the microwave. I had an hour and a half before I had to head to the harbor—again—to schmooze the owners of the parasailing boat before filming. I needed a better story line from Nick's date tonight with Kylie. Maybe the sheer terror of dangling from a parachute over water would be enough to coax some good drama out of this next date.

Chapter 6

Kylie produced no drama. She was nice. Boring. Not even vanilla. Maybe imitation vanilla. Nick tried to make something of the night, but his second date still fell flat. That made editing a pain because we had hardly anything to work with to create a "story." Our page views grew for day two despite the date, but I was banking on tonight's date, lucky number three, to produce some *real* drama and a bigger audience.

And now, a few minutes into it, I had to concede that this bachelorette would produce no on-camera drama either. She produced nothing at all, actually. Not even a personality. Which is weird, considering her name was Chelsey. Seemed to me like all Chelseys were bubbly and outgoing, like maybe if a baby was born shy but then her parents name her Chelsey, suddenly she would morph into a personality firecracker.

But not this Chelsey. Most definitely not. On the one hand, she didn't lose her mind—or footing—on meeting Nick. She walked up to him where he stood in front of the local rock-climbing gym. He gave her a wide smile, understandably, considering she was a curvy brunette with beautiful skin and striking green eyes. On the other hand, she didn't show *any* emotion. She returned his smile with a wan one of her own and then followed it up with a handshake that *looked* limp. She answered all of his questions politely but didn't add much to the conversation or ask any questions of her own.

When they pulled on their harnesses, another girl might have jumped on the chance to finagle some help with her buckles from Nick, but not Chelsey. She whipped through everything with quiet efficiency and no comment. It pleased Molly, but not me. I'd have to fill most of the video time with action shots of them on the walls, and even those wouldn't tell much of a story since her expression didn't give away anything and Nick wore a permanent amiable expression. It bored me to even think about the footage.

Yikes. "Molly," I said. She sat fiddling with the mic, which we didn't need since the reverb in the gym made sound recording too hard. She didn't hear me.

"Molly!"

Her head shot up. "I know. It's boring. What are we going to do?"

"Would it be wrong to slice halfway through her rope so it snaps and Nick has to rescue her?"

She pretended to consider the idea. "It would only be wrong if she broke a bone. Or, you know . . . died."

"Fine." I sighed. "No sabotage." I watched them climbing side by side but not at all together as they worked up the wall. Chelsey's face was a study in concentration. "I blame you." Molly had recruited Chelsey for the date. In the application video, she'd smiled wide enough to flash her dimples and spoke freely about her passion for the outdoors and her desire to meet "Mr. Right."

"I should have predicted that she would act completely differently than I've ever known her to. My bad." We watched in silence for another minute or two before Molly spoke again. "Let's do an early check-in and find out what's up."

"You think she'll say anything on camera?"

"Do you have a better idea?"

"Nope," I said, climbing to my feet. "They're about to belay."

A few minutes later, they reached the ground, and I stepped up with a bright smile. "Hey, guys. We're going to do your check-in interviews, see how things are going so far. Chelsey, you'll be with Molly."

"Okay," she said, again with a robotic smile.

I led Nick to the empty upstairs bouldering section and turned the camera on. "How are you enjoying your date with Chelsey so far?"

He smiled. "She's a beautiful girl."

My eyes narrowed. "Uh-huh. But how are you enjoying the date?"

He weighed his words until he found some he liked. "She's enigmatic."

I paused the recording. "If by that you mean impossible to get to know, I agree. Sorry. Her application video was so fun. I'm not sure where *that* spunky girl went."

"It's okay," he said. "It's not like I expected all twenty-one dates to be perfect. Am I allowed to make faces now? Because this date deserves it. Like this one." He yawned widely.

"Mean," I said.

"But true."

I studied him. "Do you expect any of these dates to go well?"

He opened his mouth to answer, but I held up a finger while I pressed the record button again. When I nodded to go ahead, he cleared his throat. "I definitely came on *The Mormon Bachelor* to connect with someone."

I grinned. Well, my job just got easier. Despite the rough start of his first two dates, we had some amazing girls still to come.

"Do you think Chelsey could be that someone?"

His practiced smile appeared. "We've barely been hanging out for an hour. Maybe I can get to know her better over dessert." His smile slipped. "Could you stop recording again?"

I did and lowered the camera. "What's up?"

"Honestly, I want to be a team player here, and I promise you I'll work hard to come up with something by the next check-in, but at the moment, I've got nothing."

"All right. Maybe Chelsey's check-in will shake something loose for her. Thanks for being a good sport."

He shrugged. "No problem. It's good material, at least."

"For what? Future acting roles?"

He paused a split second before answering. "Pretty much."

"Back to climbing, dude. Pretend you're Spider-Man. Maybe the practice will make you the surprising long shot for when they remake it. Again."

He rolled his eyes and headed down the stairs. Molly and Chelsey already stood at the highest wall, Molly looking bemused. The first signs of life since she showed up flickered over Chelsey's face when she saw us coming. "Chase said this is called the Skyscraper," she said, referring to the wall and pointing to the guy who stood by, ready to belay her. "You want to take it on?" The light of challenge gleamed in her eyes, and after a startled glance at me, Nick grinned back at her.

"Race you to the top?"

Without another word, Chelsey's elusive dimples flashed, and she grabbed her first handhold, gaining a six-foot vertical lead before Nick could clip in and follow. "It's not going to hurt your feelings when I smoke you, is it?" she called down to him. My jaw dropped, and I turned to stare at Molly. She shook her head.

"Nope, because that's not going to happen," Nick called up then grunted and reached for the next handhold. I zoomed in for a tight shot of the muscles flexing in his shoulders then zoomed back a bit so the ladies at home could enjoy the fine work from his calf muscles before widening the shot enough to show the progress of the race. My lack of camera experience had been a big negative coming in, but hours of reality-TV consumption had wired my brain for how to capture at least the basic kinds of shots, thank goodness.

When they were a third of the way up the wall, I signaled for Molly to lower the boom mic.

"What voodoo did you do?" I demanded.

"I asked her why she was being so weird. That's it."

"And?"

"And she said that when he showed up in the video yesterday as the bachelor, one of her friends in LA called and warned her about him, and it freaked her out."

"Warned her about what?" I could think of his less-than-stellar character traits but nothing that required an alarmed phone call, definitely not for a first date.

"Her friend said that LA guys, especially the actor types, are superficial. Like at notorious levels. And that Chelsey should be on her guard because he might be put off by her 'pleasant plumpness,' I think was the phrase."

I stared at the curvaceous Chelsey and then back at Molly. "Her *friend* called her plump? What is wrong with people?"

Molly shook her head. "Beats me. But I set her straight. Told her Nick's face lit up when he saw her, that he seemed confused by her standoffishness, that he's a genuinely nice guy, and so on. Told her we would have a hard time making her look like anything besides a zombie if she didn't relax and have fun with him."

"Bless you, my child," I murmured as we watched them some more. "Although, I don't know about the 'genuine' part."

"What do you mean? He's been way nice."

"But you don't think he's kind of fake? I mean, he's got professionally highlighted hair and muscle shirts. Doesn't he come off as arrogant to you?"

She shrugged. "He did at first. I don't know. He's growing on me. He's better when the camera is off and he lets his sense of humor out more." She squinted up at our subjects. "What really matters is Chelsey's opinion, and I don't think she's got any issue with him at all."

I followed her gaze up to the couple. The energy crackled between them now. Chelsey's face shone with determination and then amusement, and Nick laughed every few seconds at something she did or said. I couldn't wait for them to get back down to gauge their chemistry for myself. About twenty minutes later, I got my wish and my answer: they were gelling very, very well.

Nick made it off the wall first, and as soon as Chelsey touched down, he held up his hands for a double high-five. When she reached up to give it, he brought his hands down to wrap her in a quick, hard hug. "All right, Spider-Girl. You beat me to the top. You win."

"We should have bet something," she said.

"It's not too late. We'll make it a retroactive bet." He pretended to think. "I was going to bet a victory hug. Too bad I lost."

She poked him. "I bet the same thing. Good thing I won."

"You want to go again?"

"You can ask for a hug, you know. You don't have to scale a thirty-foot wall every time you want one."

He grabbed her and squeezed her once more. "I'm so glad I didn't have to earn that because my shoulders are killing me. Will you think I'm less of a man if I suggest a break?"

She rolled her eyes at him. "Come on, drama queen." She reached for the carabiner securing her to the rope, but he beat her to it.

"I can get that," he said.

She blushed as he helped her unhook.

Seriously? He was being so obvious. I glanced at Molly, but she watched their exchange with wide eyes and a half smile.

They headed to the bench in front of the rental harnesses. "Grab a seat, and I'll go whip up something from the vending machine," he said.

"Sure," she said. "I like—"

"Wait! Let's make it a test. Let's see if I've figured out enough about you in the last hour to guess what you want. Dare me?"

She leaned back and stared at him through her lashes. "I dare you."

"Cool."

I followed Nick with the camera. "Talk me through your decision-making process here," I said when we reached the vending machine. "I'm sure the girls at home would love to know what makes you so confident about her snack preferences."

He studied the choices behind the glass for a moment. "Granola is the right call personality-wise, but do you think she'll take it the wrong way?"

"Nah. True granolas don't care if you call them that."

"Says the not-granola."

"What? I like the outdoors and organic stuff."

He turned to look at me, his eyebrow quirked. "You're not a granola. It's not a bad thing."

"If I'm not, then you're definitely not."

"What's that supposed to mean?"

I pointed to his hair. "No granola has ever had the love affair with hair product that you do."

His hand darted up to brush his bangs. I smirked, and he dropped his hand again. "What's wrong with having nice hair?"

"Nothing. But you don't have nice hair. You have salon-perfect hair, like you're about to shoot a Pantene commercial for dudes."

"So you want me to take my grooming less seriously?"

"No, I want you to take your hair less seriously."

His mouth thinned, and guilt pricked my conscience.

"Sorry," I said. He didn't answer, and in the silence, I caught myself chewing on my thumbnail. I shoved my hands into my pockets and offered him a smile. "Really, I'm sorry. The girls are loving you, so obviously I don't know what I'm talking about. What would a clueless granola know about hair?"

He shoulders dropped a fraction. "I told you you're not a granola."

"What am I, then?" I asked, relief at the change in subject washing over me.

He didn't answer for a long moment. "Not a granola," he repeated before turning back to the vending machine.

"You could give her the 100 Grand Bar and tell her it's only a fraction of what's she worth."

He groaned. "That's worse than one of my jokes. Quiet while I think."

"Fine, but talk it out for the viewers," I reminded him before shutting up and letting him work.

He inserted his dollar bills, and then the granola bar dropped, but he didn't stop there. Soon a package of peanut butter cups joined it. He retrieved them and moved to the soda machine, where he selected a bottled water and a sports drink.

Without another glance at me, he headed back to Chelsey.

"A granola bar?" she asked, curiosity on her face.

"Definitely. You've got a completely down-to-earth feel about you," he said. Her expression turned slightly brittle. "Plus a very natural glow," he added, and her expression softened again. "But I brought these too." He held up the peanut butter cups. "Remember that old commercial about the two great tastes that taste great together? That's like you. You're down-to-earth and fun, but you're gorgeous too. The perfect combination."

I wanted to throw up a little from the cheese factor, but the look on Chelsey's face suggested that he'd hit a home run. Smiling, she took the Reese's cups.

"You did pick one of my favorite candies."

He handed her the bottled water. "This is me cheating," he said. "I'm keeping the Gatorade so it gives me a chance to beat you on the next climb."

She laughed, and they sat eating and talking for another twenty minutes. The conversation flowed well between them. As *TMB* producer, I loved that we had such a skilled social navigator. It impressed the heck out of me personally. When we were dating and he stopped and talked to everyone in a room, I interpreted it as one step short of social climbing. Gotta make the next connection, have to find the next professional hookup. But then again, we were always at "industry" parties full of Hollywood types who wanted to connect with Nick for the same reasons. Watching him with these girls who had no interest in building acting careers cast him in a different light. He had worked hard three nights in a row to put them at ease and not be "the star." Maybe he truly worried about them having a good time?

He and Chelsey climbed for another hour, and then we headed to get gelato, me filming and Molly following in her Mini. The downtown shop had a handful of customers, and all of them stared at our crew.

"Are you the news?" a small boy asked me.

"No, dummy," his taller brother with the same curly hair said. "They would have TV channel numbers on the camera. Bet it's a movie."

Their mom turned to get their orders and caught sight of Nick standing behind her. Her eyes widened. "Oh, you're that pirate!" she exclaimed.

Nick smiled, but he looked uncomfortable. "Yeah."

"Oh my gosh. Can I get a picture with you?" She scrounged through her oversized handbag, and I heard clinking. The girl at the register stared right past the woman to Nick with a starstruck smile and thrust her phone at him. *Click.*

"So cool!" The counter girl's squeal grated on my nerves. "The owner said some people would be filming in here, but we didn't know it would be you!" She slid open her phone and tapped out a text.

The mom glowered and pulled her phone from her purse. "For me too, please?" she asked, handing it to Chelsey and stepping between them to slide her arm around Nick's waist for a photo. Chelsey regarded her with bemusement. "You don't mind, do you?" the mom asked.

"No," Chelsey said. "Why would I?" And a smile peeked out while she snapped the shot.

No one else in the shop approached Nick, but they stared and whispered. He and Chelsey stepped up and placed their orders, ignoring the sidelong glances. When they sat down at a small corner table, I filmed while Molly fought with the tripod so we could leave them in peace.

"Is it weird to be recognized?" Chelsey asked.

"Only when I'm on a date," he said. "Was that weird for you?"

"Super weird," she admitted. "But kind of funny."

Sure. The first few times. It got less funny a couple dozen times in.

She bit into her chocolate-chip gelato, and I tried not to drool. "I kind of forgot for a minute that you're a celebrity."

"I never remember unless other people remind me," he said. "That's why it was fun hanging out with you. You don't seem to care about that, and that's pretty awesome."

Man, he probably couldn't say the wrong thing if he tried. Chelsey ate it up along with her gelato. Deciding I'd seen enough for the moment, I jerked my head at Molly and led her over to the counter. "To really serve the client, we should sample some of these flavors."

She nodded, her expression grave. "This kind of thoroughness is why I'll follow you to the ends of the earth, boss."

The manager, a nice guy named Wes, smiled at us from behind the counter.

"Sorry about the drama," I said quietly so his starstruck employee wouldn't overhear.

He laughed. "It's okay. I was afraid it would be a way worse circus than this. Last week a couple of the Lakers came in, and the place went nuts. What can I help you with?"

"We thought we should do some taste-testing research so we know what we're blogging about."

He kept a straight face. "Anything for research." He grabbed a couple of sample spoons. "I recommend starting with the albicocca. It's surprisingly refreshing."

We each accepted the scoop of peach-colored gelato.

"Apricot!" Molly said, beaming.

And we passed the next half hour researching and occasionally pretending to think about the editing we had to do later. I polished off a spoonful of mandorla as Nick and Chelsey stood to leave.

"Time for the end of the night check-in," I said to Molly.

She scraped the last of her straciatella from her spoon with a sigh. "Why can't the fun parts of this job be the ones that last the longest?"

I grabbed the camera while she broke the tripod back down, and then we followed Nick and Chelsey out. Thank goodness. It was close to ten, and I itched to put the video together. It should go faster now that we'd done it a few times, but it would still keep me up later than I wanted it to.

Unfortunately, instead of heading back toward his car so he could drive Chelsey back to the gym, Nick and Chelsey hooked a left toward the ocean a block down. Molly shot me a quizzical look. "I guess they both love long walks on the beach," I whispered.

"And we get to take one with them? Lucky us."

"Did I mention that we picked up fifty bucks in advertising from Pacific Breeze? Because maybe if this goes well, we can make it fifty bucks *each* with a great episode tomorrow."

Molly stared up at the nearly full moon. "What the heck, right? It's a gorgeous night. Maybe we'll get a kiss shot."

"Shhh," I hissed at her so Nick and Chelsey wouldn't hear us.

"What? Does that bother you?" she asked, studying me closely.

"No."

She looked skeptical. "Whatever. Hurry up, or we'll lose them."

Right then, Nick turned around and jogged back to us.

"Hey, girls. I know filming everything is part of the deal, but can we call this as officially being off the clock? Maybe you can tape us walking off into the darkness and do some editing magic that lets the viewers draw their own conclusions."

"Are you guys going to make out?" Molly blurted, and I hit her.

"Ignore her." I took a deep breath. I wanted Nick to have a great experience and give him alone time with his dates if he needed it, but I wanted to give the viewers a great experience too. We really should be around to film a kiss, but I didn't know how to phrase that.

"No," he said. "But I'm not ready to call it a night, and I don't want the guilt of keeping you out even later when I know you need to edit. Do you have enough for a post?"

I nodded. "If we film the check-ins, we do."

"Cool."

Molly led Nick off, and I turned the minicam on Chelsey. She smiled all the way through the interview; it was funny to see how relaxed she was compared to the start of the date. When Molly and Nick came back, Chelsey greeted him with a big smile. Molly's eyebrows waggled at me, and I smothered a laugh.

"I'll ride home with Molly," I said. "Be good." I gave Nick a small wave and turned, cringing inside. *Be good?*

"Why would you even say that?" Molly asked when we had escaped his earshot.

"I don't know!"

"It was weird."

"I know!"

She hit the light at the crosswalk, and we waited. After another minute, she glanced over at me. "Are you going to be okay with this?" She held up her hand to stop my answer. "I know I keep asking you that, but you groove along like everything's cool, and then you make some comment that makes me wonder if it's not."

"I don't know what you're talking about." But I did.

"Yes, you do. But I won't point out any examples because I'm nice."

The light changed, and I hurried ahead, eager to put a few seconds' distance between us. She caught up to me in front of Beach Sport Warehouse.

"I'm not going to give you any examples," she repeated like I hadn't done a near-sprint to avoid her, "but I need to know a few things."

"About what?"

"About where your head is with all this."

I stopped and turned to face her. "My head is totally in this," I said. "My loan from Matt is your insurance policy against me doing anything stupid."

She said nothing, but her eyebrows climbed, arching up behind her bangs.

"What now?" I demanded.

"Are you saying you've considered doing something stupid, but your financial obligations held you back? And what stupid thing did you consider? Sabotaging all of the dates or something? Hurling hideous girls at Nick to keep him from getting attached?"

I stared at her in disbelief. "Have you lost your mind? No, I haven't thought of anything like that. What is wrong with you?"

"Absolutely nothing. But you're off, and I'm trying to figure out why. I know I'm supposed to be the artsy designer and creative partner, but every minute I work for you is another minute I have to wait tables so I can make the bills. In fact, I think I have about one more day of filming like this in me, and then I'm going to have to tell the café to put me back on the schedule."

I sighed and gave her a half smile. "Let's get back to the condo, and I'll see if I can explain my crazy head better."

We spent the rest of our trip home discussing how to edit the date while I tried to figure out what I wanted to say when we got there. The conversation had to wait a minute, or thirty, once we walked through our front door to find the sofa littered with Autumn and a half dozen of her friends.

"You're here! Tell us everything that happened tonight," Autumn said, bounding off the sofa. She grabbed us each by an arm and guided us to seats on the cushion that she jerked her head at two friends to clear. We squished between two more girls, our equipment heaped on our laps.

Autumn dropped Indian-style onto the carpet in front of us. "We want the inside scoop. We know he went out with Chelsey because Traci told us." She pointed at Chelsey's roommate. "But we haven't gotten a text yet from Chelsey, so you have to tell us how it went."

"You better not get a text from Chelsey," I said. "The girls can't talk about their dates until they air."

"Good thing we've got you," she said. "How did it go?"

Calls to spill it chirped around me.

"No way, peanut gallery. You can watch it at home like everyone else tomorrow."

Groans. I grinned and struggled to my feet then helped Molly up. "And there's no way we're getting it posted if you guys don't let us work."

We headed to the dinner table and cleared it to make it our desk again. I set up my laptop while Molly booted up her Mac.

Autumn heckled us from the floor, her jibes floating over the sofa. "What is the advantage of being your roommate if I can't have the inside scoop?"

"Ha!" I called back. "At least three of you sitting over there rejected your chance to be a bachelorette."

"Oh, so this is payback?" Autumn demanded. "What's it going to take to change your mind, Lou Lou Belle?"

"Not that stupid nickname."

"Chocolate? I've got a Godiva truffle I've been saving for when I finish my 10K this weekend, but it's yours if you share the dirt."

I considered it but then rejected the offer. "Nope. Molly and I are equal business partners here, and she won't buckle for half a truffle, so I won't either."

"Yeah, crinkle a bag of Funyuns under my nose, and we might have a deal. Now let us work," Molly said, disappearing behind her wide monitor.

"I would have done it if you said it was the pirate," one of the girls from the ward piped up, a funny redhead named Beth.

I turned around. "It's not the pirate. It's Nick. You know Colin Firth isn't really Mr. Darcy, right?"

"Duh. But I don't care about their names. I care about yummy eye candy."

"That's it," I said, standing up. "I can tell we're not getting anything done tonight without an intervention." I leaned over the sofa and grabbed the remote, turning on the TV. "Netflix comes to the rescue with a Ryan Gosling movie. Step into my *other* office?" I asked Molly.

She followed me to my room, where we both plopped down.

"Short meeting, please," she said. "If I spend too long anywhere near a bed, I'll crash."

"It is," I promised. "I want to make sure you know that this whole thing will work. Don't worry, okay?"

She studied me for a minute. "Why did you guys break up in the first place? All I know is that you watch every single thing Nick's in, and his IMDB profile probably gets more hits from you than any other computer."

I flushed. "That's morbid curiosity. More evolved Facebook stalking since he happens to act. You guys all do it with ex-boyfriends. No big deal."

"But, I mean, can you explain your breakup? I haven't seen any red flags in him, so why'd you dump him?"

I sorted through my words carefully. "What you see from Nick now? That's what you get. It's *all* you ever get. He's never dialed in to *you.* Or me, back in the day. When we dated, he paid attention to everyone else in a room except for me. He said it was because when you're at a function with people in the industry, you always have to be 'on' because you don't know when an interaction with someone can lead to booking your next role." I leaned back against my headboard and studied the poster on the wall behind Molly's head. The framed print showed my favorite stretch of beach in the world, a section of Ehukai along the North Shore of Oahu.

"How about when you guys were alone?"

"We had good chemistry," I said. "Liquefy your bones chemistry. And I still had this massive crush on him from when I was a teenager and watched his show. That might be why I stuck around longer than I would have otherwise. That sounds so shallow."

"You can't spend ten minutes with someone you find shallow, much less six months. And I've seen him be charming, but you don't fall for charm either."

I sighed. "I was stupid. I was twenty-one and about to start my last year at USC. I thought I'd be planning a summer wedding by then, but I hadn't dated anyone in the ward for longer than a month. No one clicked for me. And then I go to a party, and there's Nick, and we're electric. But I played it cool, and later he told me that was a big reason he was into me at first. We talked that whole night, one of those times when you're almost falling asleep during your own sentences but you don't want the conversation to end."

I looked down at the comforter on my bed and traced the blue hibiscus next to my knee. "You've seen how easy it is to talk to him. After the first night

I met him, I thought I was on the verge of *the* relationship. For three months, I thought that."

"So what changed?"

"I'd go for weeks having the best time with him, and then I'd realize I couldn't name one substantial conversation we'd had the whole time. Sometimes we talked about serious issues, but it was more global politics kind of stuff. Never how he felt about anything."

"That would frustrate me," Molly said. "So he was fake all the time with you?"

"No. Just 'on.' Always entertaining. He was hard to get to know."

"Even after six months?"

I nodded. "Every now and then we'd have a conversation where we connected emotionally, like he'd let the real him come out. I'd think we were moving to the next level, but then he'd go back to being on stage. You said you like him better now than you did three days ago. But do you *know* him any better?"

"No." She shook her head. "I see what you mean."

"But . . ."

"But what?"

"You know how Nick told Alicia all about serving in Guatemala? That was way more than he ever told me about his mission. He'd talk about how it was nice to be in a place where no one recognized him for two years, but that was kind of it."

"And if he told you about the kids and the soccer and the weird food but didn't have some big testimony or baptism stories to tell you because there weren't any, what would you have thought?" Molly asked.

"I don't know. The point is that he never did."

"What if he didn't feel like he could? What if he thought he had to have deep spiritual stories to tell you, and he worried that he didn't?"

"He could have said that."

"Yeah?"

I frowned at her. "I tried to understand him better. I'd talk about something that came up at church and how I connected to it, and he'd say, 'I respect your testimony so much,' and then that was it. No further thoughts from him about anything."

"At least he didn't follow that up with trying to grope you. I get that a lot."

I snorted. "No, he's not *that* guy. But I grew up with all these ideals of what the perfect husband should be, and he didn't fit the important ones."

She quirked an eyebrow at me. "Maybe that's the problem for those of you who grow up Mormon; you think there's a perfect husband. There's not. God did not use a cookie cutter for perfect men and then shower them on YSA-infested areas. Give up the myth, Lou. You'll feel better."

I laughed and flopped back on the bed. "I only mean I had in mind the perfect guy for me." I had been raised with the strong sense of self-worth that comes when your mom does a great job of communicating that you're a daughter of God. Then my dad made sure I formed and defended strong opinions about everything. And then Matt made sure I had the confidence that comes from being athletic and good on a surfboard.

"Who is that, Louisa? The perfect guy for you? You sure it's not Nick? Did the attraction evaporate between you or something?"

"No. He's still hot. But I need so much more than that. The perfect guy? I don't know who that is. I figure I'll bump into him in the hall at church one day and he'll be carrying a sign with my name on it, like those chauffeurs at the airport." Heaven only knew that it hadn't worked for me to try to *find* him, whoever he might be.

I inched back up and smiled at Molly. "Want to play shrink and tell me why I'm always dating and never falling in love?"

"No."

"Come on. No guesses?" She shook her head, but something in her face made me press her. "I think you do have a guess. Tell me."

"How about I think it over and give you my doctoral thesis when I come up with an answer? Because we've got to get this editing done."

I smacked her foot. "I'm so messed up it's going to take a dissertation? Give me a hint."

She sighed. "How come Autumn let you finish making the bundt cake?"

"The bundt cake?" I'd given Autumn my mom's recipe the week before when she'd asked for it. She'd wanted to make it for our weekly Sunday girls' dinner, but I'd seen from across the kitchen that the batter's consistency was wrong, so I offered to help. "She got frustrated with it and wanted to make a salad instead, so I baked it for her."

"That's how it happened?"

"You were there. Do you have a point?"

"No. I have a deadline, and so do you. Cowgirl up, chica. I want to sleep before morning."

Chapter 7

Four a.m. Not crack of dawn territory, so we were improving, but the month of filming stretched ahead of me like a long, unbroken chain of empty Mountain Dew bottles, my only coping mechanism for the insane hours I would be keeping.

I set my alarm for nine and squeezed a couple of bizarre dreams into my five hours of sleep. In one, I was a mermaid stranded on the beach, and no one would throw me back in the water. In the other one, I grew a hand out of my back. It wouldn't take Freud to analyze those. I was out of my element and needing more help. Duh.

I shuffled to the kitchen for a pick-me-up glass of water. Pricey soda would have to be in-case-of-all-nighter-emergencies only. When I sat down at my laptop, I already had eleventy-million messages waiting for me. Facebook and Twitter notifications, a few blog comments. I cleared through the blog comments first: four more "I *love* that guy!" posts, a couple of "Is it too late to sign up to date him?" and one "This whole idea is stupid, he's stupid, you're stupid, I hate you" rounded the whole mess out.

"Be calm, be cool, be the grown-up. Be cool, be calm, be the grown-up," I muttered.

Personal messages from friends congratulated me on a great idea and promised to tune in. The site meter showed over seven hundred views in the last twenty-four hours. Not viral, but it gave me a great baseline for week one to see where our audience grew from there, and I could live with that. I'd wait another week before I decided whether I should freak out.

I opened the e-mail I'd saved for last: Nick's blog post. With a deep breath, I dove in. It would help me out tremendously if he would stay the superficial guy I'd dated way back when, but I had a feeling his connection with Chelsey would produce a blog post that took me further into his head than I wanted to go. And I might even find out exactly what happened after the camera left whether I wanted to or not.

The beginning described meeting a "reserved" Chelsey and feeling uncertain of what she thought of him. I smiled. That vulnerability would score more points with the audience. He described the awkward first hour, the change in tone after their check-ins, and then he got to the walk on the beach.

"I think at the end of the video today, you'll see me walking off down the beach with Chelsey while the camera stays behind. And I don't think it matters whether I tell you what happened next or not; you'll speculate either way, I bet. So I will neither confirm nor deny whatever it is you guys are thinking. But I'll tell you this: having a meeting of the minds with someone is an amazing thing. I love that click that happens when I hit the same wavelength as someone, and it happens so, so rarely. I can't believe what a rocking chick Chelsey is. I know it's only my third date, and I know I have eighteen great girls left to meet, but I'll go ahead and make a bold statement. This is not the last you'll see of Chelsey."

I knew way too much and nothing at all. Did they kiss? I had no idea. But he'd publicly committed himself to a second date with her regardless of whom else he met, and he wouldn't have risked that unless he'd really been feeling it. Not unless he was an idiot, and one thing Nick Westman had going for him besides movie star good looks was a super smart brain.

The wavelength thing caught me. What wavelength were they on? An instantaneous recognition that they were meant to have children together? Or something more like a mutual love of vending machine snacks?

I drummed my fingers against the tabletop and then shoved away from it in disgust. My dad, a political junkie, used to spend hours researching every new law proposed on the California ballots during each election. His particular obsession was what he called "the law of unintended consequences." He said figuring out what a law was intended to do and what would actually happen was a lot like playing chess; you had to think several moves ahead of the law's authors to try to forecast reality.

Unintended consequences had just taken me out and kicked my trash. I had spent half of the last seventy-two hours either filming or editing Nick to show him in the best possible light, and suddenly, I was seeing him that way. Worse, I was having flashes of insight into his emotions and thought processes that I had struggled to find through our entire relationship.

Only none of these revelations was intended for me. And that was fine. Just because Nick showed some hints of change, it didn't mean he and I should reconnect beyond this work collaboration. This finding-him-a-new-girlfriend collaboration.

I hit the "schedule post" button and slammed the laptop closed before heading for my closet. Maybe I couldn't run every time my brain fogged up, but I had a half hour right now, and I was going to spend all of it pounding the pavement along PCH and thinking. More than ever, I needed to focus on producing an amazing series, because this went way beyond a job. My professional identity and Molly's liberation from waiting tables rode on this. What-ifs didn't matter.

* * *

I met Nick's date for the night outside of a bowling alley in Fountain Valley. We'd filmed eight dates already, and this would be the nuttiest by far. The bowling alley wanted to increase traffic at their theme nights, and this Friday night had people trickling past us in superhero costumes. Nick had been incredibly cool about dressing up as a superhero, considering that it was a pretty dopey thing to do. I hadn't seen him yet, but I had his promise that he would put something together. I'd tried to book a different Friday with a different theme, but since the owner wouldn't budge, I'd been careful about which girl I chose.

Meredith. Merry, for short. That made her sound all sweet and pleasant, I bet. Ha.

Other girls generally didn't like her. It had a lot to do with the way she stayed stone-faced and uncommunicative until a hot guy walked in, and then suddenly she turned charming and flirtatious. If it were up to me, Merry wouldn't be on this season. Molly insisted though. She said we had to represent all types to show the true HB dating experience, and if nothing else, it would be a good litmus test for Trentyn to see if he had depth or only talked a good game. I guess Merry had now officially become Nick's litmus test.

My only comfort came from the costume thing. Merry would hate every second of it, so that's why I'd stuck her with this date. Now, as I watched her walk toward me, I smothered a smile. "Hi, Merry. Thanks so much for doing this."

Molly snickered. As expected, Merry had gone the sexy superhero route; she wore a Wonder Woman costume with a short skirt to give herself more coverage than the original leotard would. But I doubted modesty had worried her much since she had the classic top on, with plenty of her cleavage on display. "You might have to learn how to pixelate," I whispered to Molly.

"Black censor bars will be funnier," she said. "And we're definitely going to need them."

Merry reached us. "You're Louisa?"

"Yes," I said with a smile, even though she knew full well what my name was. We'd been in the same ward for almost two years, but let her plead ignorance. Whatever.

"You didn't tell me when I signed up that I'd be dressing up in a costume," she said.

We'd been over this via e-mail. Twice. She was a good writer because the whining in her messages matched her current tone exactly.

"Try not to worry about it," I said. "You look fantastic." No lie there. She'd stand out in a bowling alley full of other superheroes, no problem. "And remember, you're going out with a guy who wears costumes for a living."

At the mention of her date— prey?—she brightened. "Is Nick here yet?" she asked, craning around me to look.

"He's inside," I said. "We'll follow you with the camera and film his reaction to seeing you. Are you ready?"

"Just a second." She shrugged off her Hurley jacket and handed it to Molly. I bit my lip to keep from laughing. "You don't mind, do you?" Merry asked.

"Nope," Molly said. I didn't trust her expression.

"Let's go."

Merry squared her shoulders, tugged her costume *down* a bit, and then glided through the doors.

"I hate clichés," Molly said as we followed. She dragged Merry's jacket on the ground behind her.

"Head to the farthest right lane," I called to Merry after a warning glance at Molly. The second Merry spotted Nick in his Aquabat costume, she drew her shoulders even further back. Molly shook her head, but Nick's hair distracted me too much for me to join the Merry-mocking. It looked different, unrulier maybe, like it did after surfing when the seawater had stolen all of his hair gel and the sun had dried it to look the way it was meant to before he tamed it. He flicked me a glance, and his hand twitched toward his hair before he caught himself. I nodded. *Nice*, I mouthed. A smile played at the corners of his lips.

When Nick saw Merry, his eyebrows rose. I didn't know what that meant because he hadn't done that for the other girls. It could be as simple as his appreciating her undeniably good looks. Merry had a beautiful Latina somewhere not too far back in her family tree, so with her olive complexion, her thick, dark hair, and her full lips smiling at him, Nick would have to be a wax dummy not to smile back.

"Nice costume," Merry said.

"Thanks. One of my friends is in the band, and he let me borrow it."

"Oh, who? My older sister used to date one of those guys."

With that, the date was off and running. The five minutes between her walking up to us and then meeting Nick set the tone for the rest of the night. Merry played the vamp, and though Nick refrained from ogling her, she got plenty of looks from all the other guys in the vicinity. And Nick provided eye candy for the girls. His chest looked impressive in the blue stretchy costume. The pair of them raised the cool factor in the bowling alley several points.

I witnessed no awkward silences or nervous giggles; Merry handled herself well, and of course, with Nick being Nick, conversation flowed. I even gave her grudging respect for not acting helpless with a bowling ball. They played two games, and she lost both of them, but not by much.

Because it was Merry and she bugged me, I'd made sure the whole date stayed in the bowling alley, including dinner. They ate some cardboard-looking pizza, and I hoped it annoyed the snot out of Merry that she didn't get to do anything cool like go for a walk on the beach. Unfortunately, she compensated for the lack of date quality with the quantity of her prancing, flashing her legs, and offering big, toothy grins.

Nick's check-in didn't tell me much. He complimented her outgoing personality, commented on her attractiveness, and generally said nothing at all about what he really thought. By nine, I caught myself yawning for the hundredth time in a row. When Merry excused herself for a bathroom break, Nick smiled at me. "Are you trying to make me look bad? If you keep yawning like that, I'm going to yawn too and look super rude on camera."

"Sorry," I said. "Just remember that after you get home from your dates, I'm up for a few more hours."

"I've been worrying about that. You've been running on short sleep for over a week now, right? Are you holding up okay?" he asked.

"You've been worried about me?" I cocked my head and smiled at him. I expected it from Matt and my mom; from Nick, it came off as kind of quaint, but his words still sent a soft wave of warmth rolling through my chest.

"Yeah. I go home and fall dead asleep. I can't imagine how wrecked you are. Not that you look it or anything," he added. "Just in case your girl brain went there first."

"It didn't," I said.

"It wouldn't," he countered. "You don't get too caught up in that."

"In what?"

"Primping, fussing, whatever. I remember picking you up for a party at that one director's house and you just ran a brush through your hair and were ready to go."

I shrugged. "Life's too short."

Molly had joined us by then. "No, I'm too short," she said. "You're a tall, blonde, tan goddess. Goddesses can swipe a brush and go. The rest of us have to primp and fuss."

Nick flashed a grin at her. "You're selling yourself *short*."

"Ha," she said before punching him in the stomach. He captured her hand and threw an arm around her neck.

"I'd be in way big trouble if I gave you a noogie right now, huh?" She stomped on his foot and he let her go, laughing. "I'll take that as a yes."

She shook a warning fist at him, but she was grinning too. "Let me answer for Lou," she said. "She's doing fine right now, but I've seen her when she's not getting enough sleep. I won't say it's ugly, because as you just pointed out, you can't describe anything about Lou that way. But I'll say it's . . . it's like she gets zombified. And slightly hysterical."

"Don't bite the hand that feeds you," I said.

"I'm not. You've put twenty-five bucks in my pocket so far, and all that's going to do is pay for the parking ticket I got last week taping the art museum date, not food." She patted my arm. "You're going to have to pay me a lot more before I start shutting up."

"That's not true," I objected. "I've sold six more ads."

"But you haven't collected yet. I'll quit sassing you when they pay up. In the meantime," she said, turning back to Nick, "I'm worried. This will be the eighth day in a row where she's up all night editing, and then while I get to sleep in, she's up again checking in with the business owners, moderating the comments, following new leads, and who knows what else. It exhausts me to watch her."

"I remember that habit from your USC days." He smiled, and I returned it, the shared memory knitting us together for a moment. During my finals, he'd stretched out on the sofa for hours and memorized his lines for an *NCIS* episode while I'd sprawled on the floor and reviewed for an anthropology final. Every time he'd nailed the dialogue for a scene, he'd earned a kiss, and every time I'd memorized all the dates and terms in a chapter section, I'd earned one. Best study tool ever.

Molly shot a glance between us, and her forehead furrowed. I could tell she was trying to work out the significance of our shared smile. But there was no significance, only a funny memory. Although . . .

A lot of those had come up lately. This wasn't the first time she'd caught us sharing a look or a laugh. And it wasn't always about the memories either. A few days ago, Nick had taken to calling me after his dates. He'd wanted to complain about a gnarly night at a bakery. He and a girl named Elizabeth were supposed to be making bread, but she'd spent the whole time trying to get him to reenact his pirate commercial.

I'd let him vent the next day because . . . well, yeah. It was a bad date. And he deserved a listening ear. We talked for an hour before I had to hang up to go sweet talk some more advertisers, and suddenly, we had an official daily debrief followed by conversations about nothing and everything.

Nick cleared his throat. "I don't know how married you are to running the camera yourself, or whatever, but I have an idea to float."

"Float away."

"A couple of friends in my ward are professional cameramen. They'd love an excuse to hang out in Huntington Beach and call it work. It'll give you a break."

I shook my head before he even finished. "I'd love the help, but we can't pay them."

"You won't need to. They'll do it for free if they can crash at Kade's house."

A huge smile split Molly's face. "Yes! She says yes."

I laughed to cover my hurt. He wanted to get rid of me? "Calm down a second. It's not that easy. I have to be on scene to set up the story and make sure we're capturing the right footage."

"Ha. You do not," she said. "I'm on scene. I know what we need."

"Where does your impending return to the Café of Doom factor in?"

"May I see you over here?" she said, dragging me off before she'd finished asking. "Take the offer."

"I can't. I don't know these guys. They might run around shooting what guys think is interesting." I waved my hand toward the bowling lane we'd vacated. "If we had guys shooting tonight, we'd end up with nothing but footage of Merry from behind."

"I'm not going to lie; I wouldn't mind having a badonkadonk like that."

"Who wouldn't? But I'll tell you who wouldn't want to watch a five-minute video of it: our target audience."

"I told you, I'll stay on scene."

"For how long? You said you have to pick up more shifts at the café. You're going to be even more tired than I am."

"I can be patient for a couple more weeks, especially if you pick up more accounts. And honestly, that's why I'm offering. If you can step away from the filming every now and then, I figure that means you have even more time to do the business-y side of stuff."

"How? We film at night."

"Yeah, but you can use that time to do a lot of the comment moderation and handle all of the e-mails, and then you can spend your morning getting us more advertisers instead."

Eight dates in, and all but one of the featured businesses from the episodes had bought sidebar ads. I'd even gotten my first glimmer of interest from a midsized hotel chain with a location downtown. They were close to running a huge banner ad with us. I could feel it. It *would* be nice to have more time to go after even bigger accounts. "Are you sure?" I asked. "I hate the idea of sticking you with all the work."

"You're not, dummy. You'll be doing as much editing as ever, and while we can both oversee the filming, there's no way I could go out and get us new business. You need to do that."

I thought it through, but I couldn't argue with her logic. Besides, I didn't like the weird swoopy thing my stomach did now when I saw Nick. That needed to stop, and that meant putting some distance between us. "Hi, I'm Louisa, and I'm a control freak, but yes, we'll have Nick pull his friends in."

"And thank him for thinking of it," Molly prompted me.

"Sure," I said. "I guess he was miscast as a pirate. He should have been in the Medieval Times commercials as the—"

"Let me guess," Molly interrupted. "Knight in shining armor? Your jokes are as bad as his."

We headed back to Nick and found Merry with him after the world's longest bathroom break. On the upside, her lip gloss looked perfect. "Let's do our wrap-up interviews," I said. "Then you guys can escape to your regular civilian clothes."

"Great," she said, slipping her arm through his and smiling up at him. "It'll be nice to get to know you without the cameras."

He smiled down at her. "Man, as cool as that sounds, this taping schedule is wiping me out. I don't think I have even twenty-four hours before the next one, do I?"

"Nope, sorry. You've got an afternoon date tomorrow."

"I better call it a night," he said. "You've been such a good sport to do this. I don't know many girls who could have pulled this off."

Merry assumed a pouty expression for a moment, and then a teasing smile appeared. "I can't hate on anyone for wanting her shot at you, so enjoy your date tomorrow. I'm sure I'll get to know you better in round two." She withdrew her arm from his and fluttered her fingers in a wave before she grabbed her jacket from Molly and sidled to the exit. Or maybe she sauntered. The way that girl moved required a vocabulary all its own. Did she practice that walk?

I hurried after her. "I'll do her interview. Molly?"

"Yeah, I got Nick."

I caught up to Merry outside. "Ready for your exit interview?"

She turned and fixed me with a distracted stare. "What?"

"Your final interview? Your thoughts on the night? All that good stuff?" Her gaze sharpened. "I'm standing outside of a bowling alley in a Wonder Woman costume. How do *you* think my night went?"

I tapped the record button. "You're surprising me. You looked like you were having a great time in there."

"I repeat: Wonder Woman costume. Bowling alley. Which part sounds like an amazing date to you?"

"If it's not your thing, then why did you agree to it?" I asked, suspecting I knew the answer. "Is it because of Nick?"

She dragged her hand through her hair and let out a tired sigh. "I didn't know he would be the bachelor when I signed up, remember? *You* put this whole thing together, Louisa."

"Then why?" I pressed again, only this time I genuinely wanted to hear her answer.

"Because I'm tired of the grind. I want a ring on my finger and babies crawling on me. And it's hard to find a guy who wants the same thing."

"Not that I stalk you or anything, but you seem like you date a lot."

"No," she said, her dark hair bouncing with her head shake. "I go out a lot. It's always guys who are like, 'Hey, let's drop in on a party' or whatever, and I'm there as some dumb prize. And I swear to you that if one of these idiots does ask me on a date, it's because they hope buying me dinner will impress me enough that I'll make out with them."

I winced.

"It's true," she insisted. "My sister is almost fifteen years older than me, and she says it wasn't like that before. It was just regular dating. People hung out too, but guys weren't afraid to take a girl out to get to know her."

I sighed as I considered her. "I owe you an apology. I kind of doubted your motives for signing up to do this."

She lifted her eyebrows. "Then why did you cast me?"

"Because I wanted you to make us look good."

After a long stare, she burst out laughing. I smiled back, but when she gestured down at her Wonder Woman getup and laughed harder, I broke down too. "Oh man," she said on a gasp. "I signed up because I thought a guy willing to do this show might be serious about dating. I put on Spandex—with spangles!—for a shot at finding the right guy. And Nick is super hot, but he's so not it."

"Why not?" I asked, still smiling.

"Wall's up, I think. A guarded guy isn't looking for someone new."

"You think he's guarded? Did you see his other dates? He's been pretty open."

She shook her head again. "Nope. You know what I think he thought of his dates? I have no idea, because he never said. He said a bunch of nice things that could mean anything. That's guarded."

I quit recording and tucked the camera back into my bag while I debated asking the next question. Merry had surprised me with her perceptiveness. Once again, I reminded myself that I had to suspend my judgment of people, especially people who I needed to portray in the best possible light for the audience. "I think he's being diplomatic. Who's really going to put everything they think out there on the Internet?"

She shrugged. "I get that he's being polite. That's a good thing. But at the same time, it definitely seems like there's a lot he's holding back, so I can't get a sense of how open he really is to the idea of falling in love. Like I said, it's not just diplomacy. He's guarded."

"Why do you think he's so guarded?" I asked the question casually, like I hadn't spent my entire relationship with him plus several months afterward trying to figure out the answer.

"I could be wrong." She paused, a speculative look in her eye as she stared past me for a moment, thinking. "All I can say for sure is that he acts nice, but he's definitely not into me." She zipped up her hoodie and turned toward the parking lot. "Thanks for trying to make a difference with this whole project though. It's a good thing you're doing," she called over her shoulder.

"Wait," I said. "We do dinners at our place for friends on Sunday nights. Want to come?"

Her face lit up with her first unironic, not-vampy smile of the night. "That sounds cool."

"We're in the ward directory. Come over around six?"

She nodded and deactivated the alarm on a Subaru wagon. I'd have pegged her for something small, red, and racy. Once again, I'd judged wrong.

Meanwhile, back in the Aquabat Cave, Nick and Molly sat chatting on a bench near the shoe rental counter, her camera nowhere in sight. She must have gotten what she needed from his date wrap-up, but Merry's observations led me to wonder if the audience would get what *they* needed when I edited it all together.

"Hey, boys and girls. I'm going to grab Molly for a second for some production talk before we call it a night if that's okay with you," I said.

"Sure," Nick answered. "I'll lie down right here and sleep until someone tells me I have to move."

"Boohoo," Molly said, poking him before she stood and jumped away from his retaliatory finger. "If only I didn't have to go home and spend a few more hours on this while you sleep, I might find real tears to cry for you."

He stretched out on the bench and laced his fingers behind his head. "Get out of here, slave drivers. You're messing with my power nap."

"What's up?" Molly asked when we'd moved a short distance away.

"How did the wrap go?"

"Fine. The usual. Merry's nice, he's a lucky guy to be out with her, he liked her willingness to go along with such a crazy date idea, all that."

She noticed my expression. "Is that bad? That's what we've been getting from him every night."

"I know." I sighed. "And Merry pointed out to me that it probably *is* bad. And now I get to go demand yet another thing from him."

"Remember to say please," she said, following me back.

I nudged Nick's foot, and he cracked one eye to look at me. "Yes, ma'am?"

I smiled. "Ma'am? Do I look like I'm about to boss you or something?"

"Yes, ma'am. What do you need?" He sat up and ran his fingers through his hair, leaving several strands poking up.

I loved that his hair slid through his fingers so easily now, untamed by product. I itched to touch it and explore the softness for myself, but my hands were smarter than my brain and stayed put. "Have I mentioned that we're super appreciative of everything you've done for us?"

He eyed me with a look that suggested he was waiting for a trap to spring. "You need something big."

"What makes you say that?"

"You're only nice when you want me to do something. The rest of the time you point and tell me where to go."

"That's not true."

"It's true," Molly said. "Very true."

"Go away," I said.

"Nope." She stuck her hands in her back pockets and rocked on her heels. "It's totally big, Nick. Brace yourself."

I smiled at him, infusing it with every bit of "trust me" mojo I could muster. "Based on feedback, viewers would love to know more about your reactions to your dates. We're getting comments that it's hard to tell if you like these girls so far."

"I do like them. I've said so on camera every night, and in the blog posts I'm amazingly kind enough to write for you."

"Yeah, but . . ." I trailed off, trying to figure out how to fill in the blank.

"Don't act like you don't know exactly what you want to tell me." He looked like he found my word search funny.

"Fine. You sound ambivalent."

"Ambivalent?"

"Yeah. Wishy-washy, unsure."

"I know what ambivalent means," he said with an eye roll. "I think you picked the wrong word. The word you're looking for is *polite*. I was being polite."

Molly stuck her hand out for a high-five, which he gave her. She sat down next to him and glared at me. "Yeah. Polite."

"We need to make compelling video if we want viewers and also cash, so you need to be on my side," I reminded her.

She hopped up and stood beside me again. "You need to be less ambivalent, Nick."

"I'm not getting any money out of this," he said. "What happened to you guys just being glad I'm doing it at all?"

Molly sat back down. "Also a good point."

"What happened to getting tons of exposure for your career?" I said.

"That's if this goes viral. Still waiting on that," he said, unperturbed.

"We've only got a shot if you quit being ambivalent." I crossed my arms and eyed him.

He sighed. "It's loud in here. Let's take this outside."

We followed him out to his Xterra and waited while he leaned against it and jingled his keys. "I'm open to the idea of falling in love," he said. "Does that help?"

My stomach twisted. It didn't help at all, but since I knew that was a personal response, I put on my professional game face. "That's awesome.

You've still got thirteen girls to meet. If you haven't met 'the one' yet, your odds are still better than good."

He nodded. "I know."

Another stomach twist. Another professional smile. "If you'd let the audience in on how you feel, whichever girl you truly connect with is going to know, and maybe it will make her even more likely to return those feelings."

"That's what it takes, huh? Spilling my guts to everyone with an Internet connection? If *that's* all . . ."

"Look at it this way," I said. "It's like being open and honest with whichever girl you choose so she can let her guard down too."

He stared at me for a long time. "There's another side to that."

"Which is?"

"These girls are putting themselves out there for people to judge. I can't imagine every comment about them has been super nice, right?"

My lips tightened when I thought about some of the rejected comments people had left, calling the girls everything from attention-hungry to pathetic.

"That's what I thought," he said. "I'm used to that kind of stuff because of my job, but I don't think there's any reason for me to point out where they're less than perfect when the whole viewing audience is going to do that anyway. It's one thing when I'm complaining to you because these dates are wearing me out, but to be honest, I hope that being on the show raises their profile with some of the slow-moving guys around here."

Okay. That impressed me.

Molly cleared her throat. "That's hard to argue with."

And yet I had to if I wanted to keep our show's long-term prospects healthy. "We don't want you to trash anyone. We just want you to share what your impressions really are. It gives the show an edge. I don't think being up front can hurt, and the audience will appreciate it."

He shook his head. "No. The audience is not on camera for everyone to rip apart. I know you have to consider your site traffic and all that, but it's not fair for these girls if I'm going, 'Nice face, dumb as a brick, no go.'"

"You don't have to say stuff like that." I should probably have been frustrated by his stubbornness in refusing—once again—to let anyone in on how he felt, but I respected it. This time. "Look, they're not getting the full experience if you're not sharing your full feelings."

He jammed his fist into his pocket, silencing his keys. "This sounds exactly like some arguments I remember having three years ago."

Thank goodness for dim parking-lot lighting; I didn't want Molly to see my reddening cheeks. Her snort at his comment was bad enough.

"Guys? Do I need to leave you alone to work some stuff out?" she asked, entertainment threading through the fake concern in her tone.

"Nope," Nick said. "We're good. Just some déjà-vu."

Déjà-vu for sure; I remembered running into this wall over and over again too, and I knew I wouldn't budge him right now. Time to go. "Think about it, okay? If you can find a way to be even more specific about your thoughts and reactions, not only is it added value for the show, but more importantly, it might keep some of these girls from dealing with false hope."

"All right. Go edit, and then go do your super-businesswoman thing in the morning. What's the date tomorrow?" he asked.

"A food festival on Main Street."

"I'll get one of my buddies down here for that."

"No, I'll do that one too. Then I can talk to the vendors there. I'm sure they're going to be interested in what we're filming, and maybe I can wheel and deal with them about what makes it into the video that goes up."

He smiled. "Good thinking. That's why you're the big boss."

I shot him with finger pistols and then twirled and holstered them. "Those were ironic finger guns, by the way."

"I know."

Molly piped up. "I'm tired. I want to go home. I want to go home before I start whining about it, so I'm saying it now while I still sound like a rational adult who is clearly communicating her needs."

Nick cocked his head at her, curiosity written across his face.

"I watched a marathon of old *Celebrity Rehab with Dr. Drew* episodes this afternoon. I think he possessed me for a second there," Molly said.

"Dear roommate, you're weird."

"P.S. You are too. Love, Molly."

"Ladies, I think you need to do a whole new web show where you guys just sit and talk to each other, because that's funny."

Molly perked up. "Yes! And I'll autotune our dialogue, and then it can be a thing."

"And I thought we had to get closer to two a.m. to have conversations like this," I said. "Seriously, I'll get her out of here before it gets weirder."

"Cool. I'll have a buddy down here for Monday, then."

"Well . . ."

"Lou, are you actually going to let me bring some help in?"

I swallowed my concerns. "Okay."

"Done. You can't change your mind now."

"I want to go home," Molly said, bouncing in impatience.

"See you tomorrow," I said. We headed for Molly's car and a long night of editing. In case I hadn't changed Nick's mind about being more forthcoming, I'd have to find some creative ways to make future dates distinct and original. Tonight's would be no problem though. Smoking-hot Merry in a Wonder Woman costume had done all of the work for me.

Chapter 8

To no one's shock, the Merry episode suddenly pulled in a fair number of comments from guys. Several of them came from guys I knew. One in particular caught my attention, a comment from a guy named Luke whom I recognized from his profile photo. "The fact that this pseudo-pirate didn't fall down and worship Merry as the goddess she is tells me everything I need to know about his IQ."

It wouldn't be going on the blog, but I might show it to Merry when she came for dinner on Sunday. I'd seen Luke around. I liked his understated hipster style, and he had a pretty cute face hiding behind his funky glasses. Maybe Merry would think so too.

The other comments from guys focused more on her hotness and demands for more girls like her on the show. Blech. Trophy hunters. These guys were by no means unique to HB, but it didn't make them less annoying. The comments from the girls surprised me though. I thought I'd have to filter out a bunch of catty remarks, but most of them either went on and on about Nick again, or else they complimented Merry for not taking herself too seriously.

I sat back and considered that. It had definitely been some catty mean-spiritedness on my part that had provoked me to choose her for this date. She'd seemed like such a boy-crazy, prissy girl that I'd wanted to embarrass her ever so slightly. I wondered how much of her behavior grew out of a defense mechanism. She'd definitely done things to alienate herself from the other girls in the ward, but maybe it was a strike-first mentality. Or maybe she'd simply given up trying to make friends with girls.

My cell phone buzzed with a text from Autumn. *At Chelsey's house for lunch. Just watched new ep. Please don't let Merry come for dinner. She seems kind of cool, and I might have to hate her more.*

I smiled and went back to the e-mails, opening one from the sailing school. "We booked our second customer from people watching your dating thing. Run us for the rest of the series, but we want a bigger ad. What do we get if we double our money?" Randall signed it, but I'd recognize his terse verbiage without a signature. I hopped up and did a happy dance.

"This is when I need a camera rolling," Molly said from the hallway, where she leaned against the doorframe to the living room. "I guess we got a lot of views?"

I continued my dance and added jazz hands. "We've already matched yesterday's numbers, and it's only been up for an hour. Go ahead and tweet though." I shimmied for my finale and then ran over and hugged her. "But the dance is because we got more advertising."

Molly hugged me back and then pushed me away. "You might be doing a sad dance next."

"What's up?"

"The café texted. They're begging me to come in for the early dinner shift. I need the money. You think we can get someone to cover for me?"

"In two hours?" I asked, trying not to flip out. Guilt pinched the skin around her eyes, and wormed its way into my conscience. "Yes," I said. I couldn't make her feel bad for needing the work. "Let me make some calls."

"Start with Nick," she said. "Maybe one of his buddies will be ready to go on short notice. It'll make you feel better if you could train whoever replaces you behind the camera, anyway."

I nodded and texted Nick. *Molly has to work tonight. Any of your buddies up for shooting the date?*

A minute later, he called. "Aren't I supposed to be meeting you downtown at four?"

"Yeah."

"What if I can't get someone down here?"

"I'll call and beg other people. Worst-case scenario is that I'll do the whole thing myself. The audio will be less than stellar, but I can make it work."

"I'll get back to you."

"Thanks, Nick."

"Later."

When he hung up, I scrolled to Ashley's number. What are future sisters-in-law for if not for pulling your bacon out of the fire? *May need you to follow some strangers around while holding a microphone all night. Could you do it?*

Her reply came back right away. *Believe it or not, this isn't even the weirdest text I've gotten today. But yes, if you need me to skip a Skype call where I argue with my sisters about bridesmaids' dresses, I GUESS IT CAN'T BE HELPED.*

I laughed. Ashley and her easy-going spontaneity suited my brother so well. I couldn't wait for their fall wedding. Except . . . *Hold strong against the lavender!* I tapped to her.

Bronze or bust, she texted back.

"Go make real money," I called down the hall to Molly.

She stuck her head out of her room. "Cool. I'll snitch a sandwich for you."

"Only if Peter lets you have it for free. Don't spend any of your tips on food for me out of guilt."

"Who, me?" She feigned innocence and ducked back into her room.

I sat down and checked about a hundred social networks to see what, if any, *TMB* buzz I could find. Our Facebook page had picked up two hundred more likes from the day before, and a few people had tweeted links to the new episode. It might be small potatoes to other people, but a little over a week ago, we'd been getting no mention at all. More improvement, then. I sagged in relief. This whole campaign would live or die by social media. With only nine episodes on air, we still had modest traffic, but it had doubled each day. Time to reach out to even more bloggers to see if we could gain more traction that way.

I stole a glance at the time on my laptop screen. Almost two. Since I had a backup plan no matter what thanks to Ashley, I decided to grab a quick shower and get ready. Fifteen minutes later, I stood in front of my closet with wet hair and a blossoming headache. I'd been in jeans and cute tops for all the other dates, but today I needed to go more business casual since I'd be chatting up merchants for potential sponsorships and advertising. I settled on black polished-cotton capris, ballet flats, and a drapey teal shirt. It wasn't fancy, but it looked professional and wouldn't upstage Nick's date.

My phone went off, and I snatched it up from the dresser. Nick. *My friend Mikey is coming down, but he needs more time. Can we push the date back an hour?*

Oh, heck yes. I let him know that was fine, texted Ashley that she was back on the hook with her Skype call, and called Anna, Nick's date for today, to let her know the change in plans.

"Oh, thank goodness," she said. "I tangled a round brush in my hair, and I had no idea how I was going to get it out in time. We don't need the scissors," she called to someone on her end. "Gotta go."

Typical Anna. I'd never seen that girl when she wasn't on the verge of some kind of klutz-induced crisis. That's why I picked a date for her that offered her a very low chance of hurting herself or others. She couldn't fall off a boat, a rock wall, or into a bowling alley gutter tonight. As long as she didn't try to walk *and* eat at the street fair, both she and Nick should be safe. Maybe.

Since I had more time to get ready, I used it to do something besides pull my hair back in my usual low ponytail. I got it mostly dry and stuck in some Velcro rollers before hunkering down to tackle more e-mails. By an hour before date time, seventy-six comments had already come in, roughly four times the total for the entire twenty-four hours after Alicia's date. Traction. Nice. I predicted at least another hour of comment moderation when I got home tonight.

I checked the time again, yanked the rollers from my hair, and with a quick swipe of mascara and lip gloss, I gathered up the camera and other equipment and headed for the car. I'd need extra time to find decent parking so I wouldn't have to tote everything too far.

I drove on autopilot, thinking through the scene shots and practicing my pitch for the business owners at the booths. I had nailed down the angle I wanted to take by the time I reached our meeting spot, the lawn in front of the small Main Street library branch. I set up the tripod and camera and leaned against a concrete planter to wait for Nick and his friend.

They rounded the corner from Lake Street a few minutes later, pausing in front of the Italian cucina on the corner before crossing the street to meet me.

"Can we let them eat street food and you and I check that place out? Because *dang*," the cute guy at Nick's side said. He had a large camera bag over his shoulder, and using my Sherlockian powers of deduction, I figured it was Mikey.

"Lou, meet Mikey. Mikey is a very smart guy and excellent with a camera, but he does all his thinking with his stomach. I'm pretty sure the food theme is the only reason he agreed to film this date."

I held out my hand for a shake. "You get a festival pass too, so you'll be eating all night. It's pretty much the only way we can pay you."

"Not the only way," he said, and Nick slugged his shoulder.

"Ignore him," he said. "Hunger makes him stupid."

"Sorry," I said, "but you'll have to work on an empty stomach for a few minutes because we're filming the meet-up here before we walk down to the fair, and Anna won't be here for another twenty minutes."

"Fine. Walk me through what you want."

I explained the pattern we followed for each date, from the initial meeting to the check-ins and then post-date interviews. He suggested several ideas for framing shots, and I decided that even with an underfueled belly, he was nowhere near stupid.

My text alert went off with a message from Anna telling me that she was coming up Sixth Street. "She'll be here in about a minute, from that corner." I pointed to the right. Mikey's laid-back jokester vibe disappeared in between eye blinks, and suddenly he was alert, camera braced on his shoulder and very, very still as he aimed it. Wow. "All right. There she is, in the purple."

Anna moved toward us at a brisk pace, wearing a super cute striped T-shirt dress with white Toms. She told me she'd quit wearing heels after her fourth ankle sprain.

"Hi!" she called out when she drew closer. "You don't make me nervous, but I'm still prone to tripping. I'm Alicia times ten. No, times fifty." Nick grinned at her easy greeting. When she reached him, she gave him a hug.

"That was for the fourteen-year-old Dex Hall fangirl that still lives inside me," she said, smiling. "And now that I've got that out of the way, nice to meet you."

"I dig your energy," he said. "Are you always like this?"

"Like what? A hot, caffeinated mess? Minus the caffeine, yeah. Crazily enough, this is all natural." She gave a small hop, and I doubt she even realized it.

He laughed, and they were off, strolling down Main Street toward the sounds and mouth-watering smells. At least Mikey's mouth watered. I think I caught him swiping drool away.

After a short discussion, Nick and Anna started with a curry place. The employees eyed Mikey and me with all our camera gear curiously. I smiled and waited for the magic question. It came as soon as Nick placed their order and they moved off to the side to wait for it.

"Excuse me, miss," an older gentleman behind their makeshift counter said. "What is it you're doing?" I loved the lilt of his Indian accent and smiled wider. Mikey signaled to let me know he'd stick with the date, and I held out a business card to the man. After introducing myself and asking if he was the owner, I launched into a breezy explanation of the show and the advertising opportunities.

"Ah, love," he said, with a smile. "My parents arranged my marriage, and thirty years later, we are still happy. Do a show about that."

"Arranged marriages? Sometimes I wish." I leaned on the counter, making sure my posture suggested an invitation to join me in conversation and not a threat to his personal space. "To be honest, that's kind of what we're doing here. I picked out twenty-one great girls who are looking for a relationship, and if he clicks with one of them, then maybe it could lead to marriage."

"Click? Do you mean like find a magic spark?" He peered over to where Nick and Anna sat chatting. He studied them for a moment. "Not with her. No magic." He smiled at me. "How did you choose her? You are a much better fit." He tapped my bare ring finger. "You arrange your own marriage to him."

I laughed. "I'm more interested in arranging some advertising so we can keep sending him on these dates. How would you feel about buying some ad space on our show's website?"

As it turned out, Mr. Patel didn't want to run an ad, but he so enjoyed the whole idea of the show that he offered to let us shoot one of our dates at his restaurant with complimentary meals and everything.

Since that at least reduced production costs for a future date, I left with his business card and a bounce in my step. The rest of the evening went much the same. I picked up two more sponsorship offers and a couple of tentative commitments from restaurant owners who wanted to check out our site before advertising. I even got a date out of one conversation—if I had wanted it, which I didn't. A couple of guys running the Bad Boys of Barbecue booth wanted to know if I was part of the sponsorship package. Uh, no.

Mikey did all of Anna's check-ins at Nick's request because he said Mikey would make him laugh otherwise. According to Mikey, Anna was having a great time. Nick's opinion of it boiled down to his opinion of his other dates. "She's a cool girl."

By the time they'd spent two hours eating their way down Main Street, I had a feeling Mr. Patel had gotten it right: I couldn't see a love match. Another hour of filming them on the sand proved it to me. They talked and laughed, but it was with the ease of friends, not like two people attracted to each other. I yawned as the sun set, and I made a mental note to grab an apple on my way home; Matt had read that they were as effective at boosting your energy as a cup of coffee.

I called Nick over while Anna examined some hand-beaded bracelets one of the street merchants was peddling. "I'll film your good-bye, and then I'll go home to edit. You ready?"

He glanced at Anna, who smiled into Mikey's camera as she modeled a bracelet.

"Is it cool with you if Mikey films the rest and then e-mails you the file in a while?" Nick asked. "Do you have other stuff you can start first, or will that mess you up?"

His request caught me off guard. Maybe I'd been wrong about their chemistry. But I yawned again and knew this was one of those moments where I had to give up some control to keep my sanity, so I nodded. "I'll be all right for a couple of hours. Let's do your final check-ins, and I'll get out of your hair."

"More like you'll get me out of yours," he said, smiling. "Speaking of, it looks great. Your hair," he clarified. "I don't know if I told you that or not, but the curly thing is pretty cool."

He reached out and tugged lightly on a strand. The slight wave in my hair only translated to loose beach waves when I played it up, so it's not like the curl did a cute spring back thing. In fact, it stayed wrapped around his finger for a second or three before I pulled away, aware that Anna could look over and take exception to the innocent gesture.

"Thanks," I said. "The closer I live to the ocean, the less I bother fighting my hair."

"Don't fight it at all," he suggested. "It works for you."

"I'll take that under advisement," I said, since saying thank you again felt stupid. Then I felt stupid anyway. I wondered if I should pay him a return compliment about his hair; I could give him a million and do it honestly. Right then, I liked the way the sun lightened the ends of it so the rich brown strands looked shot through with gold. Instead, I tucked the strand of hair he'd touched behind my ear and held up my camera. "Final check-ins?"

"Sure."

I called over to Mikey, who looked up and nodded when I explained the plan. He moved off toward one of the mural-painted alleys with Anna to shoot her confessional, and as they disappeared from sight, I led Nick toward a brick-sided building. "You'll have Mikey do the end-of-date wrap-up?" I asked him.

"Yeah. I'll punch him if he makes me laugh."

"Whatever works. Thank you again for doing this. I know it's not the most normal situation in the world and that you're giving up a ton of time. But for what it's worth, I think you've got a great shot of finding someone if you want to."

"Hey," he said, drawing me into a hug. "Quit apologizing. I started this as a favor, but it's something else now."

I loved hugs, so I stayed where I was for a minute, enjoying the smell of spray starch and salt air on his plaid shirt. "What is it now?" I asked.

"A lot of things," he said.

"Like?" I asked, stepping back and feeling the brisk night air like a slap. I wanted to crawl right back into his hug. For warmth. Oh man.

The second his arms had closed around me, I had traveled back three years in time to the perfect part of our relationship before all the trouble had started. I wanted to stay there, and that's why I'd stepped away.

"Go get some more quality time with Anna," I said. "She's a cool girl."

"She is, but I bet she's cool enough not to mind if I walk you to your car."

"Uh, no?" Why would he take time from his date to do that?

"I'll worry if I don't."

Right. "Okay, then. Thanks."

We stepped back out into the flow of people on Main Street and headed toward Pecan. "Who had the best food tonight, do you think?" he asked.

I considered the options for a moment. "That Peruvian place."

He nodded. "Yeah, reminds me of my mission." He fell quiet for a minute. "Seems like you liked the barbecue place pretty well."

"The Bad Boys of Barbecue?" I snorted, thinking about the cocky grill jockeys who'd tried to talk me into going out with one of them. "They talk big for serving average food."

Nick nodded. "Also, worst name ever."

"Yeah."

"But you seemed like you enjoyed yourself even with the average food."

I stopped and moved toward the street to get out of the other pedestrians' way. "You're not the only actor around here," I said. "Check this out." I stuck my hip out and ran my hand through my hair, pulling it away from my face while I shook my head slightly to give the waves a soft bounce. I flashed him a killer smile and then froze it and pointed at it. "See this?" I asked, my lips barely moving. "This is the smile that says, 'You want to do business with me.' I've practiced it a lot."

"From what I heard, it's the smile that makes strangers want to ask you out." He said this with a small smile of his own.

I dropped the smile and started up the sidewalk again. "You heard that, huh?"

"Yeah. They were working pretty hard to get a date with you."

"And I worked pretty hard to get them to buy advertising. Neither of us got what we wanted, but I came out slightly further ahead."

"Sounds like you scored several dinner locations for filming in the next few weeks."

"Yep."

He bumped me with his elbow, which jutted out a bit since he'd been walking with his hands shoved in the pockets of his khaki shorts. "You're really good at that," he said. "I understand why Molly wanted to free you up to do more of that kind of thing."

"Thanks," I said, warmed by the praise. People didn't always realize that it took way more than a good speech to get people to buy something like advertising. So much of building a client base rested in building client relationships, and that came down to the ability to read people. Which was why the last few minutes with Nick had me on high alert. I'd been dating pretty steadily since I turned sixteen, and I'd learned how to read signals fast—signals like the ones I'd swear Nick had been sending since we did his check-in.

But what to do about it? I knew him too well to think it was just my imagination, and myself too well to think it was a good idea to ignore it.

"Nick?"

"Yeah?"

"What is this?"

"What is what?"

"What have the last few minutes been?"

He didn't answer, and I shot a glance at him to see his brow furrowed as if he were puzzling out my question. "I give up?" he said, sounding unsure.

"You know what I'm talking about. The long extra-squeezy hug, the walking me to the car, the excessive interest in who's asking me out." I had to smack him on the arm because he started laughing when I said "extra-squeezy." "I'm being serious," I said. "What's going on?"

He shrugged and kept walking. "I'm not sure what you're getting at. What do you think is going on?"

"You watch me." I stopped. "I see you do it. I feel you do it."

"I do watch you."

I relaxed now that he wasn't denying it or trying to act like I was imagining things.

"But I watch everyone. And I hug everyone. Don't you remember complaining about that back in the day?"

I did, yes. And it embarrassed me to remember my stupid whining about it. "I was pretty lame," I said. "Can we forget that happened?"

"No," he said. "It's filed away where I keep all the stuff I draw on for creating a character."

I rolled my eyes. "I guess as long as my emotional immaturity is good for something . . ."

"You weren't and aren't emotionally immature. Where are you parked again?"

"Pecan."

He started walking. "But I'm sorry if I'm being confusing. I'm not trying to send mixed messages or whatever."

"Don't worry about it," I said. "I should have had this conversation with you last week so it would have been out of the way. But I'll say it now in case my begging you to take this gig didn't make it obvious enough: I have no lingering feelings about our relationship, and it's not weird for me that you're dating all these girls." Ha.

"Cool." He smiled. "Can I ask a favor now?"

"Shoot."

"I've got Mikey here, and my other friend Ethan will drop in to film from time-to-time. But I feel disconnected from everything, being down here and away from my house and my routines. And it's even weirder than when I'm filming for something because this is a different kind of exhausting. I'm thinking that since we're both over our past, I could definitely use another friend in the mix to keep me grounded right now. You want to take the job?"

"What are the requirements? Am I going to say yes and then find out I'm responsible for running you hot cocoa on demand or something?"

He laughed at my teasing tone. "Requirements include what you do already: talking me off the ledge when this starts making me crazy. And being my sounding board so I can tell the truth about these girls sometimes but know that it's never going to become public knowledge, okay? And I'll do the same for you."

"Sign me up."

"You're hired." He offered me an official handshake, which I returned with a laugh.

At Pecan, I hooked a left and pointed. "I'm right there. You can go rescue Anna from awkwardly staring into the camera and trying to think of things to say."

"I'm sure they're fine. Can I hug you again now that I know we're both cool and no one is going to take this the wrong way?"

Like I would refuse an offer like that.

Chapter 9

Sunday dinner rolled around, and my apartment swam in estrogen and the smell of roasted red peppers. Each of us invited someone every Sunday, but then we also had a regular group of friends who invited themselves and showed up with something savory in hand, so it wasn't like we ever told them no. Tonight we had thirteen girls in the house, including one very guarded-looking Merry. I quit worrying about her the second Lily plopped down beside her on the sofa. Lily could make anyone feel at ease.

"Seriously? No show tomorrow?" one of Autumn's friends said.

"Seriously. I had a brain freeze and didn't think through the planning," I said. "We didn't do one last Sunday either, remember? I should have figured out some Sunday-friendly date or something, but I didn't. So no date will post tomorrow."

"That makes me nervous." Molly said. "We dipped big time last Monday when we didn't put anything up. I hope we don't lose momentum."

"All I know is that time is *dragging*," Mandy, a cute blonde and also a future bachelorette, said. "I was kind of *whatever* about this whole thing until I saw Nick on the first episode. Now I'm dying until it's my turn, and I have to wait ten more days. He's totally going to fall in love with someone before that."

"Maybe not," Molly said, her tone thoughtful. "Maybe we can make the magic happen right now. You feeling cute?"

"I'm terminally cute," Mandy said with a sigh. "I couldn't be anything but cute if I tried."

"That's bad?" Autumn asked.

"Sure. Because you pat cute on the head. You don't fall asleep and dream about cute." She stuck her bottom lip out in a pout.

Molly laughed. "I actually understand that. But yep, you're cute. Totally doomed, sister. The question is, do you feel cute enough to go out with Nick?"

"Excuse me," I said, waving my hand in front of Molly's face. "I don't mean to interrupt your psychotic break, but . . . what the what?"

"I know it's a long shot, but I think we need something to post tomorrow." She waved her hand to encompass everyone sprawled on the sectional. "We've got a room full of girls who can help figure out a cool, Sabbath-approved date."

"I don't even know if Nick is around," I said. "He usually does Sunday dinner with his family. I didn't see him at church, so he probably went back to Malibu."

Turned out he'd moved up there from Santa Monica the year before.

"Text him and see. If he's up for it, I'll film it. Will you do it, Mandy?"

Before she could answer, Merry piped up. "If she won't, I'll go again. It would be nice to do something not in Spandex."

I'd been wondering how she would take all this talk about the guy she'd been out with two nights before. If the small tremor at the corner of her mouth was any indication, she was taking it with a pretty good sense of humor. Then again, I knew what to look for and the other girls didn't, so her declaration launched an awkward pause grenade into the chatter. It lasted until she burst out laughing.

"I'm kidding, guys. Good luck to whoever gets him. He seems great, but we're not a good fit."

More laughter, the relieved kind, met this admission. Ever since she'd walked in, I'd watched the other girls treat her politely, but no one had pressed her about the date the way they had Chelsey. Autumn jumped in. "So give us the dirt, yeah?"

"Wait," Molly said. "Dirt in a minute. Date right now. Seriously, Mandy, are you up for it?"

"But I'm not dressed right," she said. "And I would have done my hair differently."

"I'll glam you up," Lainie Jensen said. "If the flip-flop girls let me play with their make-up and stuff." The ward knew our place informally as "the flip-flop hut."

Since Lainie was a highly sought-after hairstylist and make-up artist, Mandy perked right up.

"Worth it just for that," she said.

"Whatever you guys need," Lily said.

"Me too," Autumn said.

"Lou?" Molly asked, her eyebrow arched with a distinct do-not-defy-me curve.

"How do you do that with your eyebrows?" I asked.

"Pure attitude and a fantastic waxer at my salon," she said. "This is all on you now. Should we make it happen?"

I pulled out my phone. "Let me text him." I started to tap out a message and then stopped. "What would I even be telling him he'd be doing on this date?"

"Leave it to us," she said. "This brain trust can figure something out by the time he gets here."

"*If* it happens," I said, finishing my text to Nick. *Are you in HB today?*

He answered a few moments later. *Yes. What's up?*

"He's here," I said. A chorus of squeals rose from the peanut gallery. "I didn't ask him about the date yet. Don't get all excited." I tried to think of the easiest way to explain our idea and then realized I had no idea what our idea was. *Up for a date?*

Seriously?

Yes. It'll be fun. Could you be at my house in an hour?

A long pause followed, and the girls all sat waiting with expressions ranging from amusement to excitement painted on their faces. My phone chirped, and Mandy flinched.

How should I dress?

I looked up at the expectant faces. "He wants to know how he should dress."

Cheers erupted.

"Let's go," Autumn said. She hopped up and sped down the hallway, Mandy and Lainie right behind her.

Molly snapped her fingers to break up the remaining girls' babbling. "What are we doing for a date?"

"Dinner on our patio!"

That came from Cambry, our neighbor across the hall. White fairy lights covered their backyard fence, and their outdoor café table made a great hangout spot. "We'll pull the extra chairs, throw out a tablecloth, and serve up two plates full of stuff from this potluck."

"Do you mind taking care of that?" I asked.

"On it," she said, climbing to her feet with her roommate Tessa right behind her. "See you in an hour."

I texted Nick with my address and a warning. *Dress casual. Come hungry and text me after you park.* He didn't need to walk into a condo full of gawking girls. He might get a post-traumatic stress disorder flashback to his sitcom days when he couldn't go anywhere publicly without security due to obsessive teenage fans. Poor Nick and his first-world problems.

"I'll get the food ready," Lily said, heading into the kitchen. I heard a cabinet open and the cheerful sound of clinking dishes as she rummaged through them.

Six sets of eyes still watched me, or my phone, expectantly. "Girls? Plan a date. You've got fifty minutes." I pointed at Molly. "And you and I have to figure out shots and stuff."

"I'll shoot it," she said. "You need a night off."

"Great idea, but you still need someone on the boom mic."

"I'll do it!" Lily said, poking her head out. "Autumn has some meeting tonight, but I'm free."

"There you go," Molly said. "Stay home and recharge."

I walked into the kitchen to help Lily get the food together. She looked slightly alarmed to see me but moved on to sort through the silverware drawer for matching utensils.

"You know it's killing me to stay out of this, right?" I called to Molly.

"Too bad. You can't burnout, or I'm doomed at the café forever, so leave this to me and enjoy dinner with the rest of the girls."

I shrugged. "I'll take a break, but I'm definitely checking this out before it goes up on the site."

"Duh. And breathe," she said. "You have no idea when you'll get a break like this again between now and the end of this mess—I mean, great social experiment."

"Funny," I said. "I'm going to short-sheet your bed now."

"Sweet. I'm going to check in on Cambry and Tessa."

Lily had moved on to choosing glasses. I examined the place settings she'd picked out. The simple white plates were fine, but she'd gone with the more ornate utensils of the two sets of silverware in our drawers. The curlicues on the handles made the plates seem even plainer by comparison. I swept the pieces off of the counter and swapped them for the cleaner modern design of the other silverware pattern.

"What are you doing?" Lily asked.

"Don't worry about it," I said with a smile. "I love what you're pulling together here. I'm tweaking it a little, that's all."

Lily put the glasses she held back in the cabinet. "Why don't you go ahead and choose these too?"

"Sure," I said.

She sighed and left to join the girls in the living room. I stared after her for a moment. She wasn't mad, exactly. But what was that all about?

I finished off the place settings with a clean set of cloth napkins and our chrome salt-and-pepper shakers before moving on to fill both plates and bowls with selections from our potluck. By the time Nick texted that he had parked, I had transported the whole meal across the hall and the girls had an "activity kit" all assembled.

"I can't believe you let them plan the whole thing," Molly said.

"Why wouldn't I? They're the viewing public. Let them decide what kind of date they want to see."

Which apt do I want? Nick texted.

Head to 25, I said. *Those are my neighbors. Date starts there.*

We're not meeting at your house? he asked.

Nope. Believe me, I texted with a quick glance at the nine girls all jockeying for premium spy position around the two windows facing the neighbors' place. *I'm doing you a favor.*

Ten seconds after I sat down, a knock sounded. Autumn jumped to get it.

"Whoa," she said after opening it.

"Is Lou here?"

Nick.

I hurried to the door. Molly stood behind him, looking confused. "He didn't know we were filming."

"Oh. Uh, what did you think we were doing?"

He looked over his shoulder at Molly and back to me, and a faint flush washed over his cheeks. "Nothing. I misunderstood."

"Nick . . ." I gestured Molly into the condo then stepped out and closed the door behind me so no one could overhear us. "Did you think I meant a date with me?"

"I mean, yeah. That's why I was confused."

"You agreed to a date, thinking I meant me?" I repeated, trying to process it. "But . . ."

"Awkward," he said. "I know." He shoved his hands into his pockets and rocked back slightly. "I thought I was going to have to come over here and have another define-the-relationship talk with you about being friends. Turns out my ego was just raging again, that's all. Glad I'm off the hook for an uncomfortable conversation. Who's my date tonight?"

"Mandy. She's cool. We're moving her up in the rotation. Molly's going to film, and I'm taking a break for the night. And don't worry about a blog post. I'll do one and make sure you're cool with it before sticking it up." It was hard to speak normally when embarrassment that he'd thought I wanted to date him threatened to choke me. He must have spent the whole drive over here thinking I was still hung up on him and pitying me for reading his signals so wrong.

"You don't need do the blog post, okay?"

"It's no big deal, I promise," I said. I could almost predict what Nick would say before he said it. "It won't take me that long, and I'll e-mail it to you to check before I post it. I don't mind doing it since I know you were planning on a day off."

"It's not that." He hesitated like he was trying to figure out what to say. "Sorry. I'm not trying to make a big deal out of this. It's just that because of my job, other people put words in my mouth all the time. Whenever and wherever I can use my own words, I'd rather do that. I know you're trying to help, but I'll feel better if I say it my own way."

"Sure," I said, taken aback. "I didn't mean to offend you."

"You didn't," he said, smiling. "But you really think you could sound like me?"

"Yep. Watch, I'll do a sample blog post without even watching your date, you write yours up, and we'll compare notes."

"You're on," he said.

"No, you're on. Go be the city's most eligible bachelor."

"Bye," he said, but then he stood there. "It's weird that you're not going to be on this date."

"A minute ago it was weird that I *was* going to be on the date," I said, hoping the teasing would restore our normal balance. "You should be glad to be rid of me. Enjoy the breathing room."

"All right." He pulled me into a quick hug and then turned toward Cambry and Tessa's door. I walked back into my condo and set off an immediate flurry of questions and comments from my friends.

"Holy smokes, he's hotter in person!"

"I should have tied up Mandy and taken her place."

"Lou! I hate you for not making me do this."

I ignored them. The chatter got on my nerves, but I didn't want anyone reading anything into my annoyance. "Can we have our own dinner now?"

"Amen," Merry said. Her tone of long-suffering made me smile.

No one moved from the window.

"He knocked!"

"She answered!"

"He gave her a hello hug!"

That bit of date narration made my stomach clench. So, so stupid. Me, I mean. For caring. Especially since he'd made it clear that it was a relief not to be going out with me tonight.

"She sees us!"

"Guys. Hush," Autumn said. "They'll hear us and take it inside, where we can't spy anymore."

"Too late," someone groaned.

"Dinnertime," Tessa called, and a wave of girls converged on the table.

I scooped up extra mashed potatoes. I had a strong need for comfort carbs.

* * *

"'Mandy is a fun girl with a great personality,'" I read out loud to Nick over the phone from his blog post.

"'She's a great girl with an attractive personality,'" he read in reply from mine. "Fine, I get it. I'll fine-tune it and have it to you by the morning."

"Great," I said. "Did you have fun tonight?"

"Yeah," he said. "Generic descriptions aside, she's cool. Fun. And a good sport."

I brushed aside the jealous pang that sparked in my stomach. "Thanks for doing this so last minute. I'd promise not to drop anymore changes like that in your lap, but I'm not sure I'd keep it. It's one of the things that frustrates me about not being in charge of the whole universe."

He snorted. "I'm staying loose, Lou. When someone tells you to climb on their crazy ride, you can't be surprised when it's actually crazy."

"Tomorrow should be calmer," I said. "Low tide is around lunch, so you're going over to the Corona Del Mar tide pools, and you'll have a picnic on the beach."

Silence greeted that.

"Nick? You don't like that idea?"

He sighed. "How old and lame will I sound if I complain about sand in my food?"

"How cool and romantic will you look if you do the beach picnic?" I countered. "Remember, this is about building your image as the perfect leading man. Keep your career in mind, and smile when you crunch down on the grit."

"Right. Image, grit, smile."

"And I'll make the lunch," I said. "Don't sweat it."

"I'll do it. I've taken up cooking in the last couple of years. Who's my date?"

"Jenny J," I said. "She's blonde. You'll meet Jenny D later. She's a brunette."

"Blonde Jenny," he said. "See you at the tide pools tomorrow."

"No, you'll see Mikey at the pools tomorrow. He's filming."

"Wait," he said before I hung up. "Why are you in such a hurry to go?"

"I'm not," I said. But I was. I didn't want to talk about the bachelorettes or surfing, our regular subjects. I mean, surf talk would have been okay, but I wasn't in the mood to talk about his dates.

"Good, because I want to ask your opinion on something."

I stifled a yawn. "Blue. Wear blue. You always look good in it."

"Thank you, but that's not what I was going to ask."

I straightened. No girls, no surfing, and no tell-me-what-to-wear conversations? We'd never covered anything else in our post-date debriefs. "Then what were you going to ask?"

"It's about a project I'm thinking of taking on."

"A new role?"

"Kind of. Is it possible to portray contemporary Mormonism in film without the Mormon being a punch line?"

I leaned back in my chair and ran through my mental file of Mormon references and characters. "Can it be done? Yes. But I've never seen it. We're always the punch line, which I guess is better than being shown as religious zealots."

"Yeah, I think we're past that stereotype now. But I'm trying to figure out if there's a way to play a Mormon on screen in a way that shows us as real, everyday people."

"I don't know, Nick. Maybe we don't want to be shown that way. I mean, the point isn't to blend in. Define *real* and *everyday*."

"I don't know if I can. It's like what you're doing with the show, giving people a look into the reality of Mormon courtship." He laughed. "I use *real* loosely. But I've been thinking you're on to something, pulling back the curtain on something that isn't that much of a mystery when you look at it closely. Then again, pop culture isn't that interested in nuance. And maybe our normal is so odd to everyone else that we can only ever be the punch line, anyway."

"Is someone offering you a Mormon role? I can see the ad campaign now: I don't just play one on TV . . ."

A smile warmed his voice. "It's just something I'm considering."

"Sorry. I don't think I helped much."

"Of course you did. You always do," he said. "I'll let you go now."

We hung up, and I stared at the phone for a moment, wondering if his words or the battery made it feel so warm in my hand. I set it down and turned to Molly. "You ready to overview tonight for me?"

"Sure," she said. "No love connection, so it'll be harder to edit, but not too bad."

"No connection on which side?" I hated how much the answer mattered. I hope she'd seen what Nick reported: an easy rapport and nothing more.

"Either, I think. Mandy was nervous, and that seems to keep Nick on edge. Or as on edge as he gets. You know what I mean?"

Yeah, I did. His baseline was always pretty laid back, but he showed more relaxation with some dates than others, especially with the ones who showed an ease with themselves.

"Go away and let me work," she said. "Love you though."

"Can't go away. I've got comments to read. But if I fall asleep on my keyboard, wake me up to see the final cut, will you?"

She waved a hand at me that might have meant agreement. It for sure meant she was in a groove, her earbuds in while she listened for the right song to put with the video. An hour later, I finished wading through the day's comments, but Molly hadn't finished the editing. I snoozed on the sofa, and she shook me awake near midnight. "I got it. Come watch it and then go to sleep in a real bed."

I sat down in front of her screen and pressed play. The first slate read "Nick + Mandy's Super Sunday." The music came up, and I settled into the chair to watch their date.

Something about seeing it this way, stripped of my own perceptions based on eyewitness evidence, made me see Nick differently. Even though he took the same diplomatic approach he had with all of his dates, the tiny changes in his expression communicated so much more to me than I'd seen when I filmed and edited. Maybe it was because I wasn't projecting my own interpretations from having been there myself. Whatever the reason, sitting here and watching his check-in in the much-tighter camera shot Molly used made the one-on-one feel more like a one-on-one with the viewer. Me.

I saw almost imperceptible hesitations, split-second pauses, flashes of concern before he answered a question that spoke far greater volumes than his words did. It added up to a picture of a guy who was guarded with his feelings, not to protect himself but because he wanted to be as kind as possible to Mandy.

My heart fluttered.

This wasn't good.

No wonder the e-mails piled up in a digital logjam for him; if every girl watching saw and sensed the same things I did, then we'd go viral in a matter of days. No one could resist this sweetness in his character, and the more people who posted and tweeted about it, the faster others would pick up on what a cool guy he was. It would be easier to sell advertising, and every time our viewership jumped, I could charge more for the ads. Even better, each ad was an opportunity to show the advertiser what Hot Iron could do graphically and conceptually. If we were lucky and very, very good, we could start cashing regular checks as soon as our page hits reached the tipping point that took us from a local sensation to bona fide viral smash. And we were close. I could feel it.

But . . . crud. I scrubbed my hands over my face. The first guy I was interested in since Nick was Nick. And he'd made it clear he was now open to love, but with whom? He hadn't given me a name in any of our conversations about his dates. The lame part of me that imagined him flinging himself at my feet and confessing that he was sorry he hadn't recognized a good thing when he had it had been silenced by his discomfort when he'd thought I was his date tonight.

I paused the playback. How dumb would I be to go down a road I knew would dead end?

So dumb.

He'd obviously already figured out something that I still needed to get through my head. Maybe Nick had matured since we broke up. Maybe I had too. But we were pretty much the same people at our core, and those two people did not work in a relationship. I pushed the what-ifs aside and pressed play again. Molly had edited him so well that anyone who hadn't fallen for him yet would be helpless before this perfect digital specimen of a man. I'd limit my enjoyment of him to this and let the rest go.

Chapter 10

Leave it to Nick to take himself to the next level without any help from me. I climbed out of bed before eight, determined to visit businesses and follow up on several new contacts. I didn't want just date sponsorships. I wanted advertising clients. The kind that paid.

Nick's blog post waited for me in my e-mail. His first line captured me, and the rest of it wouldn't let me go.

"Instant magic. I think that's what I want when I go on a date. I think it's what anybody wants. I think it's what keeps some of us getting out there even when the constant disappointment threatens to grind us down."

Instant magic? I'd seen for myself that he hadn't found it with Mandy. Where was he going with this?

"A magic show is an illusion. It's not like the magician is really sawing anyone in half. It's a trick. So does that mean that I or anyone else should get cynical about finding magic in dating?

"No. Not cynical. But we need to get real, to define what that magic really is. I want to believe that lightning can strike, that it can hit someone—two someones—so hard and fast that the air sizzles. I've had that before, and I worry that it won't strike twice. But I have to believe I'm wrong, because if not, there isn't a point in me trying. There's no point to ever going on another date, ever opening up to another girl, ever believing that the magic other people find can find me.

"But I also know that my parents' marriage of twenty-eight years wasn't built on magic tricks and daily fireworks explosions. It was built on simple principles that are hard to practice. But they practice them, and that's why after three decades, it looks like magic.

"I hear there are complaints that I don't say how I'm really feeling about every girl I date. We're in a partnership, you and I. You watch to be entertained, and part of that entertainment is getting the inside scoop on how I and these awesome girls really feel about our dates. But I won't sit and tell you every single thing I think if it might hurt someone's feelings. You'll hear pretty much the positives of each date. If I can be straightforward without hurting or embarrassing anyone, then I will be.

"Here's the thing. Even though we all know the magician is somehow tricking us, they still amaze and delight us, but I'm not the magician here. I'm looking for the magic the same as you are, but I want the real kind. So be patient.

"If you want my take on last night's date, here it is: Mandy is awesome. Our interests are too different for us to be a long-term fit. She has an incredible ability to stay grounded in reality, and while she keeps it really fun, she keeps her practical lenses on. I admire that. But I'm one of those artistic types who wanders down philosophical trails and worries about the abstract, and the fact is, over time, I would drive Mandy crazy. I wouldn't punish her with a second date, but I doubt I'll get the chance. Some very smart guys out there watching right now are going to be blowing up her phone, and maybe . . . magic will happen."

Holy cow. If every unattached girl out there watching hadn't already fallen in love with him, he'd doomed them to it now.

I dug this new, open Nick so much. So, so much. Insanely much. My what-ifs returned to taunt me.

Things always looked bleak when you tried to figure them out in the middle of the night. What if I was wrong? What if we had both changed enough to make a do-over work? Maybe he only needed a tiny nudge to move me out of the friend zone.

Time to talk to Molly.

"I come with gifts of juice," I said, sticking my head through her door and waving her carton of OJ in front of me.

"Enter, peasant."

I plopped down on the end of her bed and folded my legs. "My brain is wound tight with a bright, new, shiny idea right now."

"Some good ideas come out of your brain pan. Let's hear it."

"Remember how you were asking me if I was over Nick? And I said yes? And you looked at me like I was a big fat liar?"

She scooted up against the headboard and wrapped her arms around a pillow. "Yep."

"I'm a big fat liar."

No response.

"Should I see if it's a mutual thing? I've probably lost my stinkin' mind, but I think . . ."

"You think what?" she asked, her voice sharp.

"I think maybe he likes me too. Or that he could."

"Why do you think that?"

"I don't know." *He changed his hair for me; he calls me all the time; he touches me constantly when we're together.* "Woman's intuition. Let's call it that. So what do you think I should do?"

"Not a dang thing. It didn't work three years ago; why would it work now?"

Her curt answer surprised me. I thought she'd suffocate me in a cloud of smug over being right, high-five me, and then help me figure out which bachelorette I should be replacing to take a shot with Nick. "It's different now because he's different," I said. "The things about him that kept us from progressing before are changed, I think. I want to find out for sure."

She set aside her pillow and leaned forward, concern etching a crease in her brow. "News flash: you're half of the equation. And a changed him plus an unchanged you does not equal success."

I winced.

"I'm sorry," she said. "But it's true. You're pretty wonderful, but you being the exact same you as you were with him before only sets you guys up to fall into the same traps."

"You and I have only been friends for two years. How do you know if I've changed or not?"

"Have you?" she demanded. "Have the hang-ups you brought into your relationship with him magically disappeared? You guys already crashed and burned once. You really want to take twenty-one other girls' chances with you this time? You jumping into this mix only makes everything confusing. Nick will seriously consider the idea, and by the time he's figured out you guys still won't work, he'll have lost his chance with several great possibilities. So don't do it."

I stared at her quilt, unwilling to meet her eyes because I didn't know whether confusion or anger or hurt would win out in my expression.

She pressed her point. "To be even more blunt, now that this is actually going viral, I'm definitely scared of putting that paycheck at risk. This has been a hard week. There are going to be more hard weeks ahead while we film. I don't want to waste it all because you want to gamble."

She crawled over to me and sat with her knees touching mine before putting her arms around me in a hug. "I love that you're so spontaneous, and I love that you're willing to take risks, but I think this is too big of a risk for infatuation."

"What if it's not infatuation? What if it's real?" I mumbled into her shoulder.

"Then it has to be real on both sides. If it's meant to be, he'll be a single guy in a month from now."

I wiggled out of her hug. "Fine. But if I never get married because I was supposed to be with Nick all along, it's your fault."

"I accept that. Now go do business-y things and work some magic."

I groaned. "Don't say magic."

"Huh? Why not?"

"Read Nick's blog post for the morning. And remember that you're the one telling me to leave him alone." I walked into my room and headed straight to the closet. I pulled out something work appropriate but cute. I'd head out to more businesses, definitely.

But first, I needed to see the best free therapist I knew.

* * *

An hour later, I found Mom's behind sticking out of a hydrangea bush in my parents' large backyard. The space was mostly concrete hardscape that ended at the harbor, where their small electric boat bobbed in its dock slip. Flowerbeds surrounded the perimeter inside their low iron fence, and the profusion of blossoms had my mother's touch all over them. No gardeners for her in their fancy harbor neighborhood. Since Matt and I were out of the house, my parents had "downsized" to this place almost nine months ago when they got back from their mission, but it sure seemed like they were doing as much puttering as they had at their big place while they whipped this new one into shape.

Then again, they seemed perfectly content to do it. Mom especially loved a project.

"Mom? That's you, right?"

She jumped and backed out of the bush. "Did the hot pink garden clogs give me away?" She climbed to her feet and pulled me in for a hug. A long hug. That kept going. And going.

After a full minute, I patted her back. "This is because I don't come over enough, huh?"

"You bet," she said, still squeezing. "Don't know when I'll get to do this again."

I squeezed her back and wiggled away. "I was just here."

"Two weeks ago," she said, peering at me over the top of her sunglasses. "That's pitiful. Let me clean up, and then you sit and tell me how your web series is *really* going."

I trailed after her into the kitchen, where she rinsed the dirt from her fingernails.

"It's going great," I said.

She patted her hands dry. "Really?"

"Don't you watch it?" I asked. "How does it look like it's going?"

"Oh, it's wonderfully done, honey. Very entertaining. But it's Nick."

"So?"

"Your Nick," she said. "Tell me what I'm not seeing in your five-minute videos." She pulled out a pitcher of lemonade and two glasses and led me back outside to sit in the sun.

"We're getting a ton of traffic. More than I even hoped for at this point, and I think when today's episode goes live, it's going to explode."

"Ooh, was it a scandalous date last night?" she asked, her face eager.

"Mom!" I laughed at her mischievous expression. "No scandal. But Nick's blog post will get some people talking, I think."

"That surprises me. He hasn't been letting on to much."

"I know. That's why this one is different. He pulls back the curtain on his feelings way more this time."

She set her drink down on the small glass-topped table between us and leaned forward. "Which brings us back to how you feel about him doing all of this."

I sighed. I'd avoided coming over for the last week because I didn't want to have this conversation. I'd shown up this morning specifically because I did want it now. That didn't mean I looked forward to the truth telling Mom would do, no matter how lovingly she delivered it. But I needed it. "How come I'm not married?"

Her eyebrows shot up. She opened her mouth to say something but closed it again and leaned back in her chair, looking out over the harbor instead. Her sudden forehead wrinkles meant she was considering the question carefully.

"You don't have to sugarcoat, Mom. Just tell me."

"You're too picky," she said.

"But I date a lot. I'm always hopeful. I go out with the best of intentions. It's not like I think I'm too good for anybody."

One of her eyebrows crept up again.

"You think I think I'm too good for people?" I asked, stung in spite of myself.

"No. I wouldn't put it that way," she said, reaching over the table to take my hand. "But sometimes you think they're not good enough for you."

I let that sit for a moment, and she squeezed my hand. Then I said, "I don't think I'm better than anybody. But I also don't think I should marry someone just because I'm twenty-four now. I want to be with a guy who has his life in order. And—whoa."

"What?" she asked, startled.

"I can't believe this," I said, grabbing my hand back so I had both of them free to rub over my face. "I haven't been getting nearly enough sleep this week."

"I'm confused, sweetie."

"Sorry." I pushed myself up and walked down to the gate. Mom stayed right behind me, even when I took the ramp down to the short dock and sat down at the end of it. A spotted stingray glided past, and I wished I could slip into the water with it and outswim my stress.

Mom's hand drifted up to rub gentle circles on my back. "Are you going to throw yourself in? Because I'll only fish you out again, so you'll need to choose a different dramatic gesture."

I laughed. "No. I might need to stick my head in the water for a minute to clear it, but you don't have to go all *Baywatch* on me today."

"Good. Talk to me, Lou."

"Last night, I thought I had an epiphany. I was watching the playback from Nick's date, and since I didn't actually film it, I had fresh eyes, right? So things have been feeling kind of sparkish between us for a few days, and then I thought I was seeing all these nuances in his expression. And I'm thinking, 'Man, out of all these girls, I'm the one who really gets him.'"

A small smile played on her lips. "Oh."

"Except I bet every single girl he's been out with this week thought the same thing. And the truth is, I know he and I have chemistry. Great chemistry. We've had it since the last time we dated. And he's gotten better at opening up about how he feels. Heck, I think he's better about feeling, period. He seems to connect with stuff more, not be kind of removed from it like he used to be."

"That all sounds encouraging considering your frustrations with him in the past," she said.

"Yeah. That's why I forgot something important in all of this."

"Which is?"

"I hate his job."

"Sweetie, I'm listening to you, but I am so confused right now. I keep saying that, I know, but I mean it more every time."

"So it goes like this: ex-boyfriend is back in my life by invitation. Ex-boyfriend and I are still attracted to each other. Ex-boyfriend has made personal changes over the last three years that make him even more attractive. I don't get enough sleep for a week and a half, and suddenly getting back together sounds like a great idea."

"But it's not because . . . why?"

"Because regardless of all his personal changes, he hasn't made any professional ones, and that's a problem." I hadn't realized how big of a problem until I'd said it out loud. It shocked me that I had so easily been sucked back into the Nick mystique, caught up in the heat I felt every time he got within six feet of me, tricked by the hope that some changes—an important one, even—meant that everything was all better.

But how changed could he be if the things that most defined him had stayed the same? Like his job. And the environment that it placed him in constantly.

I loathed the Hollywood scene. I'd loved it up until I'd lived in it during college, and *then* the loathing had started. As a freshman, I'd researched which ward I wanted to be in. I'd heard the stories about good little Mormons who came to LA for school or work and then fell off the radar forever. Despite it being way farther from USC, I picked the Santa Monica Third Ward because it had a reputation for being more active than the small USC student branch.

Two dozen other freshman started at the same time I did. By the end of the semester, only ten of us were still showing up to church, and less than that to institute. When I got called into the Relief Society presidency during my second semester, I took my first look at our rolls and saw exactly how high the inactivity rate had soared in our plastic corner of Zion.

Maybe the kids who came out to Hollywood always intended to drop off the Church radar. Maybe being in a culture that hated organized religion generally, and Mormons specifically after the Prop 8 fight from years before, made it hard for them to stick it out. Or maybe the difficulty of finding values-friendly roles did. Maybe if you played characters that behaved and thought and believed totally differently from you for long enough, it colored your perspective permanently. All I knew was that I saw the ranks thinning every single Sunday.

True, Nick hadn't fallen away yet. *Yet.* A very big three-letter word. He would always be hungry for that next role, always schmoozing for that audition or callback. And what happened when he wasn't a marketable actor anymore? Would he transition to theater and go on big national tours that took him away from home for weeks and months? And what if he didn't even have that option? I wanted to stay home with my kids. Maybe his trust fund would always allow us financial stability, but I couldn't imagine being married to someone who worked at such a family-unfriendly job or maybe didn't work at all because he had never developed a skill set to do anything besides act.

"What am I doing wrong, Mom? You told me to have high standards. I've had them my whole life, for everything. I thought living by those standards meant I would be blessed. That's the rule, right?"

She sighed and held out her hand for me to take it again. I did, comforted by her warm grip. "You expect a lot from other people, and you should. Your dad and I have always told you to hold out for a man who's worthy of you. And we've taught you that you're worth a lot. But you can't demand the same perfection from others that you expect from yourself."

"I'm getting tired of the word *perfection.*"

"That's a clue about what you need to pay attention to, then." She squeezed my hand. "When you say to someone, 'This is the standard I expect you to achieve,' sometimes it looks impossibly high."

"So then I should *lower* my standards?" I asked, loading the question with my frustration.

"Of course not. But it wouldn't be a bad idea to see if you can love people exactly as they are already."

"But . . ." I couldn't think of how to explain my objection. I didn't expect people to be perfect. But I expected a guy my age to be done with school. I expected him to have a testimony. I expected him to be doing what he was supposed to be doing. And we needed to have some kind of attraction to each other. "It's not like I expect Ryan Reynolds to appear on my doorstep, converted, shiny, and waving a temple recommend in his hand."

Mom laughed. "Even if he did, you'd reject him for being an actor."

I slumped down in my chair. "I chose the wrong example," I said, pretty much to my lap.

"I know what you meant." Another hand squeeze. "I love you. Pray it out. You'll get it right."

"I've been praying it out for years," I said. "That's how I knew Nick was wrong for me in the first place."

"Patience, Loulou-girl. Have more patience. This will all come together when it's meant to."

We sat in silence, and I soaked in the sound of the sea birds trying to pillage the neighbor's koi pond, the sunshine breaking through the morning inversion. It also broke my funk. If the clouds were burning off, it was later than I'd meant to stay, and I had business to go out and win.

* * *

I hustled into a quiet carrel on the third floor of Central Library, stoked to pull out my iPad and take advantage of the free Wi-Fi. Actually, I didn't hustle in. I floated in; two awesome phone calls in a row can create a cloud of happiness thick enough to ride. The first call was the manager of a new karaoke lounge opening downtown, confirming that the owner had greenlit some advertising on our blog. I had promised to bring in a ton of business by organizing a Mormon night on their typically slow Mondays. Since Autumn happened to be the FHE coordinator, I knew I could deliver on the promise while accepting the thanks of a grateful roommate for coming up with an activity idea. Classic win-win.

The second and even happier phone call went to Molly. Not only could I tell her we'd gotten an ad buy for a thousand bucks, but the Lizard's Lounge had expressed interest in retaining our services for future marketing consulting beyond the web show if they saw a positive response to their *TMB* ad. The manager dug the strategies I shared with him, and the thrill of victory flooded my veins.

When I logged into my e-mail, I whooped and a head shot up on the other side of the study desk, a pair of bloodshot eyes glaring at me over the top of the carrel while I blushed. "Sorry," I mouthed, not wanting to aggravate the annoyed woman opposite me with even a whisper.

Thirty-two comments awaiting approval. Thirty-two! And we'd been live for only ten minutes. Thirty-two comments would represent a fraction of our unique visitors in those ten minutes.

Viral.

We are viral! I texted Molly. *32! No! 35! 36! Aaaaah!!!!*

I blew through the approvals as fast as I could. Few of them mentioned the video; almost all of them focused on Nick's blog post, his heartfelt cry for what he wanted. It had already been shared nearly two dozen times on Facebook. My phone vibrated in my hand with a text from Autumn.

Loved it! Love him! Make him be mine!!

Several more texts came in from friends over the next several minutes as I worked to clear the e-mails and get the comments up. Ashley texted. *Why did you break up with him again? B/c possibly it was as dumb as me breaking up with Matt last year. Love you, dummy.*

I winced. I didn't want to spend the emotional currency on analyzing that yet again.

I cleared all but two of the comments that came in. One wanted to sell me something. I guess. The characters were Asian, not English. The other one knocked Mandy. I flipped the cover closed on my iPad and shoved it back into my bag. Time to drop in on a string of spas in the area to see about drumming up some ad business there. Our blog attracted the perfect demographic for them.

When my car purred to life, it revved my determination up too. I'd spent hundreds of hours preparing for and then launching *The Mormon Bachelor* to do exactly what it was doing right now: getting the attention of people who wanted a creative approach to selling their products, services, and businesses. Molly and I had made a pie, and now people wanted a piece of it.

Well, I'd be offering the next piece of pie to Galina, a beautiful Slavic woman who had told me to come back after she'd had a chance to watch the show. Her spa offered a service I thought would make for a great date, a mud treatment that could translate into hilarious footage. Nick would go for it, I knew. His mom and sister used to drag him to the spa with them so often that he'd grown to like pedicures, although he'd sworn me to secrecy about that. If Galina agreed to advertise with us, I would offer to film a date there and show yet another novel idea to our viewers. I had the data now to prove that it would be a smart investment of her resources.

I pressed down on the accelerator, enjoying the quick surge of the engine. Talk about humming along nicely. The only potential hiccup in this whole thing was me, but as I'd thought through my conversation with Molly and my realization that Nick was still entrenched in the grind of the entertainment industry, I knew I wouldn't be the one getting in the way of my own success.

More importantly, if Nick truly wanted love out of this, I wouldn't be an unnecessary distraction. The giddiness of that old infatuation had almost derailed me, but I had myself straightened out now. I'd stand way off to the side while Nick tried to find love and then stick the whole thing online and land a slew of new accounts while everyone cheered on his fairy tale.

* * *

"New plan for tomorrow," I said to Molly an hour later.

"Are you hands-free?" she demanded.

"Yes, Bluetooth Nazi. Want to hear the plan?"

"Shoot."

"So, Nick and Macy are supposed to go to the indoor bounce house tomorrow night, right? And we picked that date because Macy's so spontaneous?"

"Yeah."

"Do you think she's spontaneous enough to play in the mud instead?"

"Macy will do anything if it's legal. Or illegal, if she knows she can't get caught."

"Cool. Tell her to dress dirty and meet us at Galina's."

"You want to rephrase that?"

"Yes, please. Tell her to dress in clothes she doesn't mind getting dirty and then meet us at Galina's."

A beat of silence followed. "Galina's?" Molly asked, the question rising on a note of hope.

"She totally wants to advertise with us, and she loves the idea of us filming a mud treatment. She can't wait, actually."

Molly whooped. "How many shifts can I skip with this account?"

"It should keep you out of the café for at least two weeks."

"Yes!"

We hung up, and I spent the afternoon moderating more comments and interpreting the analytics on the blog. I did pretty much anything that distracted me from thinking about Nick and Jenny J and their potentially romantic date at the tide pools. I didn't know her well, so I had no way to predict how this one would go. She'd sent in an application video and said she was from the YSA ward near Long Beach. She came across as fun, but she got the gig because Trentyn thought she was hot. I wondered how Nick would like her. Then I made myself not wonder and focused on the blog again.

At first, most of the IP addresses visiting our site were from California, specifically Orange County. Now we had visits coming from everywhere, but a large chunk of them were coming from Utah and Salt Lake counties. Huh. Time to Google businesses in the area for potential advertisers on *TMB*.

By late afternoon when Molly strolled in waving an SD card at me, I had cold-called several Utah businesses, from photographers to clothing boutiques, and had a couple of promising leads. Like Galina, they wanted time to review the site before making a decision, but I knew I'd given them a strong pitch. I could almost smell the dollars in my grasp, and they smelled like whatever the absence of stress smelled like. Maybe something distinctly unoatmeal and un-Top Ramen scented. Ramen smelled like poverty. College-broke poverty.

"How does it feel to know you don't have to stay up till midnight to get this one done?" she asked.

"How does it feel to know that I'm on the verge of getting you out of even more café shifts?"

She sat down across from me and smiled. "See? I knew freeing you up to do your sales voodoo would work."

"Do you really not mind having to do all the filming?" I asked.

"No way. It's fun." She hopped back up and headed to the fridge. "Check out what I bought myself after you said we got Galina's account." She pulled out a six-pack of Diet Coke with lime. "Living the high life, baby. It wasn't even on sale."

I grinned. "Try not to spend the money I haven't even given you yet all in one place. How did the tide pools go?"

"Good. Should be pretty easy to put together a video."

"Meaning what? Really good chemistry or none at all?"

"None. It'll be interesting to see how Nick squeezes a blog post out. You're mostly going to want to show action shots of them scrambling over the rocks because the picnic lunch was a long string of awkward pauses."

She held up a hand. "Instead of asking me a million more questions, why not watch it? I worked out a visual shorthand for you. Anything I think you'll want to include, I did a thumbs up in front of the lens. You can fast forward until you see one of those, and then you know to rewind and watch that scene."

My jaw dropped. "Genius. How did we not think of that before?"

"I don't know, but at least we've got a system down now."

"I don't even feel the need to procrastinate. It's almost too easy."

"Maybe, but it isn't automatic. You can't sell ad space for segments that don't air. Heeyah!" she said, miming a cracking whip. "And now I'm going to go take a nap."

"Cool, but are you good with working up a couple of layouts later for the new sidebar ads?"

"Yeah, boss."

I opened the video file on my computer and watched the date. Jenny J seemed nice enough, but she had some of the reserve I used to sense in Nick. Maybe this fascinated some guys who then took it as a challenge to chase her, but Nick reacted in kind. At first he tried to get her to open up with questions, but when I cued to the one-hour mark and stopped to listen to the awkward lunch conversation Molly mentioned, I could tell he'd made an emotional retreat at some point. It left them with only strained courtesy.

I backed up to his first check-in. I'd avoided it at first because Molly's penchant for shooting him in a tight close-up created an intimacy that made me twitchy. Now more than ever, I wanted to avoid that, so I fortified myself against the short interview by opening my bookkeeping program. Priorities. I had them, and paying back my debt to my brother definitely ranked ahead of indulging a stupid crush. Or so I repeated to myself a dozen times before pressing play.

I wondered how much worse off I would have been if I had tried to watch it without psyching myself up for it. It was bad enough as it was.

Molly's voice opened the check-in with the standard first-impression question.

Nick gave it the same patient consideration he had every time. "Jenny is a very pulled-together girl. She carries herself well. But she comes off as reserved."

"Is that a problem for you?"

He shrugged. "Maybe. I'm emotionally stunted myself. Two of us in a relationship could be challenging."

I winced. I'd called him emotionally stunted several times in our breakup conversation. At first I said it calmly in an effort to get some real communication going. I think by the end, I had nearly yelled it at him as an accusation.

I fast forwarded to the next check-in, which did exactly what I feared it would. It reminded me that Nick was pretty awesome and way less stunted than he used to be. By now they'd been jumping around the tide pools for an hour, checking out the sea stars and other ocean life. When Molly pulled him aside this time, her close-up of his face showed tired lines around his eyes that suggested the strain of keeping a polite surface conversation going was wearing him down.

"Jenny keeps a lot of what she thinks to herself. On the one hand, I understand that impulse. It's a safer place to be. But it makes this situation trickier because I'm a guy trying to find a connection with someone, and she's hanging back."

"Do you think it could be that she expected a different guy?" Molly asked.

He hesitated. "I need to think about that." He stared off camera, and I wondered what or whom he was studying so intently. When he answered, his tone matched his tired eye lines. "Yes. People assume that I get to point at a random woman, crook my finger, and she'll come running." He demonstrated and then laughed, but he didn't sound like he thought it was funny. "Some of them do. Does that sound obnoxiously cocky? But they usually want something from me. The girls who are cool and down-to-earth, they definitely don't come running. I think they hate my job."

Another ouch. I hated his job. And even though I did, even though I knew he couldn't give me the future I saw for myself, I wanted to reach through the screen and hug him, wrap him up in a cocoon of friendship, and then kiss him until he felt better. Or until I did.

But I kept my behind glued to my chair and cracked my knuckles instead. Time to click and cut and caption because I could *not* keep having this same debate with myself and stay sane. Molly was right; I had no right to drag us down a rabbit hole when I knew we'd get the same end result.

And having said that to myself for the thousandth time, I dove into the editing, more infatuated with Nick than ever and equally as determined to keep my distance for both of our sakes.

* * *

"Lou!" I barely heard Molly holler over the sound of my hair dryer.

"Yeah?" I said, shutting it off and turning myself upright. My hair formed a giant poof around my head. If I could maintain a third of that volume for longer than a minute, I'd be a happy girl. I frowned at my reflection.

"Peter is weeping into my ear," she said, waving her phone at me.

Uh-oh. Peter managed the café. "Eat a biscotti, P!" I called to her phone. "You know carbs make you feel better."

"He needs me to come in," Molly said. "He sounds pathetic."

I heard an objection squawk from the phone.

"You do," Molly said into the mouthpiece without listening. "I gotta go. You have to film, but I swear to stay up as late as I need to help with the edit."

"Go," I said. "You're supposed to hit Fantastic Fromage at five, right?"

"*Oui, oui*. It's Ethan on camera duty tonight, so it should go well." She ducked out of my room.

Ethan was another friend of Nick's who'd gotten pressed into camera duty. I didn't know what our volunteer camera guys got out of it, but they were a super-size blessing in this whole process, so I would never voice my one complaint about their work: I wished they would take over filming check-ins from Molly. She did an exceptional job of getting Nick to open up in those interviews. From a business standpoint, it was perfect. From a personal standpoint, it made for emotionally exhausting nights as I edited. Those check-ins sucked me in.

Sucked in everyone else too. Two weeks into this and we had hit over fifteen thousand page views a day. If I had one more advertiser ask for space on the page—and I had every intention of making that happen—I'd have to start rotating the ads to give everyone equal exposure . . . unless they paid a higher premium for permanent placement. I defined that as "sitting pretty."

Better yet, I'd lined up my first midsized account only three hours before. The karaoke place *loved* the turnout for the FHE activity Autumn put together, and now they had hired Hot Iron to do a grand-opening campaign starting immediately. Thinking about *anything* besides *TMB* and Nick represented a breath of air so fresh it practically intoxicated me.

But my *Matrix*-style bullet-dodging skills had run out. I'd have to sub for Molly, and I couldn't think of a date I wanted to film less.

Tonight was Cara.

Tonight was Cara and a fine arts gallery and a fancy grape-and-cheese platter at a private table overlooking the ocean.

Tonight was the date I'd most wanted to have with Nick, only he'd be with the girl I'd known all along would be the one to snag him.

Fantastic.

Although it had thrilled Trentyn when I cast her, she outclassed him significantly, and Trentyn was already a class-act kind of guy. But Cara just . . .

Molly once told me that girls like herself wanted to be like girls like me. I thought that she meant tall, but she meant confident and happy and pretty. I beat some sense into her with a pillow when she told me that because her tiny frame bristled with edgy energy that some quirky, perfect guy out there would love. But I kinda got it. I wanted to be more like Cara: more confident without being conceited, more beautiful without looking like I was trying, more educated from a more prestigious university. Plus Cara made everyone feel like her best friend. She lived in San Diego—taught an English lit course at one of the universities down there—and dropped in on the Beachside ward every now and then. Often enough to make the rest of us shrivel inside while our souls sucked on lemons of jealousy and long enough to make us feel wretched about it when we remembered that she was genuinely a cool girl.

Cara. Cara on *my* dream date with *my* dream guy.

Fine. Dream guys are by definition a daydream because that's all it makes sense for them to be. It's not like I loved Zac Efron through my teen years because I secretly believed we would end up together.

Because he's an actor, for one.

I blasted the hairdryer into my face again, hoping to blow the stupidity out of my brain cavity. I eyed my yoga pants and broken-in Surf Shack T-shirt in the mirror. So much for a scroungey night of comfy clothes and a bag of Doritos. I had a couple of hours to degrungify and be fabulous for this date. I'd start with my hair, and since it wasn't quite dry yet, I still had a chance to do the beach waves Nick liked. I pulled out my vintage eyelet sundress with a soft peach cardigan and gold sandals for an understated romantic look. Out came my special-occasion mascara and the perfect coral lip gloss.

I walked out the door looking like a soft-focus portrait of a sun-kissed beach girl. I may have to hold a mic all night while Ethan filmed the date that would shut the door on my Nick daydream for good, but I didn't have to be beige background paint while I did it.

* * *

When I was little, my mom took me to the mall, and I fell in instant love with this tiny Yorkie in the pet store window. I mean, we locked eyes and that was it; I knew it was meant to be mine. But my mom wanted to get church pants for Matt for the next day because he was growing through a new pair about every two weeks, so she herded me past the window, and my seven-year-old heart ached for an entire month.

Here I stood again, five minutes after Cara showed up at Fabulous Fromage, my nose pressed against the pet-store window staring at something that would never be mine. I said nothing, putting all my energy into looking without seeing so it wouldn't bum me out as much. Ethan, a low-key guy, seemed fine with my limited interaction. Molly had mentioned before that even more so than Mikey, Ethan lasered in on the filming. He spent the evening watching intently, his muscles tensed in high alert.

Me too. But for different reasons. My antennae had gone up the second Cara rounded the corner in four-inch wedges and a summer dress that I instantly loved better than mine. I was TJ Maxx to her Nordstrom. A genuine smile washed over Nick's face as she walked up, and she cracked a joke that made him laugh his *real* laugh. He opened the door and rested his hand against the small of her back to guide her into the cheese shop.

The first check-in with him was torture. When Ethan led Cara off to do her interview, Nick stepped forward and gave me a long hug, resting his head on top of mine and sighing loudly. "Hi, Lou."

"Hi," I said, hugging him back because I couldn't help it. Because it felt so good. Because he was so warm. Because I was so stupid.

"I feel like it's been forever since I saw you."

"Yeah." I wiggled away. "It's been busy. You got my e-mail that the page views are in the stratosphere, right?"

"I got that e-mail." He nodded. "And your replies to my other e-mails and texts. You don't pick up the phone and talk anymore?"

"Does anyone do that anymore?" I joked because it was easier than telling him the truth. I wanted nothing more than to sit and talk to him, and that's why I couldn't let myself do it. Laughing with him, listening to his ideas, hearing his opinions—it all hurt. I needed bubble wrap around my heart, but he had a way of popping the bubbles with every joke and smart observation he made.

"How's everything going?" he asked, his easy smile in place. "I miss you. I've had about a million things to tell you."

I patted the video camera and pressed the record button so he'd see the red light shining. "I'm supposed to ask you that. So, how is everything going? What do you think of Cara?" He shot me a puzzled look but switched gears with me. I held my breath while I waited for his answer.

"You couldn't have picked a more perfect girl."

I gritted my teeth and smiled at him. "Tell me more about that."

"She's cool." He stopped and considered that. "That sounds kind of generic. I thought she was beautiful as soon as I saw her, and then when I listened to her, she became twice as cool. And man, she's smart. But humble smart. That's so rare to find."

I wanted to burrow into my peach cardigan, but I listened to him describe her some more. Cara was funny and nice and a good listener. Blah, blah, blah. I'd have opposite the usual problem in editing today: toning it down so we didn't give away to the whole audience whom he would pick right up front. I wanted to snap some of the toothpicks from the cheese samples and jab them into my eyeballs. Somewhere, a frustrated groan rose and popped out as a hiccup.

"You okay?" he interrupted his Cara-bliss to ask.

"Yep." I asked him a few more questions. When he wound down and I stopped recording, off in the distance, Ethan and Cara were still talking. Which meant I had to keep Nick busy. Which I didn't know if I could do without giving away how much I wanted to reach over and brush his hair out of his eyes and then slide into his arms again and stay there. Permanently.

Nick glanced over at them and smiled. "I don't know how much longer they'll be at it, but we might as well enjoy the cheese. Have you tried a sheep's milk cheese before? My mom gets this Basque one all the time." He held out a toothpick to me.

I accepted the cheese. "Are you sure you don't want to wait for Cara to sample these with you?"

"No, it's fine. She tried a few already, and I'll point her to any good ones you and I stumble across."

We sampled cheeses for nearly ten minutes before it occurred to me to wonder why Cara still hadn't made an appearance. Even then I probably still wouldn't have noticed she was missing except that Nick fed me a piece of honey-dipped Belgian cheese and his finger grazed my lip. I trembled. His eyes darkened for a second, and I took a quick step back. I wrapped myself up in "professional distance" like it was a flame retardant stunt suit and nearly dove through the front door of the cheese shop.

"Lou, wait . . ." Nick called behind me, but I barreled down the sidewalk without looking back. Ethan and Cara still sat on their bench, though Ethan had set his camera down.

"We need to get this date back on track," I said to Nick when he caught up with me. "Too much interview time and not enough date time."

"But—"

"Trust me," I said, trying to wrestle my smile into feeling real. "I'm a completely inexperienced producer making this up as I go along. I know these things."

He shoved his hands into his pockets and sighed. "You're doing great. Everything in its place."

"Thanks. Let's go interrupt." I turned my back on him again and walked up to Ethan and Cara. "You guys ready?"

"Ready." Ethan stood and hefted his camera. We meandered back to Fabulous Fromage, Ethan and I trailing behind Nick and Cara as they walked side by side and he laughed at everything she said. I wanted to punch both of them and then kick my own behind for caring. I dealt with another hour of torture before the cheese shop put together a selection of cheeses and crackers for them in an impressive to-go package.

They wandered out into the Laguna Beach evening air and up PCH toward the art galleries across from the art museum. One of them, Vierra Fine Arts, had agreed to host the happy couple. The owner greeted them and gave them a guided tour of the exhibit. Mr. Vierra came across as oilier than the paints on the canvases, but he gave them great background information on the sculptures and paintings.

Trudging after them, leaning in with the mic to capture every scrap of sound, forced me to notice that they already looked and acted like a couple. Finishing each other's sentences, arguing in total comfort. I stewed about that through the first three paintings, but then I decided to embrace that observation. That way it could strengthen my flagging resolve to keep my emotional distance from Nick.

I left with the memory card full of footage. Nick insisted on walking me to the car again even though it wasn't even a block away. I endured his good-bye hug.

No, not true. I squeezed him back, trying to sneak a tiny bit of closeness as a trade-off for all the closeness I was denying myself in the whole scheme of things. And again, it was amazing. But then I pushed away and slipped into my car with a tired wave and an apologetic smile. A "Sorry I'm so tired. And lame that I can't even be around you. K, bye" finger flutter.

* * *

I slept well. I woke up refreshed.

I crumbled again the second I read Nick's blog post.

"You ever go to a movie where you walk out and every one of your atoms is happy because it was the best story perfectly told by exactly the right actors and it has a happy ending? That's what meeting someone like Cara is like. It's like an instant renewal of your faith in the practice of dating.

It's worth it if it leads to someone like this. Every rejection, every bad date, every define-the-relationship talk that ends with you alone and wondering what happened—still worth it."

I read through the whole thing, and nausea-tinged despair filled my chest. I forced down my oatmeal. Whatever. It didn't matter. This would be another big lift in ratings as it proved to viewers that this process could work.

I'd spend an hour moderating comments for the blog, and then I'd go out and recruit business. I'd stay out all day and work as many contacts as I could and not let myself come home until I signed a new client to Hot Iron for a renewing account, not just as an advertiser on the *TMB* blog. *That* goal could easily keep me out for days, but I needed something besides this to think about. I shot Molly an e-mail and then noticed another message from Nick sent right after the blog post last night. I squinted at the time stamp. Or was that the wee hours this morning? Had he hung out with Cara so late, then? Molly had made a deal with him that as long as she had enough footage and he gave her a good night scene to film, he and his flavor du jour could hang out for as long as they wanted to without our camera dogging them. Maybe he'd done that last night.

I opened the e-mail.

Since I know you won't pick up the phone and call, I'm hoping you'll at least read this e-mail. I wanted to thank you for the chance to be the bachelor. It's opened my eyes to so many things. I thought the opportunity would be in the exposure, but it hasn't been the exposure I expected. I guess I'm realizing the benefit of exposing myself emotionally.

But that's all kind of boring stuff that's in my head. I'm realizing how many quality girls are out there, and it's renewing my faith in dating. I mean, I say the same thing in my blog post, but it's totally true.

The biggest thing though . . . is you. I'm glad we've had a chance to repair our friendship. I've regretted not having been a better boyfriend, and I hated that you were so angry when you ended things. I thought a lot about that, about the things you said. I've thought about it off and on ever since, to tell you the truth. And I've tried to internalize it and become better for it.

The hardest part of everything was feeling like I'd closed that door, but seeing you again and being around you has made me feel like our friendship is back in a good place. I need that so much right now. (Have I mentioned it seriously bums me out that you won't pick up the phone sometimes? Did you know that anything said in parentheses is officially off the record? So can I say that it's pretty tough to go out on so many dates so many days in a row, and it helps when I have you to bounce my reactions off of and to think things through? And then can we pretend I never said anything so unmanly? I feel like if I write my blog post like I'm e-mailing only you about what happened, it's therapy or something. You didn't even know you were being that good of a friend, did you? And now I'm about to close the parenthesis, and you can't ever tell anyone what I said here.)

I don't want to fall into my jerkwad habits from before of taking you or anyone for granted, so this is me saying thanks for hooking me up with this whole experience. It's changed everything about the way I see love and romance and girls and what I want, and it's awesome.

When had he started getting everything right? The right words, the right jokes. It needed to stop so I could catch my breath and function like a human being again. But this e-mail wouldn't do it. In fact, it kind of took my breath away. Or maybe stopped my heart. I wasn't sure yet which organ was suffering more under the incredible pressure squeezing my chest right now. Here I was trying to keep my distance, and Nick turned around and told me how much he needed my emotional support and how much he depended on me. So, yay me, the queen jerk.

And how come he didn't sound like a gigantic wimp when he made that confession? I skimmed back through it. Seriously, if anyone else had written that e-mail, it would have sounded needy and way too "modern man" for me. Which, yes, made me a hypocrite. Definitely. I'd complained for the last half of our relationship that Nick didn't open up enough, but I was quick to judge a guy who opened up too soon or easily. The difference here was that if Nick were an emotionally needy guy, I'd be dealing with it all the time. He'd be in my space or constantly seeking validation. But here he was, trusting me as a friend that he could vent to.

I reread the blog post and then the e-mail. I felt borderline desolate about the blog post and then weirdly torn between guilt and pleasure over the e-mail. The fact that he had clearly forgiven me for being so harsh when I broke up with him made me happy. Or at least lessened my guilt over that epic temper tantrum. But then I had new guilt for not being the friend in my heart that Nick believed me to be.

I heaved a sigh and dialed his number.

"I'm not going to talk about my feelings," he said when he answered. "It was in parentheses, so I don't have to."

"I'm not calling about that. You need to meet me for lunch at South Coast Plaza."

"What? Why?"

"Because a truly good friend wouldn't let you walk around in those dumb-looking tight T-shirts."

"You don't like my shirts?"

"I hate them."

"But the stylist on one of my photo shoots said they're what girls like."

"Nick Westman, you should worry about what *you* like. We're going shopping, and you're going to invest in something besides shrunken cotton. And then you're buying me lunch."

"Yes, ma'am."

I hung up the phone. Once again, I would fall back on the fake-it-till-you-make-it strategy. Only this time, I would fake feelings of friendship for him until that's truly all I felt. Even if it killed me.

Which . . . yeah. It most likely would.

* * *

"This one?" Nick stepped out of the fitting room, and I nearly swallowed my tongue.

"That one's good." Brownie point for not squeaking at the sight of him in a soft blue button-down. It accented his chest and shoulders without looking like it was trying to squeeze him until he popped. "Is that cotton?"

He nodded, rubbing it between his fingers. "The nonshrunken kind. Feel." He guided my hand to his sleeve. I resisted the urge to squeeze his bicep. Barely.

"I'm normally against paying extra for things that are artificially vintage-ized, but I think you have to get this shirt. Super touchable."

"Prove it."

My fingers itched to touch him again, and I flushed. "Isn't that what I just did?"

"Guess I'll get it."

"That makes six shirts," I said. "Do you have enough normal shirts at home plus these new ones to get you through the rest of the dates?"

"Yeah. You could have told me earlier to change the shirts, you know." He slipped back into the fitting room and closed the door.

"I've overtaken your entire love life. It seemed bossy to do your wardrobe styling."

A snort sounded inside the fitting room. "Yes."

"Yes? Yes to what?"

"To bossiness and overtaking my love life." I had a comeback ready to zing at him, but he kept talking. "It's okay though. No, actually it's good." He stepped back out from the fitting room in the Hurley T-shirt he'd worn into the store. "And I'm serious about telling me stuff. No one else would tell me my shirts are stupid and drag me to the mall. This is what I keep saying: you keep me grounded. Quit ducking my phone calls."

I avoided the ducking accusation. "I didn't say your shirts are stupid."

"It's what you meant. The thing is, that's what I thought the first time that stylist told me to get more of them, but wearing them is such a habit now that I forgot I thought that. So I repeat, stick around. I love that we have honest conversations and that everything feels so normal when I'm with you. And keep telling me the truth about myself. People never do that, and it gets old."

There were so many things wrong with that speech. Honest conversations? How could he not see through me? The effort of holding back my crazy, mixed-up feelings for him nearly choked me on a daily basis. Picking up his calls was Russian roulette, where a moment of weakness might let all my emotions break loose, and boom. Game over. None of the possible outcomes besides the insane daydream of him confessing his love for me ended well.

"Fine. I'll tell you every time your shirts look dumb. You're pretty easy in the friend department."

We reached the register, and he slid a credit card from his wallet to hand to the cashier. "It's not just that. It's the truth you tell me about other stuff too." He angled his head and studied my face. "Why do you keep dancing away from this?"

"I'm not dancing away from anything," I said. Tap, tap, tap and kick-ball-change. "I just can't concentrate on serious friend stuff when I'm hungry. You promised me food."

He laughed. "All right. Food." He took his bag from the counter. "Let's go hunt for wild burritos. I hear they hang out at a watering hole near here."

I followed him from the store and kept my sigh of relief very, very quiet. Another bullet dodged. For now.

Chapter 11

"No way!"

Molly clapped her hands over her ears, wincing. "Too loud!"

"I don't care." I didn't yell it this time, but I meant it just as much.

"Why not?" she demanded. "You're the one who wanted a chance with him in the first place. You make no sense."

"And you're the one who reminded me why that would be crazy. *You* make no sense." Date number nineteen, Jenny D, had just e-mailed me to cancel because she'd been diagnosed with mono. "I'm not filling in. You know we can easily find someone to replace her," I said.

"In two hours? Without vetting? No."

"Yes. Put it on Facebook. It'll be fine."

"No way," she said. "What if an advertiser caught wind of it and thought we were all disorganized or something?"

"You're making less sense the more you talk. How does it look any more professional for the producer to show up on camera as a date? That's weird."

"Think," she said, hopping up and patting me on the head. "It's perfect if we spin it. We say some bit about how you guys have this history and how after watching him for these last three weeks, you wanted a chance to see if there was anything left between you."

I brushed her hands away and stood up. "I'm not going to go on camera and spill my guts."

"Fine. We don't spin it that way. We make it funny, like how you and your assistant producer," she pointed to herself and flashed me a fake smile, "had a bet and you lost, so now you have to step in."

"I'm not doing it. I'd rather risk putting it on Facebook. Or send out a mass e-mail to friends who might want to date him. Seriously, why are you pushing this?"

"Because I don't know what else to do. There are a lot of people waiting for us to fail, and I'm getting tired of it. Putting it out on Facebook is going to be a crack in the dam, for one. But the thought of putting up an unvetted bachelorette makes me want to pull my hair out. What if we end up with something not fit to air?"

"Are you even trying to think of a real reason?" I demanded. "Because that's dumb. It's going to look just as bad if I show up. Why can't you see that?"

"Look, I don't like the idea of you going out with Nick for real. But if you both know it's not real, then under the circumstances, that's our only viable option right now. You know we can't publicly scramble with so many people paying this close attention to what we're doing. Is it really going to kill you to hang out with him on camera for once? Let's ask Nick what he wants to do. He deserves some input after eighteen dates."

"Whatever," I said, knowing from the stubborn glint in her eye that she wouldn't let it drop. "You call him. I have e-mails to deal with." One of the first things I would do when we'd had a regular revenue stream for three months would be to hire an assistant who could sort through and answer a lot of this stuff. Of course, by then we wouldn't have over two hundred comments a day to moderate for the blog. I wished I could take that restriction off and let people comment freely, but a small fraction of the comments still skewed negatively. Since I didn't want any of the *TMB* cast feeling badly, I couldn't lift the restriction.

Molly called Nick and wandered off to explain the situation to him. A few minutes later, she marched back in. "He wants to talk to you."

"Tell him we'll find him someone good for the date."

"That's not it," Molly said, grinning. She shoved the phone at me.

"Hi," I said.

"Can we observe a moment of silence to honor the fact that I am wearing one of my new shirts and it's not cutting into my armpit?"

"I'll be silent, but don't be offended if I fall asleep in the middle of it."

"Let's skip it. You need to go on this date with me."

"Uh . . . no?"

"Yes. You have no idea how exhausted I am. The idea of hanging out with someone I know feels like a lifeline. You said you would be my friend. Be my friend, Lou."

"I thought you were having a great time on those dates."

"Yes, but they're wearing me out."

"Okay, not to be all weird, but when you and I first started dating, we spent at least this much time, if not more, together every day, and you were working way more than you are now. Are you getting old?" I asked.

"Huge difference. This is a first date every single day. I have to have my game face on all the time. It takes way more energy than hanging around with someone you gel with day after day. That gets more relaxing as it goes. This gets more stressful."

"Sorry," I said, meaning it. "I know you told me that already. You should have reminded me."

"I would have. But I went to e-mail you a couple of times and it sounded so whiny that I deleted the e-mails and then punched myself in the face."

I laughed, and he pounced on the sound. "That's what I mean," he said. "I don't have to worry that you're getting my sense of humor. Come out tonight. I need some kind of mental health break, and you could make sure your show's talent is surviving. Win-win."

I smiled again at his use of one of my favorite phrases. "I've got too much to do today with researching some stuff and putting together some other stuff for my new accounts."

"First, congrats on your new accounts. Molly said you're tearing it up. Second, 'stuff'? That sounds suspicious and excuse-ish. Seriously, I need a break before I have a psychotic meltdown on the next date and become a viral sensation for all the wrong reasons."

"I wish we were on Facetime so you could see me roll my eyes."

"No, you don't. It would probably do that weird freeze frame thing it always does right when you rolled them, and then you would look like a freaky zombie, and then I'd be convinced I'd already had my psychotic meltdown, and it would be all your fault."

"Nice," I said. "But if you think you need a break, you should take Molly on the date. Ow!" I glared at Molly, who had charged across the room and kicked me. "Molly kicked me. Is this your fault? Did you make her hate you?"

"It's my fault. I don't know why, but I'll accept the blame."

"Why did you kick me?" I demanded.

"Because you're working me to death, and now you're trying to add even more to my duties? Unfair labor practices."

Nick laughed.

"He's laughing at us," I informed Molly. "Why are you laughing at us?"

"I've never had two girls fight so hard to not go out with me," he said. "Everything my mother ever told me about how I'm a great catch is a lie."

"Don't take it personally. I'm going nuts with this business stuff, and I need to stay on top of it. I can't do a whole evening out for a date."

"I don't think I can do a whole evening out, period. Diva fit alert: if I have to do one more blind date, much less with someone I wasn't expecting, I will lose my mind. It will be ugly. It will not be the kind of thing that entertains your viewers, so don't even think about it," he warned.

I'd totally been thinking that.

"If you need to get something on film, come out with me so I can get breathing room. If it doesn't matter, let me stay home and regroup. Seriously, playing Kade's Xbox will do more for me than therapy."

I sighed. "We have advertisers who are paying a higher rate to be on the home page for every new date we air, and we can't afford to lose that money."

"*I'll* buy the ad space. I don't care how much it is. If it lets me stay home one night, it's going to be worth whatever you charge me."

"Stop! You're making me feel so guilty! I wish I could let you skip out, but unless it's massive traumatic injury, we need to do this."

He was quiet for a full ten seconds. "That's it. I'm going to go fling myself in front of a car."

"Oh, knock it off. If it's so hard on you to go out with an amazingly cute girl, then you can go out with me instead."

Molly hooted, and I blushed. Nick jumped on my inadvertent self-insult. "Don't be so hard on yourself," he said. "I'd say you're amazingly cute."

"Great," I said. "I guess I'm your date tonight."

"Yes," he said, not so much as a celebration but as a sigh of relief.

"Fine. See you at Color Pots." I hung up. "I'm losing my mind."

Molly accepted her phone from me and reached up to pat my shoulder. "It's for a good cause. He's been pretty much a rock star through all of this. I don't think Trentyn would have held up nearly as well."

"Help me pick an outfit." I turned and trudged toward my room. I hated that a big part of me, much too big, couldn't wait to see Nick. There was something about smelling and touching him that I craved. The Nickness of him, I guess.

"You can't be all Eeyore on the date," she said. "The viewers don't want to see that."

"I'll be perky. Don't worry."

"Perky is not you. Be you."

"I'll be me. Help me find something cute to wear."

She grabbed a pair of red skinny jeans and a white blousy cotton top. "These," she said. Then she crouched down and rummaged through my shoes for a moment before handing out some yellow wedges. "And these. Done. Brush your hair. Do your make-up."

I grabbed the red jeans and put them back. "I'm not getting paint on these. I'll just wear my Old Navy skinny jeans."

"Smart. They look good, but they're cheap to replace." She nodded. "Now get dressed."

I shooed her out and changed clothes. Tonight's date would be painting ceramic pottery at a place down on Main. I checked the clock, but I had plenty of time before I needed to do my hair and make-up. I decided to sit and visualize how to act so Nick wouldn't guess how I felt about him.

Before meeting Cara, he might have been interested in the possibilities between us, but not now. The two of them had been electric, and the audience sensed it too. My e-mail had gone crazy with the comments, but so had my phone, Facebook, and Twitter feeds. Ashley even texted me. *Glad you're over Nick, or that would have been brutal to watch. Good job picking a winner for him. They'll be cute!*

It was my fault. I'd insisted there was nothing between us, and everyone except Molly had taken me at my word. So yeah, time to figure out how to act. Or no, not act. An actor would see straight through acting, right? I'd have to be me, but the unsmitten me, the "I'm cool with you" me, the friend me.

* * *

By the time Nick showed up with Ethan a couple of minutes after Molly and I arrived, I'd figured out the perfect approach.

"Hi," I said, stepping into his hug so he wouldn't start off wondering why I was ducking him or being weird.

"Hi, yourself," he said, wrapping his arms around me. "Thanks for doing this."

"I think that's my line," I said. "Sorry I was so hard-nosed about tonight. You've been an incredibly good sport, and we appreciate it."

"I think I mostly get the better end of the deal," he said.

"I have an idea for making this date look good on camera." I stepped back and smoothed my hair down. "The viewers will want romance or the possibility of it, and it might be kind of boring to watch us hanging out, so I thought we could introduce a story line."

Molly stared at me like I had sprouted daisies from my ears.

"A story line?" he repeated, sounding as baffled as Molly looked. "What kind of story line?"

"We could explain that you and I used to date and that after watching this season with you, I decided I wanted a chance to see if we had anything left between us."

Silence met this. I tried not to fidget. Molly lifted an eyebrow at this theft of her idea. Nick cleared his throat. He cleared it again. By now I'd learned to recognize it as a nervous tic. "Interesting story. Is it true?" He studied my face closely, not blinking.

"Well, no. But it would explain why I'm here."

"Or the truth would. How about you have Ethan shoot me doing the open and see what you think. If you hate it, we'll trying something else. Like your . . . story line."

"What are you—" I started to ask, but Molly clapped her hand over my mouth.

"Sounds good. You on it, Ethan?"

He nodded and hoisted the camera to his shoulder.

"Move to your left two steps, Nick," she called. "Then we can see the name of the store on the glass behind you." She turned to me. "We've gotten really good at this. I have no idea what he's about to say, but like he said, if you hate it, change it. Since I'm producing tonight, I'm putting my foot down: no talking every single part of this to death. Take orders and be quiet. Love ya." She turned to watch Nick.

Ethan held up his hand and counted down three fingers then pointed to Nick in a signal to start. He smiled into the camera. "Normally this is the part of the date where you guys watch my face as my date walks up so you can check out my first reaction to her. Tonight's date is different. If you wanted to catch my first impression, you'd have to go back in time three years.

"We had a last-minute change of plans when my date for the evening got sick, and the producer of *The Mormon Bachelor*, Louisa Gibson, was nice enough to let me choose her replacement. This will be a familiar face if you look over in the sidebar at the *TMB* staff photos because the replacement is Lou herself." He crooked his finger at me, and I walked over to join him, a smile pasted on my face.

"Lou and I dated a long time ago, and I knew her pretty well. When she called me up to ask me about taking on this bachelor project, I trusted her judgment enough to jump in. But everything took off so fast that I never had a chance to touch base with her about how these three years have treated her, so tonight you guys are going to get a special treat: you'll get to know the incredible brain behind this whole brilliant project, and maybe you'll get to see a side of me that's hard to share when I'm trying to be on my best first-date behavior." He smiled and held it for a couple of moments until Molly said, "Cut."

Ethan lowered the camera, and Molly practically launched herself at Nick to give him a big smacking kiss on the cheek. "Perfect! Genius! Couldn't have thought of a better set up! It's honest, and it still creates interest. We're going with this." She said the last part like a warning to me, as if I would argue, but I didn't. She was right. Nick had created a perfect setup for the night.

"In we go," he said, holding the door open for me. Ethan turned the camera on again, and we walked into the shop. I loved the smell; it zapped me right back to my eighth-grade art classroom. Shelves full of plain white ceramic objects lined the open studio. Everything from light-switch plates to salad bowls sat perched and waiting for aspiring artists to pluck them up and beautify them.

"Here's something I don't know about you," I said to Nick. "Are you good at art?"

"Depends on the kind. Not paint-type art."

"What kind, then?" I asked.

"Painting with words, maybe."

"Oh, because you act, and that's its own kind of art?" I said, grasping the metaphor.

"No, actually." He colored slightly. "I write now. I mean, not right now. But I write. Nowadays. When I'm not working." He cleared his throat and laughed. "I'm not doing a great job of proving we're super comfortable with each other, am I?" His gaze swept across the display in front of us, and he reached out to pick up a cluster of ceramic grapes. "I'm so tempted to do these," he said. "Seems kind of hard to screw up."

"Or so easy to make cooler," I said, taking the grapes from his hand. I had no intention of letting his "word art" remark drop, but I allowed him to distract me for the moment. "You could paint these unexpected colors. Or draw creepy faces on each one."

"Sick," he said. "And awesome. What are you going to paint? No pressure, but you've only got about ten thousand choices."

"I already know what I'm doing." The choice had been easy the second I saw the simple bud vase sitting on the shelf. I picked it up and turned it over, sensing its dimensions and possibility. "I think this will be the perfect keepsake for whichever girl accepts this from you. She can put the winning rose in here."

"We're really doing a rose ceremony?" he asked. "Like the real show?"

"Yeah. I mean, feel free to get down on one knee and propose if you feel strongly about your final choice, but I thought ending the show with you giving a rose would be a better symbol of starting a new journey."

"Cool. But you're going to have to make that a high-class vase," he said. "I don't want to be handing someone a homely craft project."

"I'm nothing if not high class. You're going to have to fight the Getty to keep this when I'm done."

"In that case, I have a challenge for you. I've decided I'm painting this puppy up." He snagged a soup bowl from the shelf. "I could live on clam chowder. They have the best chowder shack by my house. You gotta try it sometime."

I wish. And not likely. "Sounds great. I remember you being a soup fiend."

"One of the few things that hasn't changed," he said. He turned and followed the employee with the Color Pots apron on to a table set up with paint supplies. Nick set his bowl down and pulled out my chair for me.

"What things *have* changed?" I asked.

"You really haven't noticed? Hold on a second," he said, putting up his hand to stop my explanation. "I need to muster some Academy Award–worthy tears." Fierce concentration crossed his expression, but then his face smoothed out again. He looked at me with forlorn eyes. "I can't cry on cue. Do I look sad enough though?"

I made a big show of scanning the shelves. "I'm trading my bud vase for an Oscar statuette. If they have grapes, they should have one of those, right?"

Nick laughed, and I leaned back in my chair. "Another thing that hasn't changed is your avoiding questions."

His expression morphed to chagrin. "That was definitely unintentional. You want to know what's changed?" He picked up a paint brush and stabbed it into some orange then smooshed it onto his bowl. It was a unique approach. "You could pick almost any area of my life, and I feel like I could point to where I was then and where I've grown to now."

Up to this point, I'd made a point of ignoring the camera. The best date footage always came when the girls with Nick forgot about the filming and talked as if it were only them and Nick. But it suddenly seemed super uncool to say, "Tell me about your spirituality," when we had our friends plus twenty thousand viewers tomorrow hanging on the words. It also seemed like none of my business, and as much as I wanted to know about how the deep-down parts of him had changed, I didn't have the right to ask. I went the safer route. "Tell me about your career," I said. "You were trying to line up some pretty major projects before. Are you still interested in breaking into film?"

I hoped so. Because then I could for sure stay distant from him.

"Yes," he said. And I breathed a sigh of relief. "But not in acting."

The breath caught in my throat. "Oh. Then as . . . a director?" Seemed like a popular choice for people who loved the craft but didn't get the parts anymore.

"No. I've been working on a screenplay." Then he stopped and laughed. "That sounds like it should be a punch line to a joke. Everyone in Hollywood is trying to sell a screenplay. But it's the truth. That's what I want to do."

When I was teenager, my obsession with the Harry Potter books led to my adopting and exhausting the word *gobsmacked*, but I'd bring it out of retirement to describe my reaction to this. "You want to get out of acting?"

"Yeah," he said. "It's too hard to find the parts that line up with my standards, you know? And that makes absolutely no sense to casting directors. That's how I end up as the guest star on so many random shows. I get pretty regular offers for series, but there's always something in the long-term story arc that I know I can't do."

"Wow." I thought of all the times I'd seen this conflict drag LDS Hollywood newcomers off into the woods never to be seen again. "So you're switching to screenplays."

"I love the storytelling. I think in movies. It's how things unspool in my mind. I like acting, but it wasn't until I took my screenwriting class at USC that it all came together."

"You went back to school?" He'd done a few semesters toward a degree by the time we'd started dating, but his erratic schedule kept him from finishing.

"I graduated last year. You're looking at the bona fide owner of a fancy piece of paper that says I've got a bachelor of fine arts in screenwriting."

"Nick! That's great!" I leaned over and hugged him. "Good for you."

"Thanks," he said.

"You're working on a screenplay now?"

"It's what I do in the long hours between dates when I'm waiting to see what you'll throw at me next."

"Funny, because all I do in those long hours is think about what to throw at you. It's a delicate balance. It has to be something that will make you uncomfortable but not your date. I have to tap my evil-but-not-too-evil side."

He grinned. "Mission accomplished."

"Thanks," I said, faking modesty. "I try. What's your screenplay about? I don't even know what to guess for your genre."

"Now you have to do it. Guess, I mean. What do you think I'm writing?"

I sat back and studied him. "Something with vampires and a love triangle?"

"Of course. Someone has to ride that gravy train."

"For real, what is it?"

He didn't answer for a moment, instead leaning down to examine the bowl closely, maybe to ensure that the section he had just painted looked as bad as the rest of it. When he looked up, his eyes met mine with straightforward intensity. "Maybe it's Hollywood burnout, but I've become much more interested in what's real."

"So an LA film noir, old-school detective style?"

"Closer, and yet completely wrong."

"I give up. What is it?" My curiosity intensified by the moment.

"Romantic comedy. But more from the bro side."

"The bro side?" I was too dumbfounded to do anything but parrot him.

"Yeah. You girls get your chick flicks. This is a version of that, but it's stuff dudes would get."

"So you're writing a romantic comedy but from the guy's perspective?"

"Yeah. Basically."

I sat back. "Has this been done before? Because it's pretty genius, and I can't believe someone hasn't done it already."

He shrugged, a pleased smile twitching around his lips. "I could point you to a few, but they're pretty dated. I want to do something fresh and maybe more indie-feeling."

"Is it for a general audience? Because I have a hard time imagining you trying to do some sex-and-alcohol fueled buddy comedy."

"See?" he said, pointing an accusing finger at me. "Stereotypes about modern guys like that are the exact reason we need movies that show what the inner life of a dude is really like."

"Based on what? The Mormon point of view?"

He sat back and crossed his arms across his chest, grinning. "I'm sensitive about my art. You're hurting my feelings right now by not turning all fan girl and squealing."

I smiled. "I'm honestly fascinated. I'm always walking a line between the morals I try to live by and the products I have to sell in my line of work. That's part of what appealed to me about opening my own firm. I don't have to go after the accounts that make me uncomfortable. If I don't want to put together a campaign for a bikini bar, I don't have to. It's interesting to hear how you find that balance too." A thought struck me, and I sat up straighter. "Oh man. I bet I was sounding super judgmental, wasn't I? Like I was judging you for making secular art or something."

I leaned forward and touched his hand. "That's not it, I swear. It's just the balance thing. I've been thinking about it a lot lately. Everybody wants something sexy to sell their product, and I want to stay away from that whole 'sex sells' cliché if I can avoid it."

"You mean like a sexy pirate to sell a family pirate show."

A split-second of panic flared, but there was no way he could know I was behind that. I shrugged. "Don't be so hard on yourself. I'm sure the money was good."

"It was, but I wasn't talking about me. I was talking about how it was your idea." He sat back and tilted his head, an unspoken challenge to deny it.

"You, um . . . you know about that?"

"Yeah. I know about that."

"Who told you?" From the corner of my eye, I could see Molly edging behind Ethan. My hand crept toward one of the paint-muddied water bowls because I was fully ready to drench her with it.

Nick reached over and pressed my hand against the table. "Molly did the right thing. The question is why *you* didn't tell me."

"Because I didn't want to die young?"

His eyes narrowed, and he rose slowly from his seat.

"I didn't tell them to cast you!" I blurted. "I didn't even suggest it, so it's only a little bit my fault. You're the one who said yes to the job."

He plopped back in his chair. "True." He rubbed his chin then sighed and faked deep thought. "I guess we've both learned a lesson from this about the importance of money versus arrrgh-tistic integrity."

I giggled at his piratical growl. "Yep. I say no to sexy pirates now."

Nick laughed, and I couldn't stop giggling. This time he stood and pulled me up from my chair. "Arrrgh! Say no to sexy pirates!" he sang sea-shanty style and hooked his arm through mine to execute a sloppy jig. My giggles erupted into full-blown laughs, and it wasn't until I saw Molly's mouth hanging open that I tugged my arm loose and sat back down. I'd forgotten about the cameras far sooner than most of Nick's dates did. The plus side of knowing him well already, I guess.

"Sorry about the commercial," I said, the flush of jigging and laughter still hot in my cheeks.

"Don't be," he said, taking his seat again. "It kept me from having to work for two months. I made a lot of progress on my script."

"Can you tell me the plot? I love the idea of it."

"You know how *500 Days of Summer* was more the guy side of a breakup? Think that. Similar indie feel. Quirk, irony. All that."

I smiled at him. "All the good stuff, you mean. It sounds awesome. Is it your first screenplay?"

"No," he said, an embarrassed smile reappearing. "I wrote some in my college courses. And I've already sold a different one."

"No way! That's so cool. What's that one about?"

"It's no big deal," he said. "It was this concept I played with about the annual Mormon Duck Beach migration."

"The big Memorial Day thing on the East Coast?" I asked.

He nodded.

"Comedy or drama?"

"I guess you haven't gone to one before, or you would know that the correct answer is 'both.'"

I laughed again. "I've heard enough stories that I should have guessed that." We settled back into painting. The silence blanketed us like a well-worn sweatshirt, warm and comfortable.

I turned my vase this way and that, wondering how the glaze after firing would affect the colors. So far, I liked what I had.

"That's cool," Nick said, glancing over. "It reminds me of the pottery I saw in Provence. You have a good eye for color."

"Thanks. I can't paint actual shapes or anything, but this I can handle. Hope you won't be too embarrassed to hand it off to the winning girl." I hesitated, not sure I wanted an answer to my next question. "I'm going to make Molly edit out the next part of this conversation, but do you have any idea who you're asking for second dates yet?"

"Yeah. The choices have been easy," he said.

That meant Cara for sure.

"Hey," Molly said, gesturing to Ethan to stop taping. "No shop talk. If I can't use it, I don't want to film it. Give me a date, guys. You were doing great up until then."

I rolled my eyes but nodded. "Let's be date-y, Nick. We can act like it's an improv."

"I'm down. Couple reconnects a few years after a rough breakup. They agree to meet so one of them can get closure. That can be me," he said. "For the sake of making the improv work."

"Thanks," I said. "I appreciate your artistic generosity." In truth, it would be a stretch for me to play someone getting closure since being around him gave me anything but.

"Action!" Molly called.

Nick grinned. "So how have you been the last three years? I'm shocked that you're not already married with a kid on the way. Is there something wrong with the guys in the Beachside Ward?"

"That's such a loaded question," I said. "Because the answer is yes, but I'll get myself into trouble if I explain all the reasons why. So how about if I shrug and look confused?"

"Sure. But I'm being serious about the marriage thing. It blows my mind that you're not all settled down."

I could hear the curious implied question. *Why aren't you?* "I got a great job when I graduated," I said. "It kept me pretty busy. So that explains the first six months after I left LA." I frowned. "After that, I don't have any great insights or anything. I'd love to get married. I've dated. A lot, sometimes. But it never works out."

"Why not?" he asked. He'd quit painting his mangled-looking bowl and sat studying me, his brush forgotten.

"Don't hang on my every word," I said. "It's weird."

He propped his chin on his hand and smiled. "Too bad. Go ahead."

I sighed. "I have this roommate who is pretty great, except for she's super nosy and she thinks she knows everything about how my brain works." I heard an indignant squeak from Molly. "The annoying thing is that sometimes she's right. And she's been hinting that I have issues with perfectionism. I expect a lot of myself—"

"You do," he said. "True."

"But she says I expect just as much from other people and that most people aren't neurotic overachievers like me. She supported her theory with some lame story about how I micromanaged baking a bundt cake." Another squeak from Molly.

"What do you think about that?" he asked, his voice giving no indication of whether he agreed or not.

I didn't answer. I picked up a piece of sponge and dabbed at a spot on the vase where the blue didn't look quite right. Nick watched and said nothing. A minute ticked by. I set the bud vase down and scowled at it. Then I scowled off camera at Molly. Then I scowled at Nick. "I think she's right."

The jiggle of the boom mic overhead alerted me to Molly's silent fit of laughter off camera. I scowled at her again. "But only because my mom said pretty much the same thing. And then I thought about it, and it turns out, it's kind of hard to argue with mountains of evidence."

"Perfectionism." He pointed from the vase to the sponge in my hand. "Yep."

"But it looks better now," I said.

"It looks exactly like it did before you started messing with it."

"I admitted that I have issues. The answer to your question is that I'm not married because I'm a seriously damaged person."

His smile faded. "That's not it. Expecting a lot from the people around you isn't a bad thing. Maybe sometimes it's the only way to get them to step up their game. I know Kade doesn't go out looking to scrimmage with the weakest players on the beach."

"You know who the most boring person in this room is? Me. Let's talk about you. In the interests of our improv, you need to do a dramatic monologue about the last three years for you."

"May I stay seated?" he asked, pretending to take my direction seriously.

"You may."

He nodded and thought for a moment before picking up his bowl again. "The last three years. I've dated. I've not dated. I've dived into my screenplays and not come up for air. And then I've dated some more. I had kind of a rough breakup, unfortunately. It came at a good time though. If being dumped by a cool girl ever comes at the right time, I guess."

I didn't breathe. I pretended to paint, but really I was dabbing my paintbrush in random colors without any purpose. I desperately wanted to find out what kind of girl could break his heart. Could it be me? I mean, we'd been together for six months. Except he'd never seemed heartbroken after our breakup. There'd been no wistful phone calls or requests to talk about it or anything. He'd more or less shrugged and said, "All right. If that's what you want." And then he'd let it drop completely. Not the behavior of a heartbroken man. Or at least it wasn't compared to the ones I'd seen, like Matt when he and Ashley had broken up for a while.

"Anyway, enter soul-searching," he said. "I backed out of a role I had coming up and hopped on a plane to hang out with my aunt and uncle in Kenya. My uncle was serving as mission president there. I was going to stay for a couple of weeks and clear my head. I stayed almost five months." He smiled at me. "It changed my life."

"When was that?" Maybe three years ago?

He shrugged. "Awhile back. Ever since then, I've been doing my writing thing, trying to break into the industry that way, acting to pay the bills."

I smiled and hoped it covered up the weird sense of loss eating at me. In those moments back in the day when we'd connected, even though they were hard to come by, I'd never felt so dialed into another person, never felt so understood. I'd thought Nick lacked the emotional capacity to sustain a real relationship outside of those isolated moments, but obviously, I was wrong. He'd found someone he loved enough that he had to go bury his heart in Africa to get over her, and as good as it would be to pretend, I knew it wasn't me.

Molly stepped into the shot. "Let's do some check-ins."

Good timing. Sitting and listening to Nick talk about loving a girl so much it broke his heart made me feel sick to my stomach. I got up to follow Molly, but she shook her head. "Nick doesn't do the check-ins with his friends, remember? You're with Ethan."

I swallowed a protest and smiled at him like it was no big deal. "Right. We're about to get to know each other pretty well while you dig around in my brain for a few minutes, huh?"

He smiled back. "I'll get to know you better, at least."

Great. I followed him out of the store and to a nearby alley. They lay around like abandoned pick-up sticks in downtown HB. He squinted up at the waning light. "This should work," he said, but he took a small device out of his camera bag and held it near my head before moving slowly up and down the wall as he examined it.

"What is that?"

"A light meter. I want to make sure we're getting the best shot."

"Oh." Color me impressed. Eventually, he pointed to a spot six feet farther into the alley.

"Here is better if that's okay with you," he said.

"Sure." I moved and then stood, waiting for him to indicate that the interview had started.

He pointed at a small red light. "You're on. Why don't you tell me what it was like seeing Nick after so long?"

"This isn't the first time I've seen him since we broke up."

"I know," he said with a patient smile. "I think you should talk about the actual first time you saw him post-breakup."

I leaned back against the wall. "Why?" I asked. "Not trying to pull rank here, but from a production standpoint, that doesn't really matter to the narrative tonight."

"Not trying to be insubordinate here," he replied, "but you might be a little close to the situation. I've done this several times now. Why not relax and trust me? Molly will edit out anything you don't think fits." I squinted at him, trying to get a sense of his expression despite the camera partially obscuring his face. Not a muscle twitched. "Fine," I said. "What did I think when I first saw him? That these three years have been good to him, I guess. Not surprising. I can't get through a month of prime time TV without running into him on some show or rerun."

"Why did you decide to use him for the show?"

"Desperation. I told him that. But he's better at handling unpredictable social situations than anyone I've ever known. And I knew the audience would love him. He always connects that way. It was a no-brainer."

"Did it make you nervous to ask him because of your history?"

It was on the tip of my tongue to say no, to be glib and gloss over it. But that wouldn't be honest. "Yes."

"Talk to me about that. Why did it make you nervous? Were you afraid he would say no?"

"Yes." I knew he wanted longer answers, more thoughtful responses, but I didn't feel comfortable offering them up.

"But isn't rejection a huge part of your job? Why did it matter if Nick said no?"

"It mattered if Nick said no because I had a lot on the line. It could have put this whole project at risk, and I had to make a big play if I wanted to save it."

"So you wouldn't have contacted him unless it was a desperate situation?"

"I guess not," I said. "He already knows this, and I don't think the audience is nearly as interested in my reasons for asking him as they are in his reasons for doing it. Maybe move along to another line of questioning?"

He ignored the suggestion. "The more footage Molly has to work with, the better. Most of this will get cut; you know that. But at least she'll have options."

I sighed and lifted an eyebrow at him. "What next?"

"What's it like being out on a date with Nick again?"

A smile jumped to my lips. "Familiar. It feels familiar to hang out with Nick again."

"Do you feel the same connection you guys had before when you dated?"

I stared at him. Like I was going to answer that. "That is definitely not part of the narrative. Why don't we focus on stuff that Molly can use? Look, I'll ask myself the questions and give the answers." I flashed a bright smile at the camera. "Being out with Nick is always fun. He has a great sense of humor, and it's easy to keep a conversation going with him." I dropped my voice an octave to mimic Ethan. "Do you feel any chemistry with him?" I spoke normally again. "Nick is a handsome, handsome man. Handsome Nick. I should get him a shirt that says that. Only a dummy wouldn't find him attractive. A dummy with a stone-cold heart. Any other questions?" This time the smile I flashed at Ethan was brittle and clearly fake.

He sighed, and the red light blinked off. He lowered the camera. "I've been told I have a pretty good feel for capturing stories. If you'd be patient with me and follow where the questions lead, you might find yourself with some interesting layers on your hands."

He wore a resigned look as if he knew that wasn't going to happen. Something about the way he phrased the questioning, the way he suggested an approach with an air of authority, sent my antennae up.

"What did you say you do out there in Lala Land?"

"Film stuff. And I guess we're done here. Let's go see if Molly and Nick are done."

I trailed after him back to the store, a twinge of guilt for being so difficult fluttering in my stomach. Then again, I wasn't part of the story. There was no point in putting all my thoughts and feelings out there when I had nothing to do with Nick's journey on the show.

We rounded the corner and found Molly and Nick on the sidewalk.

"Ready to put the finishing touches on?" Nick asked.

"Sure."

Ethan hefted his camera again, and they followed us into the store. Back at the table, we painted and laughed some more. At first, I made a determined effort to ignore the camera and Ethan and his wannabe filmmaker vibe, but soon Nick had me laughing so hard at his impersonation of a Hollywood starlet he'd worked with that I genuinely forgot about Molly and Ethan.

Another forty-five minutes passed, and then the smocked employee came over wearing an apology on her face. "Are you guys nearly done? Because we have people with reserved studio time coming, and I don't want to make them wait."

"Definitely," Nick said, standing and smiling at her. "Don't stress. We're ready to go."

"Okay. Um—" She blushed and fumbled in her back pocket for her phone. "Would it be okay if I got a picture with you?"

"Sure," he said, still smiling, but it didn't look quite as natural as before.

"I'll take it," I said, reaching for it.

"No way," he said. "You should be in the picture so she can remember the full experience."

The girl's smile turned polite, but she didn't argue. I shrugged and handed her phone to Molly before stepping next to Nick on the other side. This was so weird. Most of the night had felt pleasantly nostalgic, but this had never happened before. In the past when I'd objected to girls snapping pictures with him, Nick had always tried to placate me by telling me it was part of the job.

He dropped an arm around each of us, and I smiled until I heard the quiet click that said we were now a permanent part of this girl's digital collection.

She retrieved her phone, and after a moment a big grin split her face. "Thank you!" she said, giving Nick a quick one-armed hug before scurrying back to the front desk with her nose glued to the photo.

I laughed. "Oh, the memories."

"Yeah," he said. "Memories." He smiled at me, and I ached, actually *ached*, at the familiar curve of his lips, the smile that wasn't his public smile but his genuinely happy smile that I used to work so hard to coax from him.

I looked past him to the wall, looking for something to break the spell settling over me. As narcissistic as actors can be, they're insanely good at interpreting other peoples' emotions when they want to. "Part of the craft," Nick once told me when I'd complained that he read me like an open book. I'd avoided giving him that chance for almost three weeks now. No need to undo all my clever evasions by leaving my thoughts naked on my face. "I can't believe I did a vase when I could have painted *that*," I said, pointing.

He followed my finger, his brow furrowed. "Jerk," he said, grinning when he figured out what I was pointing to.

I sauntered over and picked up a clown mask, holding it in front of my face and peering at him through the blank eyes. "Still scared of clowns, Nicky?"

"I'm trying to be here and present with you, but you are super creepy right now."

I stuck my fingers through the eyeholes and wiggled them at him. He shuddered. "You know what they say about payback, right?"

"No, what?" I asked, returning the mask to the wall.

"It takes the form of gourmet ice-cream sandwiches," he said with a sigh. "It's hard to threaten you when I know I have to take you to get ice cream next."

I wondered if he saw my smile slip. "Have to?" I said, keeping my tone light.

"Yeah. There's a schedule to this stuff, you know." A condescending note crept into his voice. "Certain people have worked hard to put this all together, and we can't go around messing with schedules. If ice cream is on the schedule, we eat ice cream."

I smacked his arm. "I *do not* sound like that."

He laughed and drew me into a hug. "Seriously, ice cream sounds awesome to me right now. Want to?"

"Let's go."

We walked out of the pottery studio with his arm still draped over my shoulder in the same friendly way it had been during the helper girl's photo op. I stayed put instead of trying to fake a reason to move away from him. I wanted to be there. I liked how warm he felt when we stepped out into the cool sea air. I liked how he felt next to me, period. He wouldn't think anything of me returning his friendly embrace with an arm around his waist. Friendly-like. Just friends. Yep.

The ice-cream shop I had lined up was a knockoff of a famous dive in West Hollywood called Didi Reese. Day or night, you could go to that place and still end up in a line the length of the block, patiently waiting your turn to order your cookie (white chocolate macadamia nut) and ice cream to fill it (butter pecan). Surprisingly, this new place, Tony's, had a line too. Not as long as Didi Reese's but long enough for us to expect a wait.

We took our place, and I shivered. "I can't believe I didn't bring a sweater or something. It's like I haven't lived here my whole life. Duh." A slight breeze kicked up as I spoke, and I shivered again.

"How about I be your friend-jacket?" He turned me so that my back rested against his chest, and he wrapped his arms around me. "I know I'm invading your space, but this way we each have a personal space heater. Can you live with it?"

"Sure," I said, relieved when I didn't choke on the word. I was afraid the heat radiating from my body would betray exactly how good it felt to be standing there wrapped up in him, but I forced myself to relax and lean against him.

"Do you know what you're getting yet?" he asked. "Wait. I don't know about the cookie, but I'll put money on butter pecan ice cream."

"Smart bet," I said. "I can't believe you remembered that."

He said nothing, but I felt a rumble against my back. I tried to interpret it. Did he laugh at me? Why? Or maybe it was a nervous throat clearing. Again, why?

Before I could obsess over it too much longer, he asked me a question about how the Hot Iron side of things was going. "That's going to bore the viewers," I said.

"Maybe, but I'm interested. I'm sure Molly has more than enough to work with. So tell me, because I want to know. I'm so impressed that you're making this all work."

"It's hard." I craned my head to meet his gaze. "Still sound interesting?"

"Lay it on me."

I told him about why I'd left Dane-Cooper, the loan from Matt, and all of my stress. I told him about dreaming up this idea when I couldn't crack any big accounts. I told him everything, and I couldn't understand why the words fell out of my mouth without my usual instinct to sanitize and arrange them perfectly to create the impression I wanted him to have. That's only what my whole career was about.

"I had no idea," he said, and the vibrations of his voice near my ear made me shiver again. He wrapped his arms tighter, tight enough that I hoped he didn't notice that the hug buckled my knees the tiniest bit.

Why on earth wasn't I dating this guy for real again?

I needed space to clear my head, to think this through, to see if maintaining my emotional distance made any sense. But since I had no intention of slipping out of his warm arms, I struck a compromise. I wouldn't say or do anything drastic, like turn around and lay a kiss on him before yelling, "You're my destiny!" but I'd do a painful self-analysis later when I got home to figure out what the heck was going on in my head. It's like monkeys were in there randomly pressing buttons to activate different emotions. I needed to exorcise the monkeys.

Within a few minutes, we had reached the door of the shop, and I eyed it in annoyance. Once we got inside where it was warm, I'd have no reason to cuddle with Nick. I'd pretend not to notice he was still wrapped around me, kind of like when you forget your sunglasses are on your head and you wear them all day. Then I could stay right where I was. This might be someone else's exclusive privilege pretty soon, and I planned to make the most of the moment.

Unfortunately, it ended as soon as we stepped inside the shop. Nick let go and took a step back. I turned to smile at him. "Thanks for your service as a coat tonight," I said. "You can go home and give yourself a gold star."

He whipped out his phone. "Nah. I keep a checklist on here. I can cross off 'be awesome' for today."

I laughed and snatched the phone from his hand. "Are you one of those guys with a million apps?" I asked, scrolling through his home screen. "Games, three different navigation programs, a constellation finder," I read off as I spotted them. "Yeah, you're that guy." I paused at his picture folder. "I'm totally going to peek at your photos."

"That's a bad idea," he said, grabbing the phone back.

"Oh, so you're storing blackmail material on there?"

"Something like that," he said, smiling.

We reached the counter and ordered our ice-cream sandwiches, Ethan and Molly doing the same behind us. Nick handed the cashier the voucher that covered all of the desserts, and he shot me a chagrined look. "I feel like the clueless dude that takes his date for buy-one-get-one-free anything on their first night out."

I laughed. "No one thinks you're cheap. The girls all know the businesses are sponsoring your dates."

"I still feel like an idiot. We haven't talked a lot about how next week is going to go," he said. "Can I put the four dates together myself?"

He had two more first dates to go, and then we'd take a few days off while he picked who he wanted a second date with. Then the whole thing would start over on Monday. Molly and I had scrambled to find interesting stuff to post on the four days we wouldn't be showing any dates. She'd come up with the idea of a mocktail party like they did on the real *Bachelor*, where everyone dressed up and mingled. I'd vetoed it on the grounds that the more conservative viewers might be offended by something so close to a cocktail party, but the concept was sound. We'd be doing a mixer on Saturday night, where any of the viewing public who wanted to come could hang out and meet Nick or any of the bachelorettes.

It would also give him a chance to touch base with them again and firm up his choices. Nick would choose three of his dates, and the audience would choose the fourth through an online poll. That winner would be announced at the mixer. Since it was mainly Molly's idea, she insisted on running with it. I didn't know too much about the details, but I'd learned to trust Molly over this process, and I knew she had it under control. I had to step back and be okay with that since I was getting busier with other accounts.

But the following week with the actual dates was my responsibility again, and Nick's question made me nervous. "You want to plan the dates yourself?" I asked. "What did you have in mind?"

"I don't know yet," he said. "But it would make me feel less cheap if I could pay for them."

"You don't have to do that," I said. "I've got two sponsors locked up already. It would be pretty lame to ask you to sacrifice all this time and then make you pay for the favor you're doing us. I can handle it."

"I know you can. That's not my point. My point is that I'm choosing girls I connected with, and I feel like I know them pretty well already. I want to plan a date that shows each girl I was thinking of her when I put it together instead of being a puppet for some business."

I hated so many things in that small string of sentences. That he had connected with other girls, that he wanted to do something special for them, that he was insulting my livelihood as "some business."

The counter guy called Nick's name, and he fetched our ice cream before leading us to a corner table that a busboy had cleared for us.

"I don't like what you said about being a puppet," I said, unwilling to let the dig slide. "Maybe it's not the normal thing to have businesses throw free meals and bowling and cheese tasting at you, but I'm proud of the way all of this has worked out, and it's translating into business dollars. We can't all do everything for art."

He straightened in his chair. "Whoa. I'm not giving away my screenplays for free. But I've bought into this whole process now, and I think it would take the show concept next level or whatever if I got more hands-on for the second dates."

I heard a snort, and I glanced over to see Ethan trying not to laugh. Nick rolled his eyes. "Not that kind of hands-on, idiot."

"It would definitely take the show next level," Molly said, pretending to consider it.

"It's like dealing with sixth graders," I said, and Nick laughed. I smiled, but I didn't really feel it. The thought of him doing something special for four other girls made me grit my teeth so hard my jaw ached. I forced it open wide enough to slip in a bite of consolation ice cream.

Molly lowered her mic and gestured for Ethan to cut. "It's not a bad idea," she said, slipping into a seat at our table. "It could give the audience a better sense of Nick."

"But we need advertising dollars," I said.

"Come on, Lou. This isn't rocket science," she said. "You either contact the places Nick chooses and see if they want to advertise, or you do what's already working and sell ad space to other businesses in the sidebar. You're being weird about this." Her perplexed expression mirrored Nick's.

"It's not more weird than usual for a total control freak," I said. "Sure, let's go with it. But I'm going to need your ideas as soon as you have them so I can clear filming on the premises, plus see if any of the places you pick want to sponsor the date."

"Cool," he said.

I shook my head. "I hear guys complain about planning dates all the time, and here you are, excited to do it."

"I wouldn't have wanted to do it three weeks ago, but after all these dates you put together for the show, it gave me some ideas for new things to try."

Molly threw up her arms. "Victory! That's one of the things we wanted to do. Show people that a date isn't a movie and a burger. Don't you feel good about that?" she asked, smiling at me.

"Yep, good." I glanced around the shop. It had filled up even more with people crowding against the windows to eat their ice-cream sandwiches and shoot sidelong glances at Nick and our camera crew. "This date is about over, right? We have enough footage to do the edits."

Molly shook her head. "*We* nothing. I don't trust you to edit yourself. I'm doing all of it. And no, we're not done yet. You have final check-ins."

Nick and I groaned at the same time, which made Ethan laugh. "You guys act like you haven't had a great night. Come on, Lou. Let's go outside and find a decent pool of light to film this."

"You're bossy," I said, shutting one eye and studying him from the other. "I can't figure you out."

"Nothing to figure," he said. "I'm boring. Vanilla boring. Instant pudding vanilla boring, even."

I rose, throwing Nick a long-suffering look over my shoulder. He grinned, not a trace of sympathy in his expression. "Welcome to my life. Have fun."

I stuck my tongue out at him and followed Ethan. Ethan might be vanilla, but something about his demeanor nagged at me. Molly had gotten to hang out with our cameramen way more than I had, but even comparing Mikey and Ethan highlighted massive differences in the way they approached the filming. Mikey treated his work professionally but like a technician. He had a solid grasp of the standard shots we would need for the show, and he rarely needed direction.

Ethan, on the other hand, often slipped into the role of director himself, coming back to "narrative" often, speaking up when he saw an opportunity for better storytelling. I dug to see if I could nail down the source of the air of command that clung to him when he didn't remember to act like a regular camera dude. "Thanks for filming so many of these dates. I know it's time-consuming."

"No problem. You guys are running an interesting social experiment. I like being a fly on the wall."

"Yeah, but it's gotta be a pain commuting for these dates."

He shrugged. "I'm not here every day. It's no biggie. And if Mikey and I didn't come down, Nick would be kind of stuck for clothes and stuff."

I hadn't even asked about how Nick was handling those details. I had assumed he'd been driving back every few days to grab what he needed.

"Has he left Huntington since we started filming?" I asked.

"I don't think so. It'd be pretty hard for him to get away. Especially since he spends most of his days writing. I think he's approaching it like a writer's retreat."

I considered that. It was yet another example of how he took his career shift seriously. "How come I never see him at church?"

"In the Beachside Ward?" he asked. "He said he goes with his aunt to her ward. She lives over in Newport."

"Oh." I stopped when he checked the level of the light under a streetlight. "I hope you haven't had to miss any work to do this." Yeah, subtle fishing there.

Amusement crossed his face again. "Nope, not missing anything right now. I have time off between projects."

Huh. I stayed quiet while he positioned me under the streetlight, fussing with where I stood until he liked what he saw through the camera. He opened with the standard question. "How do you think the date went?"

I gave him a generic answer that could have covered nearly every first date I'd had in my life. He asked more questions, and I answered absently, trying to figure out his deal. I smiled or nodded and, in the meantime, wondered what Nick was saying in his check-in.

"Thanks for getting into the spirit of things," Ethan said when we finished.

He was doing it again, thanking me as if I had contributed to his project rather than him being a volunteer hand on mine. He did it without any arrogance; I doubted he even realized he'd spoken with a proprietary tone. I wanted to snap that it was *my* project, but I said nothing. I didn't have the luxury of running off my volunteers just because they had become invested in the process; that should be cause for relief.

"We better see if Nick and Molly are finished too." I held out my hand like it was an afterthought. "Might as well give me the memory card so I can give it to Molly."

"You're not as sneaky as you think you are," he said, smiling. "I'll give it to her. I heard her say she's editing this, not you, remember?"

"Just thought I'd help you out. Excuse me for trying."

"Once again, you're not sneaky. You're also not a good actress." His smile had grown into a grin by now.

"What is so dang funny?" I asked.

"You." He turned back toward the ice-cream place without waiting to see if I followed. "Things suddenly make a lot more sense to me now."

I hurried after him, and it bugged me. "Like what things?"

"I'm not on camera. I don't have to answer your questions."

"I want to kick you right now."

"Nope," he said. "You wouldn't. I'm not nice, and I'll kick back."

"You're annoying."

"I know."

We walked in silence, passing the ice-cream parlor when we spotted Nick and Molly farther down the sidewalk. I should probably have been angry, but I wasn't. Unless it was at myself. Why couldn't I be interested in someone like Ethan instead of being hung up on my been-there-done-that-and-failed ex-boyfriend? A laugh escaped me as I thought of all of the roommates I'd lectured through the years for wasting time on similarly pointless relationships.

"What's so funny?" Ethan asked.

"Me. Sometimes my own lameness overcomes me, and I have to vent it. It's laugh or cry, buddy."

"Lameness?" He patted my head. "Maybe. I'm still figuring that out."

"You are so like my brother that it's spooky," I said. "I'd have to use exponents to count how many times he's patted me on the head like that when I'm being an idiot."

"Mine was a preemptive pat. I don't know if you're an idiot."

"Thanks," I said and threw a punch at him exactly like I'd done with Matt countless times through the years.

He definitely had sisters because he anticipated it and snatched my fist before it connected with his side. By now we'd reached Nick and Molly. Without a word, he thrust his camera at Molly, who grabbed it and watched with interest as he yanked on my captured fist and pulled me into his side, anchoring me with his other arm.

"What's going on?" Nick asked, confusion on his face.

"I think I have to adopt her," Ethan said. "We already treat each other like family."

"No, you don't. Four sisters is enough," Nick said.

"Nah. I like my sisters. More is good. You're in the tribe," he said to me while tousling my hair. "Congratulations."

"You are so weird," I said, grinning. "Who says I want another brother?"

"I think this is predestined. Sorry. You're stuck."

Nick reached over and disentangled my hand from Ethan's. "I've got sister dibs," he said. He tucked me against his side and jerked his head toward Molly. "I've got that one too. Why don't you hand over the footage so you can get on the road, and then I'll walk the girls to their car."

Ethan smiled and popped out the data card for Molly. "It's been real," he said, tapping me on the nose. "Really real." He secured the flap over his camera bag and shouldered it before heading toward the public parking garage with a wave to us as he left.

Nick kept his arm around my shoulder and slipped the other around Molly's. "No way," she said. "No playing big brother so you can avoid schlepping equipment." She slid away and shoved the boom mic and our smaller camera bag at him. "You strong like ox. You carry."

"You're kind of selective about when girls get to play the helpless card and when they don't," he said, accepting the equipment. He kept his other arm around me. I wondered if he even remembered he had left it there.

"I'm not helpless," Molly said. "I'm not even pretending to be helpless. I just don't want to carry it anymore, so you get to."

"Man, just when I think Lou is the bossy one, you show this side of yourself and remind me that it's you."

I said nothing as they continued to bicker on the way back to the car. They definitely sounded like old friends, if not siblings. It made sense, given how much time they'd spent with each other over the last three weeks. But I didn't know how I felt about being lumped into the sister category. No, I *did* know how I felt. I didn't like it one bit, but I wished I didn't care.

Almost as if he'd channeled my thoughts, Nick gave me a quick squeeze. "Thanks for giving me a break tonight. I can power through now."

"Here's the good news: you have only two more dates, and then you don't ever have to psych yourself up to the first date thing ever again if you don't want to." If he found someone in all of this that he truly gelled with, by the time the next round of dating started, he may have gone on his last first date. Jealousy flooded the back of my throat like acid reflux.

"Yeah, about that. I already know who I want for two of the spots, but unless one of these next few dates shocks the heck out of me, I don't think I'm going to fill the third. Want to step into the spot and save me again?"

"Nope," I said. "I mean, I would, except that we're getting almost twenty thousand hits a day, and I'd get at least half that many angry e-mails saying I'd fixed it because I'm the producer. You'll have to go with whoever least annoyed you." Instead of relief that he didn't like a third girl enough to pick one, I fretted over the two he had locked in already. Chelsey and Cara, most likely, and I hated myself for hating them. They were cool, and he'd be smart to consider something longer term with either of them.

"Fine, then." With a smile and a gentle tug on my hair, he let his arm drop. "Make Molly do it."

"Ha!" she said. "Sorry. You'll have to pick one of the awesome girls you went out with. Try to get past the trauma."

"Do I sound like a huge jerk?" he asked and then answered before either of us could. "I do. But I don't mean to. It's just that this is a more loaded situation. A second date with any of the girls implies I like them significantly. I don't want to lead anyone on, is all. Especially not for an audience."

"Fair enough," Molly said. "But no matter who you choose, she's going to know she only has a one in four shot. Your three choices plus the viewers' pick. Don't worry about it."

We reached Molly's Mini, and she disarmed it. Nick deposited his cargo in the back and straightened up. "It was good to see you tonight," he said and pulled me into a hug. "This whole thing has been keeping us both way too busy."

I returned the hug, resting my head against his chest so I could steal the sound of his heartbeats for a minute. My morning run would fall in time to that rhythm for the indefinite future. I tightened my arms and pretended for a moment that we had shared a real date.

The slam of Molly's car door broke us up, and I stepped back to blink at her and reorient myself to reality. "Let's go," she said through her lowered window. "I've got massive editing to do."

Nick shoved his hands in his pockets. "I'll have a blog post for you by morning."

"That'll be a weird read. A recap of my own date."

"Not weirder than it's going to be for me to write."

I walked around to my side and climbed in. He stayed put as Molly pulled out and drove off. I stole a glance in the rearview mirror, hoping to see him still standing there staring after us. All I saw was his retreating back as he headed the other way.

"I'm stupid," I said out loud.

"Rarely," Molly answered.

I smiled, but it was a good thing she couldn't read my disappointment that Nick didn't pine for me in nearly the same way I did for him.

Chapter 12

I KEPT MY BEDROOM DOOR shut and locked so none of my roommates could peek in. It would ruin my low-maintenance image if they saw me standing in front of my closet agonizing over my choices. The Molly Party, as Lily and Autumn had taken to calling it, would start in about ten minutes in our transformed courtyard, and I needed to be there to greet people, bachelorette people whom Nick possibly liked a lot, bachelorette people he didn't necessarily like but who would show up looking good, and other boys besides Nick who had been invited to keep the mixer from being super weird.

Since the party was open to anyone who wanted to come meet the people they'd been watching all season, Molly figured on a high girl turnout because of our star, but she'd recruited guys to show up too so the girls wouldn't all complain that it was lame. Except it turned out that she needed to do no persuading; every guy she approached, knowing the caliber of women who'd be there, jumped at the chance to come.

She'd set it all up, pulling us and our neighbors across the hall out to decorate all afternoon. Now the courtyard of our complex glowed with twinkle lights and cozily spaced chairs, plus a table of light refreshments. Lots of blinds in lots of windows twitched as our neighbors peeked out to see what the crazy Mormons were up to. Within the hour, the space would bulge with good-looking Church folk on the prowl. I shuddered at the thought.

I had a few "cocktail" dresses from my Dane-Cooper days, thanks to all the swanky parties they made us go to. I growled in annoyance at myself and grabbed a simple black sheath in raw silk. Knee length, cap sleeve, fitted enough not to be boring. Whatever. I threw on my highest, strappiest stilettos and let them compensate for the understated dress.

I shouldn't be flustered, but this would be the first time I'd seen Nick since our date aired, hence the freak out. Since Molly had refused to let me see the video before it posted, I got to see it with everyone else.

How to explain the out-of-body sensation? Imagine your biggest crush in middle school. Then imagine someone standing on a cafeteria table and shouting about it to the whole school. And then imagine that you are not lucky enough for the earth to open up and swallow you the way girls in teen novels always wish it would. Since the sweet mercy of spontaneous death escaped me, I had sat through Molly's five-minute video and squirmed. Maybe even writhed.

She had watched me, fascinated. "What is wrong with you? You came off great."

"So far, in minute one, I look like someone with a serious thing for my ex-boyfriend."

"Are you?"

"Yeah. And I don't need the whole world to know it."

"Keep watching," she had said.

I had leaned forward and turned up the volume on his first confessional. "I forgot until I started this thing how much I missed Louisa's sense of humor. She's so easy to be around. I remember having this favorite blanket when I was a kid. I dragged it everywhere, and then I left it at my grandparents' house, and I didn't get it back for three months. I forgot how comfortable it was until I had it again. I'm probably not doing a great job of setting up the metaphor here, and if I put this in one of my scripts, I'd also write in the girl slapping the guy who said that to her, but it's the best way I know how to explain it."

I had watched the rest of the video in a funk. Painting stuff, laughing, ice-cream sandwiches. It looked like every other date he'd been on. Except worse. Other girls got to be the chick who, according to Nick, any guy would be lucky to hang out with; I got to be the comfy old blanket. Not awesome.

His blog post had given me a moment of hope, but it was that kind of hope where the lottery jackpot climbs to six hundred million and you're almost convinced you have a shot until you remember, *Oh yeah, you didn't buy a ticket.* Because it would be against the rules. And Nick was definitely against the rules.

But I had almost forgotten for one breathtaking paragraph when I read through it before publishing it. And in an unhealthy move that was becoming scarily habitual, I ran through the words I'd memorized.

There are people who are a gift in your life. Lou has come into mine twice now, and it's been exactly the right moment each time. You know how some people challenge your worldview in a way that makes you want to punch them, and others do it in a way that leads you to more self-reflection than you'd ever do on your own? Lou is the second kind of person. Just being around someone who is so together makes you rethink your own priorities and values without her ever saying a word.

A small thrill had run through me the first time I read that. Maybe he would hint that he wanted something more. Maybe he would confess that he dreamed of rekindling our romance. Uh-huh. And maybe he was sitting in Kade's living room playing "loves-me-not" with a daisy. The following paragraph nipped all hope in the bud. Like a super mean, cranky gardener kind of nipping too.

Louisa and I aren't the love match of the decade or anything, but it's been a total sanity saver to have her back in my life as a friend.

And it got ouchier and more depressing from there. I went from being a gift in his life to "not a love match."

But that first paragraph . . . it wouldn't conveniently exit my memory. If I could, I'd reach in and scrub the neural pathway it had imprinted on, disinfect the germy hope it had left in its wake when it had blazed through, but I couldn't. And so I replayed it again. And again.

I stomped to the courtyard. Time to burn some new images into my brain. I had a fun night ahead of me, watching at least a dozen girls flirt with Nick. Even better, I might get to see him flirt back.

Oh, joy.

* * *

Two hours later, I hid behind a potted palm tree in a corner of the courtyard. I felt badly about that. I should be out helping Molly facilitate the mingling. She darted from a cluster of bright dresses to a clod of khakis and button-downs, trying to encourage interaction where none was happening. Most of the people had it figured out though. It was the only way I could justify hiding. That, and I didn't want Ace Porfitt to see me. Guess what Ace did for a living? If you guessed he played beach volleyball, you'd be right.

Ace was Kade's partner on the pro tour, and now that he'd caught wind of Nick's adventure, he'd decided to crash the party and scope out the girls for himself. This was a guy too lazy to attend the Beachside Ward more than a handful of times a year, but apparently a buffet of Mormon girls without the inconvenience of actual church was irresistible. And lucky me, I think I'd become the hot commodity on the buffet table.

In a way, I appreciated that it kept me distracted from Nick. The first hour before Ace arrived and decided to stalk me had been rough. Nick always had at least four girls around him at any given moment. Several of his dates had shown up, but curious nonbachelorettes had rotated in and out of the entourage too. Every time I'd seen Cara or Chelsey near him, I'd gritted my teeth and turned away, busying myself with brushing imaginary crumbs from the food table. Luckily, Ethan and Mikey had both shown up, and the two of them hung with me a bit. But still. I had a half hour of this left to get through. After that we had to herd people out of the courtyard and shut this psychological torture chamber down per our agreement with our neighbors.

Not that anyone else looked tortured, really. Everywhere I looked, I caught bright smiles, heard tinkles of laughter, low, husky chuckles, and the hum of smoothly flowing conversations. From what I could tell, most of the guys had come specifically to meet the girls featured on the series. Ace had told me he'd seen my date with Nick and thought I was a cool chick. It would have been appreciated, except I knew his reputation as a player, and for another thing, something about the way he'd said it came off like he was doing me a favor. Ugh.

Nick excused himself from his fan club for . . . Cambry's place? The noise level rose as people noticed his exit. I hoped for his sake it wasn't just a potty break. How embarrassing to have everyone observe you so closely that they all knew what your bladder was up to.

Molly went to stand beneath an outdoor propane heater she'd borrowed and cleared her throat. No one looked her way. She did it louder with the same result. With a look of exasperation, she stomped over to our neighbor Micah's house and hauled his plastic patio chair back to the lamp before climbing on top of it and clapping her hands with a sharp crack.

This time heads turned.

"Ladies and gentlemen, we decided to spring a surprise on you tonight."

We did?

"As you know, Nick has been hard at work dating some amazing ladies, many of whom are here. Now that he's gone on his twenty-one first dates, the next step is for him to explore some of those connections in more depth."

Ace whooped, a silly junior high whoop for a total nonentendre. Idiot.

Molly ignored him and continued. "Tonight we thought it would be fun to give a bigger nod to the cheesy parent show that spawned our heartfelt social experiment. Ladies and gentlemen, please welcome Nick for the most dramatic rose ceremony ever!"

A wave of laughter swept through the girls as they recognized the well-worn phrase from their reality-TV guilty pleasure. Polite applause broke out as Cambry threw her front door open and Nick stepped out. He'd been wearing gray dress pants and a pale pink button-down that worked way better than it should have on any straight male. But now he'd added a suit jacket and tie that made him look more formal and painfully handsome. In his hand, he carried four white roses. Four? He was only supposed to announce the audience favorite tonight.

He stepped over to a small pedestal several feet to the left of Molly that had minutes before held a pitcher of ice water and glasses. Now it boasted a silver tray. With quiet efficiency, Ethan slipped through the crowd and herded them back to create a clear space in front of Nick. Mikey moved over to shoot Nick, and Cambry hurried over to bring Ethan his camera. That must have been hiding inside their apartment too.

Molly scampered up to me, ducking under the low-hanging palm fronds of my hiding place.

"What is going on?" I asked as Nick picked up the first rose.

"Hush," she said. "And whatever you do, play along, or I'll kill you because there are witnesses who will see everything, and I can't go back and edit you for the reaction I want."

"What are you—"

"Shhh."

Nick cleared his throat. "I think on the TV show, the bachelor usually does a speech. I figure I do enough talking when I go on and on in my blog posts, so I'll spare us all." A small laugh met that. "I'll leave it at this: I hear complaints about the dating scene after BYU or for midtwenties or whatever. All I know is that I've spent time with almost two dozen awesome women in the last three weeks, and the guys who came to meet you tonight are smart. Any guys not getting their acts together enough to get to know the amazing girls right here in Huntington are idiots." Much louder laughter greeted that and a few claps too.

"That said," he continued, his face growing more serious, "I could only pick three girls to go out with again. These three women are all so different from each other, but they share one thing in common; each of them is intelligent, comfortable in her own skin, and easy to be around. I look forward to spending more time getting to know them better. For anyone who doesn't receive a rose tonight, don't worry. My voice mail is blowing up every day with messages from friends who want to date you. I'll be putting only the cool ones in touch."

I glared at Molly. "This was a massive production decision for you to not run by me. This is completely uncool." We'd been planning to reveal the finalists on Sunday in a confessional-style interview like his check-ins, where he would name each of his choices and say nice things about them.

"Take it easy, control freak. You're going to have to have more faith in my flair for the dramatic and my professional instincts." The calm in her voice only made me madder.

"This is not okay," I said.

"It *is* okay. It's going to be better than okay, especially if you shut up and play along like I told you to."

"Cara," Nick called out so she could hear him.

The crowd parted to let her through, and she walked up to stand right in front of him. I couldn't see her face from my vantage point.

"Cara, will you accept this rose?"

"Yes," she said, taking it and giving him a hug. When she turned, she winked into Ethan's camera, and a huge smile split her face. No surprise there.

Nick selected his next rose. "Chelsey, will you accept this rose?"

Again, no surprise. Chelsey accepted it with a happy smile and a hug.

Now I was hooked in spite of myself. Nick had said he didn't want anyone for the third spot. Neither of his last two dates had seemed like anything special when I edited them. Molly had kept me up to date on the voting, so I knew the audience had chosen Cara, Chelsey, Brooklyn, and Hailey for the top four fan favorites so far. But who had Nick decided would fit number three?

"Merry?" he called.

She stepped into the space. Merry? Seriously? *Seriously?* Granted, she was much cooler than Molly and I had realized as we'd gotten to know her over the last two weeks at our Sunday dinners, but Nick didn't know that side of her. He'd gotten Merry the Vixen.

I snorted, and Molly glanced at me, startled. "We like her, remember?"

"We like her for the right reasons," I said. "Why am I so disappointed that he's suddenly being a regular boy?"

"Cut him some slack," she said. "He's been a good judge of character up to this point."

Merry had already slipped back into the crowd with her rose, and Molly jumped up and hurried to Nick, who had a furrow in his brow.

Molly stepped up next to him, looking comically small next to his tall frame. "As you can see, there's still one rose remaining. That's because we've been running a poll on *The Mormon Bachelor* website to see who the audience favorite is, and that lucky girl is . . ." She trailed off in a dramatic pause, and I supplied the rest of the sentence in my head: not that lucky. Nick didn't even want his third choice, much less this audience-chosen fourth he was about to be saddled with.

Nick had picked up the rose, and now he smiled at Molly.

"Louisa? Will you accept this rose?"

Chapter 13

"I TOTALLY VOTED FOR YOU!"

"Lucky!"

"I knew it would be you!"

I accepted all of the comments with a dethorned rose clutched in my hand and a vague smile on my lips. I'd done as Molly asked and played along with it, but the hard look I flashed her warned her that we'd be discussing this later.

For twenty more minutes, I'd stood in the middle of the courtyard and chatted with people about my rose, all the while wondering what fueled the satisfied grin on Nick's face whenever he caught my eye. The crowd thinned now that the evening had peaked with the rose ceremony. Several girls who didn't get picked had left shortly after, and several of the guys had followed them. Now only the behind-the-scenes people plus Merry remained, and my roommates had come out of our place to help clean up.

Nick wandered over with Merry right on his heels.

"Congratulations," she said, smiling at me.

"Thanks? Uh, you too."

She burst out laughing at that.

"Thanks are more appropriate than congratulations," Nick said. "I cheated and contacted Merry ahead of time to see if she'd be cool with standing in as the third date. I figured she wouldn't mind doing some acting, and then I don't have to worry about sending the wrong message to anyone."

"You both owe me," she said. "I'll pretend, but do you guys realize I have to be rejected in front of every single viewer when he picks Cara or Chelsey? So you better think of some awesome compensation."

"Like what?" I asked.

"That Luke guy," she said. "Serve him up. I'll handle it from there."

"No problem," I said, remembering his comment after her date aired. "It's not like it will take any convincing."

She smiled and headed to my condo, where several of the other girls were probably conducting a grisly postmortem on the evening.

I turned back to Nick. "You're pretty cheerful about being stuck with me again. Just so you know, you don't have to make our date a huge thing. Do something cheap and easy. Or better yet, let me plan it."

"Nope," he said. "Consider it payback for stepping in again to save me from another awkward date. And we should probably find out who the second highest vote-getter is and make her write you a thank you note for saving her from a lame date with me."

I smiled. "I doubt any of your dates would think I saved them. In fact, let's never tell anyone that Molly rigged this; that way I won't get shanked in the restroom before Sunday School or something."

"I rigged *nothing*," Molly said. "You got the highest votes. I just kept lying to you about it because I knew you would have a fit."

"Probably my mom and Matt and Ashley voted a hundred times each," I said.

"Nah. People can only vote once, and you got over sixty percent of those votes. It was a lot of votes," she added, looking pleased.

She must be confident of Nick's immunity to me, or she wouldn't go along with this so easily. I almost frowned, but I caught myself in time.

"If I gotta, then I gotta," I said. "I've been out with worse dates."

Nick rolled his eyes. "Thank you, Lou. That means everything."

"Yeah, yeah. Get out of here. Are you finally going back to Malibu tonight?"

"Yep. It'll be good to sleep in my own bed again. And do laundry. I don't even know if it's all going to fit in my car. Three weeks of clothes is a lot," he said. "I'm going to have a Mount Baldy of rank rags in my backseat for an hour and a half." He shuddered.

"Don't be so hard on yourself. You're not rank." I sniffed the air. "Maybe musty sometimes."

"That's it. I'm officially planning the worst date for you."

"Bring it on."

He laughed and pulled Molly and then me in for a hug. "See you in a few days. And the boys are happy to do all the taping."

"Good," I said. "We all know it doesn't matter, but I think it would weird out Cara and Chelsey if I were on their dates. Now that I've been out with you, I'm not really your average camera guy anymore. To them, I'm competition."

"Thank Mikey and Ethan again a million billion for us," Molly said. "They're so good. Ethan especially. He thinks of stuff—angles, questions, music—that would never cross my mind."

True. He was dang good.

Nick shrugged. "He likes it. Keeps him sharp in between projects."

That struck me. Mikey was between *gigs*. Why was Ethan between *projects* if they were both camera guys? Wouldn't the slang be the same? Maybe it was some kind of difference between TV and film. "What kind of projects does he usually do?"

Nick's eyebrows rose in surprise. "I can't believe you didn't Google him. You should." He slung his jacket over his shoulder and strolled off down the hallway toward the street, whistling as he went.

Molly and I stared after him for a moment then broke into a mad run for the condo. She beat me by slipping off her shoes, but I was right behind her. The half dozen girls lounging on the sofa glanced up when we burst through the door, but neither of us stopped until we reached her Mac. Her fingers flew over the keyboard.

"Great party," Autumn said. "I got a date."

"Excellent! Tell us about it in a minute," I said as I hovered over Molly's shoulder. Two seconds later, she clicked on a search result, and two seconds after that, my jaw dropped. "Whoa," I said. Ethan the camera guy, Ethan who had maybe a couple of years on us but bossed us around like it was a decade of experience, had more to his credit than camera experience. Like his name as director on two documentaries, including one that earned an Oscar nomination. I'd seen that one, a film called *The Dawn Patrol Girls*, an exposé on sexism toward women surfers on the pro circuit.

"What the what?" Molly said, shock sending her voice up an octave. She twisted to look up at me. "I had no idea."

"Me neither. Why in the world is that guy," I stabbed at his picture on the screen, "messing around on our stupid project?"

"It's not stupid," Lily called from the couch. "It indirectly got Autumn a date."

I hauled myself away from the computer. These girls had worked hard for us tonight, and at the very least, I could pay them back with sincere excitement. "Very cool, Autumn. Let me guess." I thought about who I'd seen her talking to throughout the party. "Kel Barnes."

"Yes! Best party ever!" She filled us in on their conversation through the whole night, and I settled back to listen with a smile.

I'd had my suspicions about whom Nick would choose, but no matter what, at least a handful of dates with potential had come out of this. Nick's point from three weeks ago sank in again: the world had gotten to see some flat-out cool girls, and at least a few guys had been smart enough not to pass up an opportunity. I knew some of our "jilted" bachelorettes hadn't escaped the party before surrendering their phone numbers to some quality guys. I felt pretty good about that.

This whole process had wrecked me. It chewed me up daily. I had a bruised heart, a new "friend" whom I wanted as something much more, and an obligation to step back and let him take a shot at a relationship that would work instead of one I'd broken with my impatience and superiority long ago. But if in all of that, a few people found love with each other, then it would all be worth it.

I guess.

* * *

We hit the wrong side of midnight before I could ask Molly the question that had bugged me all evening.

"You should have rigged it when you saw it would be me," I said. "Why didn't you? Do you have any idea how hard this has been for me?"

"Yes," she said and closed her Mac. "When Nick makes his final choice, will you really be ready to wish him well and move on?"

"Yeah. I have to be."

She frowned. "Not even you can tell yourself how to feel. I've been watching you try to talk yourself out of your feelings for him for days now."

"Then why are you pushing me toward him?"

She sighed. "Can I tell you something hard?"

My stomach dropped. I swallowed. "Yes."

"I think Nick has made his choice. You're not a threat to the show anymore. You need to see for yourself exactly how it's going to play out for you guys, or in the future, you might always have that what-if."

"You think he's made his choice?" I asked, hating how weak my voice sounded. "Who?"

"You know."

I nodded. I did know. Cara. She was perfect for him.

"I can't do this," I said. "I haven't even been able to film the dates. I can't go on another date and fake my way through it. I can't."

Her forehead creased, and she shifted in her seat. The apartment had emptied out an hour ago, and Lily and Autumn had both gone to bed. But she still lowered her voice when she answered. "Not an option, Lou. Even if we didn't post the announcement that you got the votes, too many people already know. More than that, it's the best thing for you. I believe that. You need to know. And if you don't do it, then what? Miss Runner-Up can know that not only did he not pick her, but even the audience didn't? That's not fair."

"I wish you would have told me instead of springing it on me like that."

"I knew you'd say no if I didn't trap you. I'm sorry. I know it doesn't seem like it, but I really am trying to be a good friend." She leaned toward me across the table. "Reality is that we can't undo this. Not without gossip starting or advertisers thinking we're flakes or whatever."

I plowed my fingers through my hair. "The gossip would bother me more. People are going to make up some drama between Nick and me if I don't show, huh?"

"Yeah," she said with a sigh. "Especially since almost everyone who showed up tonight is in Beachside."

"I'll do it," I said. "I'll have to practice my friends-only act."

"Maybe not," she said, considering me. "Have you gone in and looked at the comments from your date yet?"

I shook my head. I'd set them all to forward to her e-mail for approval before our date aired. I didn't want to hear the feedback, and she'd offered to take over all comment moderation after that so I could focus more on strategy.

"People liked you guys together. Way liked you."

"That's weird. We were buds the whole night. How is that interesting?"

She started to answer but stopped.

"What?"

"Nothing," she said. "But I have some theories. Nick is more relaxed around you than he is with anyone else."

"Well, duh. I'm an old, stinky blanket."

She ignored that. "Lots of girls have that 'what if' guy, and they're indulging a little wish fulfillment by cheering for you guys to get together." She pushed away from the table and headed for her cabinet, where she dug out a box of Joe Joes. "I need fuel for editing tonight. I've got another hour left in me, and then I'll have to finish in the morning."

I shook my head when she offered me a cookie.

"I'll eat yours for you." The cookie made it halfway to her mouth before she froze. "Don't do that."

"Do what?"

"Frown at me because I'm not strong enough to resist. You're Super Woman. The rest of us succumb to cookies in times of stress. We're mortal."

"I wasn't frowning."

"You're still frowning."

I was. I smoothed my expression. "I don't care if you eat cookies."

"You do. You don't get why I don't just give the box away when I'm always complaining about needing to lose ten pounds."

"I'm too tired to be reminded of my deep, unfixable flaws. You said theories. What else do you figure?"

She ate her next cookie in a single bite. "Everyone loves the in-love-with-your-best-friend story line. It's even better than the dating-the-bachelor story line. More wish fulfillment. Which means you should give them that. It's not like Nick is going to know you mean it."

"So go out with him and act as smitten as I feel? Yeah right."

"Seriously. You should. Lots of pluses. If you try to act not smitten, you're going to be stiff and awkward. No fun for the audience. Act how you feel, big win for the audience. "

"And my face is the love note being read from the top of the cafeteria table."

"What?"

"Nothing."

"Okaaaay," she said, eyeing me with slight confusion. "You give the audience what they want. You tell Nick that's what you're doing, putting on a show, and he'll never question it."

"He'll lecture me about how we have to keep it real, and he'll refuse to play along. You know he will."

"Too bad for him. Tell him it's the price he has to pay for making you take the date."

I considered it. How would it feel to act exactly the way I wanted to toward him without worrying about giving myself away? I could touch him whenever I wanted, smile at him without worrying what he could read into it. Just for a night. Molly's plan made a strange sort of sense. And I'd been a very, very good girl. I deserved it after a month of working eighty-hour weeks, watching girls falling all over Nick, patching my heart up after every video of his dates sliced it open.

"Fine," I said. "I'll do it for the show."

"Smart choice," Molly said. "It'll play really well."

Maybe. But I wanted this game to be over, and soon.

Chapter 14

I WOULD BAT THIRD IN the lineup. Nick went out with Chelsey and Merry first. For Chelsey's date, he took her salsa dancing in Santa Monica. Much like their first date, they laughed constantly and talked easily. I had to depend on dancing footage and snippets of conversation to piece a video together though. While Mikey had given me lots of great action shots of Chelsey smiling and shaking her moneymaker like she'd danced salsa before she learned to walk, the check-ins fell flat. She came off like she was having a great time, but Mikey didn't ask great lead-in questions, and it didn't give me much to work with.

Nick had been as thorough as always in his answers, but I couldn't do a ton of his thoughts and none of hers; the piece would feel lopsided. Luckily, he'd saved it with a strong blog post. He'd decided on a slightly different format for the final entries. Instead of a recap, he thought it would be good to create a sense of mystery by listing the ten things he liked best about each girl and leaving the audience to guess which one he liked the most. His list for Chelsey included things like her fearlessness and the way she embraced every experience. Pretty accurate there.

Merry's date had a totally different vibe. In a stark contrast to their superhero bowling ridiculousness, he'd invited her up to Malibu and dinner at a swanky restaurant. I nearly fell out of my chair when I got three different texts from Molly during the date to tell me which famous celebrities had stopped by their table while they ate. Merry had loved it, I knew. For one, she gushed on and on about it in her check-in, but beyond that, it was so her scene. All the glitz and glam and poshness of it. I knew her well enough by now to understand that it didn't come from a shallow place. The girl had deep roots in her; she just loved illusion and spectacle. And drama. Man, did she ham it up.

I had no idea if the audience would catch on or not, but she got dang close to falling over the top. Nick stayed his usual self, charming and complimentary and present; that was the quality I saw in him most that I'd missed in him when we dated. He'd rarely been present.

That Nick had disappeared, and this new one stayed always in the moment, always focused on his date. If he had been like that with me, not only could I not have walked away, but I wouldn't have wanted to.

His list for Merry talked about her vivacity and allure and total comfort with herself. Again, totally right. The comments on the blog ran to debates over which of the two girls he actually liked better. The audience seemed slightly more convinced that he was into Merry according to Molly's unofficial calculations. I took her word for it since I had no desire to read through the comments myself.

And yet . . . this whole second-date thing so far hadn't been nearly the soul-crushing experience I had feared. I didn't love watching all the flirting and meaningful looks between him and the girls, but I could tolerate it.

Maybe it was knowing his choice was made, and I couldn't do anything about it. It helped to keep myself as busy as ever. I had several non-*TMB*–related campaigns to worry about now. Molly had quit the café completely so she could handle shooting *and* doing graphic work, and I'd written another satisfying check to Matt. I still dropped in on my mom's pantry, but mostly to make her feel better.

But it was my turn now, and I couldn't bury my nerves about a second date under distractions anymore.

"You're nervous," Molly said, watching as my hand tapped my gearshift. We had been on PCH headed north for almost an hour, and I felt twitchier with every mile my tires swallowed toward Malibu.

"Yes."

"Why? It's Nick. You don't have to impress him."

"I'm going to stick with the friend thing."

"No way. We can't end this season with you being a boring friend date."

"Maybe I don't feel like being emotionally naked for the whole Interwebs," I snapped.

She said nothing. I took a deep breath. "Sorry."

"It's okay," she said. "But I wish you wouldn't freak out. It only matters if Nick thinks you're being emotionally naked, and he already knows you're going to be 'acting.' It's a double-reverse. No emotional nudity. He's not going to know it's real."

"But what if he does?"

"He won't," she said. "He didn't suspect anything when you guys talked yesterday, did he?"

"No." I sighed. Our daily talks had gotten longer. Sometimes I called him back from my car on the way to visit new businesses, and an hour later, I'd find myself still sitting in a parking lot chatting instead of getting out and getting clients. We talked about bachelorette stuff. Or sometimes not. Sometimes he wanted to bounce script ideas off me because he wanted the female perspective. Sometimes the conversation meandered, and we talked about nothing. I loved it, and I hated it, but I couldn't shut it down. The day before when he'd called, I told him my plan to "act" into him.

"No way. I need our date to be real, or my brain will explode. Let's just hang out," he'd begged.

But I'd put my foot down and used Molly's line about it being the price he had to pay for pinning me into it. He'd grumbled a bunch but then had agreed.

"It's going to be weird trying to act all romantic with you," he'd said.

Twelve words to shred my ego into a dozen pieces and my heart into twice that. I pressed harder on the accelerator.

"Chill," Molly said. "We don't need to hit warp speed to get there."

"Whatever. I want to get this over with." Which was only kind of true. Part of me wanted to spend a few hours with Nick under the most backward of pretenses: no pretense at all, just me and all of my sticky feelings, only he'd never know. He'd be ready to send me home with one of his People's Choice awards from his teen idol days for my incredible acting.

I pulled into the public park he'd directed me to, and Molly hopped out. "Stay here while Ethan and I get the shot set up. I'll text you when we're ready."

Almost ten minutes later, my phone went off. *We're ready. Watch for the cluster of three palms.* I climbed out of the car and smoothed down my capris, which were white denim and not one bit wrinkled. Nick had said to dress casually, so I had, topping the pants with a flowy coral shirt and a funky blue necklace. I picked my way across the grass, careful not to twist my ankle in my canvas wedges. I spotted Nick immediately. Panic licked at my stomach, and I stopped for a second, leaning down to adjust a shoe that felt fine. *Get up, idiot. Play it up, and he'll never know. Take it way more over the top than Merry did, and he'll think you're faking for sure.*

I straightened, picked up my pace, and ran the last ten yards to greet him with a huge hug, which he returned, squeezing me tightly and letting me down slowly. "Remember," he whispered in my ear, "this was your idea."

When he stepped back, he looked like a kid dying to set off a contraband firecracker. Pure mischief flickered in his expression. He ran his hands down my arms, taking his time to reach my wrists before he tightened his fingers and lifted them as he stepped back to give me the once-over. "You look amazing."

"You're amazing too," I said through clenched teeth. He quirked an eyebrow at me. I relaxed my jaw and smiled for real. Well, fake-real. "It's good to see you. It feels like it's been forever instead of a few days."

"You too," he said, pulling me in for another hug. And it reminded me of how good his acting truly was because it felt natural and right.

This is what you wanted, I reminded myself. *Quit fighting and go with it.*

So that's how the best and worst night of my life began. When he let go of me, I slipped my hand into his. "What do you have planned for us?" I asked. "And let me say right now that 'nothing' is an acceptable answer. I like just hanging out with you." The freedom to speak the truth like it was a lie made me nearly dizzy.

"Good, because that's what we're doing. Hanging out. I wanted to show you a day in my life but in about one-sixth the time."

"Let's do it."

If someone used words like *magical* to describe an evening in a movie, that's pretty much when I ejected the show and handed it to my mom to watch. But . . . seriously, we passed a magical hour following the sidewalk from the park until it petered off into a hard-packed dirt trail before slowly dissolving into the fine sand of the beach. He'd already set up a blanket and a paddleball game, which we played with blatant cheating and fake commentary.

He won by default when he described my serve as the paddleball equivalent of an Elaine Benes dance move.

"Unfair!" I accused, staring up from the blanket at his grinning face. "You know I can't resist a *Seinfeld* quote."

He dropped down beside me. "Yes. Know thy enemy. Blah, blah, blah. I win."

I righted myself, still laughing, and leaned back on my palms to watch the waves crashing. "I wish we had our boards."

"Nah. I can show you a better place to surf some other time."

Some other time. I liked pretending that we had more surfing together in our future. I drew in a lungful of tangy sea air. "Can we spend our whole date sitting on this blanket waiting for the sun to set?"

He scooted closer, his hand touching mine. I brushed his pinkie with mine.

"Once again, you read my mind, except you messed up some important details. We'll definitely watch the sunset, but not here."

"Where?"

"My house. Cool?"

I nodded, my stomach flipping. "Cool." Except not. I didn't need permanent images of him in his space, doing his thing, burned into my brain. But I pushed that aside. Today was my parting-from-Nick gift to myself; I would soak it all in. "Cool," I repeated, smiling.

Twenty minutes later, we had the blanket packed and situated in his car, Ethan in the backseat to record us while Molly followed. As soon as Nick turned the key in the ignition, Led Zeppelin's "D'yer Maker" blared from the radio, and after exchanging a startled glance, we burst into laughter.

"Let me in on the joke, guys?" Ethan prompted from behind us.

"We listened to this all the time before," Nick said. "Mostly when we were cooking or cleaning. We blasted it and sang like idiots."

"Before, meaning when you used to date?"

"Yes, genius documentarian," I said, and as if he had read my mind, Nick cranked the sound up, and we sang along at the top of our lungs.

We reached his house before the song ended, and he had to shift gears to climb the steep driveway. I faced the house and the empty space behind it. "Let me guess. Your back window looks out on an ocean view."

"I had to use my residuals for *something*. It's the least I deserve for having every one of my teenage zits memorialized forever in Nick at Nite reruns," he said, smiling.

"No argument." I watched those almost every night. I'd be sure to walk around like I owned his place since my rabid fandom had indirectly funded it. Shows didn't survive in syndication without nostalgia junkies like me.

He took me on a tour. It was plain and had comfy overstuffed guy furniture and a couple of cool paintings on the walls that he said his friends had done. The open kitchen and dining area overlooked the ocean, and light flooded in, a soft rosy glow that hinted at approaching sunset.

"I thought a stir-fry and some fresh-squeezed juice on the patio, maybe?"

"I'm in," I said. "Point me to the rice cooker." As easily as that, we fell into the routine we had followed many times when he'd come to my apartment and cooked while I studied for a final or when I went to his place and threw something together in the kitchen while I helped him run lines.

The chop-chop of his knife running over zucchini thudded in time with the pulse of memory, recalling dozens of similar stir-frys and evenings from the past.

Forty-five minutes later, we settled into the patio set, burrowing into the sofa that faced the water with our plates on our knees. "We could sit at the table," he said.

"Why?" I scooted closer to him and speared a piece of chicken with my fork. "You don't trade perfect for practical."

And then it got quiet. The good kind of quiet, broken only by the clink of silverware and the breeze. We ate and watched the dying light play over the ocean swells.

"This, right now, is my perfect day," he said. I rested my head on his shoulder and smiled. He turned and dropped a kiss on my hair.

Molly coughed, a small sound, but it snapped the mood that had settled over us. "Guys, I know you're playing up the whole 'real date' thing, but honestly, you're giving me nothing ambiguous to mislead the viewer. Every single person watching this is going to be convinced you're picking Lou, and you'll look like a total jerk when you don't. And Car—I mean, whoever you do pick is going to be mad when she sees this footage."

Nick dropped his head to the back of the sofa with a groan. "What do you want us to do?" he asked.

"Be worse fakers," she said. "Make this trip worth my while."

He lifted his head and shot her a glare that hinted at more annoyance than he usually showed. "Fine," he said.

"Trust me," she said, her voice sweet. "It's for the good of the show."

He glared for almost another thirty seconds. "For the good of the show."

That's what it felt like to be inside of a bubble. Floating one second and then flat on your behind and drenched in a filmy residue of regret and soap the next second when it burst. I grieved the lost mood the second I felt the shift, but I spent another hour channeling my "friend" vibe so Molly would have enough to work with to confuse everyone. Stupid show. The check-ins had been generic enough for her, so we didn't need to reshoot anything, but after I helped Nick clean our mess in the kitchen, I knew we wouldn't recapture the earlier magic of the day. I didn't protest when Molly suggested we get on the road. "You sure your laptop will work in the car? Because it would be awesome if I could start this on the way down."

"It'll be fine," I said.

"Yes!" She hurried out the front door with Ethan behind her, tutoring her on how to do mobile editing.

I watched them go and wished I didn't have to follow.

"Thanks for a great date," Nick said, joining me on the threshold. "I think you've got a career in acting if you ever want one."

I ached with the memory of all the good night kisses we'd shared on doorsteps in the past. His face didn't reflect the same ache. He wore only an easy smile.

"Yeah, who knew?"

"Thanks for driving all the way out. I'll see you next week?"

I swallowed and nodded. Our next face-to-face would be at the final rose ceremony when he made his choice. I only had to get through his excruciating date with Cara, plus his two final meet-the-family dates. "Good night," I said, taking the two steps down from his front porch. "It's been real."

His bark of laughter followed me to the car, which Molly had started for me. I reversed and waved good-bye before pulling out and winding my way toward home again.

"So what do you think—" Molly asked, but I held up a hand to cut her off.

"I can't even tell you how much I don't want to talk about it."

She said nothing for a long moment and then dug her earbuds out of her purse. "Fair enough. Time to work."

I nodded and concentrated on the road flowing beneath my front fender, sweeping me farther and farther away from Nick.

Chapter 15

THE BEST AND WORST PART of having our date on video was that I could replay it over and over. I could watch every expression that flitted over Nick's face and wonder if it was acting or if he meant it. I froze frames where he smiled at me and analyzed the happiness in his face. Acting? Real? Real but happy-to-be-with-a-friend? I froze frames where I thought I saw desire flash across his face. There was more than one.

It wasn't healthy to project what I wanted onto him, but I couldn't help it. I even made a stupid video file on my phone with some of the clips where I thought his eyes might be saying more than his words did. Every time I checked something off of my to-do list, a project for one of our new clients or a long run, I rewarded myself by watching my unhealthy video montage. For two days.

And then Molly posted the date with Cara, and I had my answer. Nick Westman was the most underrated actor in Hollywood. The heat that sizzled between those two, the clear sense of rightness between them ignited their pixelated love story like the low-key ease between Nick and I never could.

Molly watched my face as I watched the clip. "You okay?" she asked.

I shrugged. *No. Definitely not.* Couldn't-speak-or-I'd-cry not. Another shrug. I kept my eyes on the screen, watching them wander the grounds of the Getty Museum, stopping to talk about a sculpture here or a shrub there. Nick's eyes devoured Cara's beautiful, animated face, and mine devoured his. They looked perfect together, her dark head and bright eyes tilted up to laugh at him, his face turned down toward hers with a soft smile on his lips.

"It went well?" I asked. I'd gone to bed as soon as Molly had texted me the night before that she was on the way home and not to wait up.

"Yes," she said cautiously. "I'm sorry this is hard for you. But maybe I'm changing my mind. Maybe you should tell him how you feel. You never know. I could be reading the situation totally wrong."

"I'm falling for a guy who is falling for someone else. It's already stupid to revisit old relationships. It's extra stupid to try to persuade someone into liking you back."

"But what if I'm wrong? You know how he is. He says a lot but not everything. Maybe he hasn't seriously considered you because he didn't know you were an option." She walked over and gave me a quick hug before taking the chair next to me. "After filming your last date, I realized I've been giving you bad advice. I'm worried about how you're going to feel if you sit by and don't do anything. I'm afraid you'll regret this."

"If I thought there was a shot, I'd take it. But I do stupid things like watch videos of him all day and read secret emotions into them that I know he isn't feeling. And when I fall asleep at night, and there's the few minutes after you lay down where you're too tired to be anything but honest with yourself, then I know: if he wanted me, he'd have come after me. If he wanted me, this connection between him and Cara wouldn't be lighting up my screen."

I pressed play to watch the last few minutes of the date unfold.

"Why are you doing this to yourself?" Molly asked. "You look miserable."

"Because I'd rather watch the actual truth than the stupid one I make up when I watch my stalker files," I joked. Or tried to. "It's better like this. I need to know. It reminds me not to invent a fairy tale."

She said nothing for a while, and then she sighed. "You have the wrong actor for that. He's a pirate, remember? Not Prince Charming."

I didn't even smile.

She tousled my hair and headed down the hallway.

A slate indicated the exit interviews were coming. "Do you see this going anywhere?" the caption read. I muted the sound on his answer.

A sob tore free from my throat, and I gulped back the next one before the noise summoned any of my roommates. Nick talked about Cara differently than he did any of his other dates, but it shouldn't surprise me. She'd impressed the heck out of me in her audition video, and she'd only gotten better the more I saw of her. Nick wouldn't be dumb enough to let her go.

So why had he let *me* go?

I came back to the question that had nagged at me ever since we'd broken up, but in the past month, it had grown into a lament from a bruised place inside me. *Why? Why? Why?* The question throbbed like an inflamed splinter. I was right to break up with Nick three years ago. But he didn't try to save us. And our breakup wasn't an easy decision for me. I'd walked away from the only guy I'd ever wanted, the one who made my knees weak with a glance and decimated me with his kisses. This was the guy who lit my imagination on fire when he talked about art and his passion for film, who had surfed more waves with me in a deep, easy quiet than I could count.

It was the quiet at other key times that had broken us. He had never told me how he felt. He had never talked about the things he and I would have to build on if we weren't going to be doomed to fall apart: the gospel, our goals and dreams for the future. I always knew about the next role he wanted, but he brushed off my questions about what came after that. I didn't think he knew.

And in the last two months of our relationship, the soft voice of caution grew louder in my brain. *You need more than this for a forever kind of relationship.* So I had pushed. I had poked, prodded, even tried to pull him toward conversations that might give me a reason to stick the relationship out. "Do you want to stay in acting forever? What did you think about that talk at church today? Would you ever want to do a temple night for a date? How come you've never had a serious relationship before?"

And it didn't matter that I asked those questions slowly over time. I'd gotten past his veneer, but the second I tried to move to the layer below it, he shut down. It was subtle. General answers followed by a gradual change of subject or deflecting the question or sometimes a vague agreement and a "Yeah, let's talk about that sometime."

Three years ago, it had been easier to focus on the flaws in him that made walking away the right move. His shortcomings made the breakup *his* fault.

Yeah, definitely easier to think that way. But maybe not right. Maybe not fair. Maybe not honest. Maybe dumping him made it easier for me to ignore a truth that hurt too much to see: I had fallen for him like crazy, and he only had one toe in. And if he didn't love me back, then that hurt too much. I'd been the most perfect me I could be with him, and it hadn't been enough for him to open up and connect with me spiritually and emotionally.

I'd let my departing footsteps fall in a specific mantra designed to keep my rib cage from crushing inward: *It's not you. He's stunted inside. It's not you. He's stunted inside.*

Now I had to face reality. If that mantra was true, then I was the only person in the history of love who had never contributed to a breakup.

Except I had. I stared at Cara's face frozen in the frame in front of me. Despite her impressive professional credentials and her natural beauty, she had a graciousness about her that translated even on video. It's why I'd cast her to begin with. In contrast, Molly had hinted that if anything, I was the opposite. People sensed my disappointment with them when they didn't meet the invisible bar I set. Maybe Nick had sensed the same thing?

Add to this horrible stew my mom's opinion, however lovingly shared, that I had raised my expectations for any guy impossibly high since Nick to protect myself from another failure, and . . . and it made the worst stew ever, is what.

I clicked play and watched the rest of the Nick/Cara footage in misery. And lucky me, I'd get to hear more about Nick's thoughts in his blog post.

Even better, tomorrow afternoon, Ethan would be recording and e-mailing us Nick's announcement about which two bachelorettes he would take home to meet his family on the final two dates. I'd get to spend two days torturing myself with thoughts of how well Chelsey and especially Cara might fit in with them and how I should have understood what I'd been seeing when I watched Nick with his family and how I should have fought harder to keep my own defenses down.

So. Another twenty-four stellar hours coming up.

Chapter 16

"Guess what the following phrases all have in common," I called to Molly the next morning. "A soul for art, a radiant intellect, and transcendent beauty."

She slumped in from the kitchen and plopped down by me on the sofa. "They're in a pretentious review of Renaissance art?"

"Nope. Those are three phrases Nick used to describe Cara that he will never use to describe me."

"You're kidding. That doesn't sound like him." She squinted and leaned over to check my laptop screen. "The embodiment of truth? The grace of Pavlova?" She flopped back. "I don't know who Pavlova is, but I'm going to assume he's guilty of the same hyperbole there as he is with the rest of that list."

I snapped the laptop shut. "A special girl requires special comparisons, I guess."

Molly snorted. "I liked her better until that list. Transcendent beauty?" She pretended to gag. "For real?"

At least I knew why I had fallen short three years ago. Cara was more everything. More educated, prettier, kinder. More free of perfectionist tendencies that undermined everyone else's sense of worth. You know—the little things.

"When is Ethan sending the announcement over?" she asked.

"I don't know. This afternoon, I think." My phone rang, and Nick's number flashed up at me. I dropped my head and groaned. I so did not want to hear a rundown of his amazing day with Cara. I snatched the phone up and sent him to voice mail.

Molly's eyebrow rose. "Nick?"

I nodded. The phone rang, flashing his number again.

"You better get it," she said after we listened to it for another thirty seconds.

I sighed and hit answer. "Hey."

"Hey." He sounded relaxed and happy.

I gritted my teeth.

"Thanks for sending the top-ten list over."

"Sure." He cleared his throat. "Do you think it sounded . . . okay?"

I pulled the phone away and stuck my tongue out at it. "Yeah. Sounded great."

"Cool."

I waited for him to follow up with the point of his call. He stayed silent. "Um, do you need something, Nick?"

He cleared his throat again. "Not really. I kind of want to give you something. A heads-up about the filming." I switched to speaker phone while he continued. "I've been rethinking what I want to do for these last two family-visit dates, and I think I'm going to try something different. Ethan and I filmed a thing this morning after we surfed, and he's ready to send it over. Do you have time to take a look right now?"

I shot a befuddled-looking Molly an equally befuddled look of my own. "Yes?" I said.

"Don't worry," he said, obviously hearing my uncertainty. "If you hate it, we shot the announcement you probably wanted to hear in the first place."

"Send this 'different' thing over, and I'll call you if I have questions."

Molly looked as thrown as I felt. "You don't know anything about this?" I asked.

She shook her head. My phone dinged with an e-mail, but I opened my laptop to view it, knowing it would be the mysterious video. I downloaded Ethan's file and then scooted over to make room for Molly. Before it could play, I stabbed the pause button.

"What was that for?" Molly demanded.

"Nothing. I need a minute." I stared at the screen. A medium shot of Nick filled it, the ocean in the background. He wore his wet suit, and it set off his blue eyes. This change of his could be anything, but the stupid part of my brain had a secret hope. Maybe . . .

Maybe he would pick me as one of his final two for real, and he wanted to give me a chance to decline before it aired. Maybe he hadn't been acting on our date three nights before either.

The echoes of a *Shawshank Redemption* quote bounced around my head. "Hope is a dangerous thing." Too late. Hope had already taken up residence and multiplied inside my rib cage, pressing so hard it threatened to erupt. And it would be a super-cheesy eruption too. If Nick *did* say my name when I pressed play, I'd be a volcano of white doves to the accompaniment of angels singing.

I scowled. "Here we go." I clicked, and my heart flipped with each cycle of the buffering signal. When it finally started, I thought I would vomit due to my suppressed volcano of doves.

Nick smiled at the camera, and I breathed again.

"I'm not going to lie. I had ulterior motives for agreeing to be the bachelor, and I'm not going to share them with you because I want to spare myself the judging. But I want you to know that I've repented and reformed." His smile would earn him forgiveness from every single female who saw it. If he had paired it with a wink or a twinkly eye, he could probably have confessed to mass murder and still gotten a pass. "Despite those motives, I did at least come into this with an open mind toward finding love. I had no idea about the kind of girls I would meet. I don't even have the words to describe how awesome they are. So I'm sticking with that. Awesome. Oh, and amazing. And incredible. But you guys know; you've seen them all too."

He looked past the lens to Ethan, maybe, before addressing the audience again. "I'm probably an idiot for letting some of these women go, but this is a bizarre situation. I'm listening to my heart, and I guess the Spirit." A fleeting tension around his eyes hinted at his discomfort in discussing this publicly, but he smiled again and continued.

"After a lot of thought and prayer—think how much one guy can pray and at least triple that—I've chosen who I'd like to get to know even better on my final two dates."

Without thinking, I grabbed Molly's hand on the sofa next to me. She whipped around to stare at me, but I ignored her.

"I think these two ladies are exceptional. I know I don't have to propose at the end of this whole experience, but that's what I want do: I want to find my wife. I need to get to know them better, to figure out who I would trust to bring into my own family's circle as our relationship grows. I hope they're willing to let me into their homes to meet their families and learn more about them. I realize that's a big leap of trust for some people, but I think it's the right next step. With all that said . . ." He leaned down and scooped two roses up from the sand. "I'd like to offer one of these to Chelsey and one of these to"—

I hit pause and let go of Molly's hand, but she snatched mine back and patted it a few times.

"You okay?"

I nodded. "Yeah. I had a flash of insanity for a moment. Don't worry, I'm back in reality now." I drew another deep breath. The pressure of hope pushing outward had morphed into pain pushing inward. I knew I wouldn't hear my name. I pushed play.

"Cara." He smiled and held it for a five-count. My heart banged with a hollow thump in each of those five seconds. Then he dropped his smile and spoke into the camera. "Hey, Lou. And, Molls, if you're watching." He waved. "Call me and let me know if it'll work to go to their families instead of bringing them to mine. If not, we shot the announcement we originally agreed on, and we'll send that, but I'd rather do it this way if we can." He smiled again for a second, then the screen went black.

"Are you cool with it?" Molly asked.

He had flipped the tables here, and I wasn't sure why. Maybe he wanted to keep his own family out of the spotlight. "I guess. We're going to have to call Cara and Chelsey and run it by them."

"Maybe one of them will turn him down?"

"I'm fine," I said. "You want to take Cara, and I'll call Chelsey?"

Molly nodded and climbed off the couch to find her phone. I pulled up Chelsey's number and braced for the squealing, but it didn't come. I could hear a smile in her voice, so I took that as a good sign.

"That'll work," she said. "My parents live in Orange, so it's not like we'd have to go far or anything. And they won't mind being on camera. Mikey's good about staying off the radar."

"I'm not sure who'll be filming," I said. "It'll depend on Ethan's and Mikey's schedules. Or I might even have to do it. I don't want to assume. Does it matter who films?" I asked.

A short silence followed. "I guess not. I got used to Mikey because he filmed our last date."

"Okay, no problem. I'll see if he's around and can do it."

"Yeah, ask him, if you don't mind." She sounded like she was trying not to laugh. It bugged me, but I didn't know why. Oh, wait. *Yes, I did.* She'd taken the spot I wanted, and now she was making diva requests for specific cameramen. Nice. She was higher maintenance than she'd seemed on their first date. Not that I was bitter.

Ha.

Molly walked back in. "Cara's good with it, but we'll have to go down to San Diego."

"I can't."

"I know." She sat down beside me again. "I got it. You spend the next four days making lots of money for us to spend so you can soothe yourself with retail therapy."

"I'll get right on that."

She sighed. "Sorry. I know my jokes aren't super helpful. I'm not sure what to do. If you won't go after Nick yourself, I don't know what else to tell you."

"You don't have to tell me anything," I said. "What's there to say, you know? Do *not* feel bad. That is an order from your producer. I don't blame you for any of this."

I shoved the laptop away and headed for the fridge. "I blew this three years ago when I broke up with him because I couldn't see my own flaws. I see them now." I pulled out a jug of milk and moved to the cabinet to fish out my box of Cheerios. Name-brand cereal—another perk of positive cash flow. "This is hard. I don't like it, but I'm trying to learn from it." The Cheerios plinked into my bowl, and I sloshed milk on top. After a crunchy mouthful, I finally looked up to meet Molly's concerned eyes. "Having said all that, yeah, I'd thank you forever and promise you my firstborn if I could stay out of the filming. Not that I'll ever get married to produce a firstborn."

She nodded. "Yes. Stay out. I'm worried for your head."

I reached up and rubbed it. "It'll be okay."

I couldn't promise her the same about my heart.

* * *

I did a mud run last year near a military base farther south of us. Because my team consisted of athletic girls, the dumb half of our group convinced the smart half of us that doing the extended 10K version of the run made sense.

Even running on the sand for two months before race day didn't prepare me for the grueling reality of slogging through mud pits in a tangle of other people's limbs for what felt like never-ending hours.

The four days surrounding the two family dates felt like the emotional equivalent. The family dates didn't require much set up. Molly scheduled a night with each of them; they'd head over to Chelsey's parents' house the following night and then down to see Cara's parents two nights after that. That left a comfortable two-day buffer before the long-standing finale night we'd set up with the Wharton hotel at Dana Point. Getting them to agree to let us film the last rose scene on their seaside grounds before the season even started had been one of my greatest coups. The exclusive resort would show beautifully on camera, and I'd scouted the perfect spot months ago to film Trentyn's final choice. Molly would have to fight the event manager at the Wharton for my never-to-exist firstborn because that's pretty much what I'd had to put up as collateral, along with editorial veto, to secure the manager's agreement to use the grounds.

And now, against that beautiful backdrop, I'd have to watch the footage Molly brought me of Nick standing there gazing down with his eyes full of . . .

I didn't want to think about it. Or about Cara, who would without a doubt be on the receiving end of that look.

I stepped out onto our back patio and grabbed my short board. It had languished out there too long while I drowned in Hot Iron business and *TMB* sorrow. Fifteen minutes later, I unfastened it from my beach cruiser's bike rack and jogged to the water. Once I paddled out and had a chance to bob on the waves, I took my first deep breath in days. Maybe in the month since Molly had first contacted Nick.

In so many ways, I had achieved exactly what I'd wanted to with this project. *TMB* was unquestionably viral. Nick's announcement of his final two had generated over a hundred thousand views, over ten thousand Facebook likes, and nearly five hundred comments with people arguing over who would fit him best. Molly had with some trepidation let me know that a lot of the comments coming in were demands that he change his mind and pick me. I'd told her not to post any of them. No need to muddy the water even more.

It had been too muddy for so long already. I wanted to get through the next four days in the clearest frame of mind possible, and I owed it to myself to ask some hard questions. Did I do the right thing by stepping aside?

A perfect wave rolled in, but I ignored it in favor of sitting and thinking some more. My breakup with Nick had broken us past fixing. I could see that now. And how fair was it to expect him to pick right up where we'd left off when he'd done so much changing in three years and I'd done pretty much none at all?

Not fair at all.

He'd done the hard work of growing up, and he deserved a lasting relationship for his efforts. Falling back into an old pattern with me would be the least fair thing of all.

The biggest if-only that haunted me was this: if I had figured out my brokenness sooner and been ready to open up to him and be as vulnerable as I'd criticized him of not being for me in the past, would I be on one of those last two dates? Would we have bagged the whole season halfway through to explore the possibilities between us?

But I hadn't. I had pulled my "high standards" around me like bulletproof armor, and it had deflected everything long enough for Nick to take a long, hard look and then leap with Cara. Or maybe Chelsey. But probably Cara.

I took the next wave coming and rode it out, glad to think of nothing but staying in the sweet spot of my board before the swell petered out. I turned to paddle back out and then stopped and pulled myself up. I didn't want to be here either. I didn't want to be on the date filming with Molly right now because it would remind me that it might have been me if I'd been woman enough to be vulnerable.

I didn't want to be on the sofa tomorrow at noon, waiting to watch the playback of their date. I didn't want to be at church on Sunday listening to the excited chatter as everyone tried to guess who Nick would pick when Molly recorded the final episode at the Wharton the next day.

I didn't want to be me at all when that episode aired because then it would be undoable. Nick's choice had been made already, I knew. And that left me . . .

As alone as I had been before. But sadder about it. I had no idea how to unbend enough to let in anyone else in the future. At the moment, it felt like the last thing I'd ever want to do.

I dug my hands into the waves and propelled myself out past the break before whipping my board around and waiting, every muscle tense, for the next good wave to form. Every time my thoughts tried to drift toward Nick or Cara or work, I shut them down and stared harder at the water. When the right ride came, I took it, letting the adrenaline of carving down the face purge the stress from my system.

And then I did it again. And again. And when I caught twenty waves in two hours, I decided it had been my most epic day of surfing. A really good day meant a dozen rides, but the ocean must have sensed how badly I needed more. Tired but less tense, I trudged out of the water and back to my bike, making my way home and feeling marginally more equipped to deal with the emotional beating I would take when Molly straggled in with her footage.

One more week of this view from the bottom of the mud pit and I could forget it all and move on. This time for real.

Chapter 17

It was as bad as I had expected when I watched Molly's rough cut. I listened to Nick's check-in about how awesome Brother Sanchez, Chelsey's father, was. And her mother. And the brother and sister who had come with their kids. And their spouses. And her nieces and nephews. So awesome. All of it.

"What's the name of that dating website you use sometimes?"

Molly's head popped up over her Mac screen. "Are you serious? Are you going to set up a profile and everything?"

"Yes. Maybe?" Her surprise made me feel self-conscious. "I thought it might be good medicine. You know, like hair of the dog."

"That's for drinking, I'm sad to say I know from my wilder days. You're talking a rebound romance. You know that, right?"

"I hope it's not a rebound." I tapped my fingers on the tabletop. "I've been dealing with all this uncomfortable self-reflection crud for a few days now, and I figure the misery is only worth it if I get something out of it. Like learning how to really be in a relationship."

She stared and looked suspiciously close to laughing. "So you're already on the way to recovery from Nick?"

"You mean the relationship that never even happened over this last month? Why wouldn't I be?" I asked with false brightness. Then I groaned and dropped my head to the table. "No, I'm not. But I don't want to be in emotional limbo for another three years. So I'm going to fix this."

There was no mistaking Molly's snort of laughter this time. "Don't be mad!" she said, holding her hands up to placate me when I glared at her. "This is just so *you*. Such a methodical approach to love and self-improvement. Except for the part where it would make sense to actually talk to Nick about all of this."

"No way. This will end with him and Cara riding a paddleboard into the sunset."

"Right after you push them off of the Wharton's sea cliff?"

I smiled. "Probably. I hope she doesn't go for a beaded dress. That'll get heavy in the water."

Molly laughed again. "Look, I like LDS Lookup, but I don't think you need it. If you want to know the truth, about eight guys left comments after Nick didn't pick you saying that they would love to take you out. If they have the good taste to watch the show, I think you should start with one of them. And some of their profile pictures were cute."

"Seriously? They wanted to ask me out?"

She smiled and nodded.

"How come you didn't tell me before?"

She shrugged. "Because I've been hoping you would make a play for Nick. And even though I know you won't, I think you need to let this season end and take some time to breathe before you go wading into the dating waters."

"I'm not a wader," I said. "I'm more like a diver."

"I know. That's what makes me nervous. I think you're going to plunge right into the next relationship that comes along to prove to yourself that you can do it. Explore *all* of the options, okay? Make sure you're heart-whole."

Tall order. Fat chance. Long shot. Blah. But I nodded. "Fine. But you better forward me those e-mail comments no later than one month after the finale airs."

"Got it. For what it's worth, he's not into Chelsey. I can tell you that much."

"It's worth something that you're trying to make me feel better. But honestly, I think the Cara date will put me right back at sad."

"Say something to him, then."

"No."

"You're stubborn. Go to bed." She leaned toward her monitor, and her expression sharpened as she focused on the editing. I was off her radar now.

The front door opened, and Lily and Autumn tumbled in with dripping-wet feet from the faucet they'd rinsed in outside. "Towel!" Autumn demanded cheerfully.

"Chocolate and a movie!" Lily added. "And don't say no because we're only going to sit on you and force you to watch. You've been blowing us off too much lately."

"Says the girl who spends all her free time with her boyfriend," Autumn said. "Towel!"

I hopped off the sofa and grabbed towels from the linen closet in record time. "No argument. Here's your towel; give me my movie. And make sure all the sand is off before you take a step in here."

Autumn, the worst offender for tracking in sand, grinned and rubbed vigorously at her feet. "All right, bossy pants."

I snatched *The Avengers* off the shelf. "This is a preemptive strike against any romantic comedies." I settled back into my spot.

"Captain America! Yum." Lily curled up beside me.

"I'm a Thor girl," Autumn said as she stretched out on the other side of the sectional. I fast-forwarded through to the opening sequence, desperate to immerse myself in superhero reality and drown out the soft clicks of Molly's mouse as she worked to make Nick and Chelsey look perfect for each other. That reality I couldn't handle at all.

* * *

"I told you," Molly said over a turkey sandwich the next day at lunch. "They get along great, but it's not a love match."

"Why . . ."

"Why what?"

I couldn't think of how to phrase my question, but I knew I'd be frustrated until I understood the lopsided video she'd posted. "Why is there so much Chelsey and so little Nick?"

She took another bite of her sandwich instead of answering. I waited her out without saying anything. I didn't want to offend her, but from what I'd watched, her excellent editing skills had fallen apart big time with this date video. We couldn't afford to change our pacing and delivery at this point in the season.

"You missing your man?" she asked. "Wishing there was more of him?"

"The audience will wish there was. What happened?"

"Mikey," she said, no longer kidding. "I swear I thought he was getting more of both of them, but I don't know. He was off his game. I ended up with a lot of Chelsey somehow."

"And check-ins? Didn't you film Nick's?"

"Yes, but it's like I told you. He's not into her like that."

Then why didn't he pick me?

"It's pretty obvious who he really wants, and I figured we didn't want to give away the mystery." She shrugged.

I winced.

"Sorry," she said.

"It's okay. But try to get more tomorrow night, okay?"

"Change of plans. Cara texted me twenty minutes ago to see if we could move their date to tonight. If everyone is game, we're heading down to San Diego in a few hours."

My phone went off. "It's Nick," I said, checking it. He'd left two messages the day before, but I'd avoided returning them. I knew he'd want to talk about his date with Chelsey, and I wasn't feeling like a good friend. More like a jilted ex-girlfriend. I sent it to voice mail, even less eager to talk about his big night with Cara's family. Thirty seconds later, a text alert went off. Nick again. *Call me. RIGHT NOW. Or else.*

I hit his number. "Or else what?" I demanded when he answered.

"I don't know. I figured I wouldn't have to think that far if it got you to call back."

"Lame."

"Yes, but you didn't return my calls yesterday."

"I texted you that I was busy."

"For sixteen hours straight? There must have been some time in there you could have called."

"Not one single second." Not when I was painting my toes. Or watching Dex Hall reruns. Nope, not a spare second.

"What did you think of the date footage?" he asked.

I stifled a groan. *Kill me now*, I mouthed to Molly. She shook her head and headed down the hall. "The date looked fun. Chelsey's family seems nice."

"They are. Super down-to-earth. I'm more nervous about meeting Cara's family. Her dad is a big-shot corporate guy. They live in the same neighborhood as the Romneys."

I paused to let that process. "You do realize your family is loaded and lives in a huge house too, right? You have millionaires over all the time."

"My parents do. And those are entertainment types. I don't know if 'Hi, I have a decent address' is going to impress a businessman. What if he thinks I'm the flaky artistic type?"

"It matters that much, huh?"

"Well, yeah."

My heart sank. "You're going to be the coolest guy who ever ate dinner at their house. Seriously. You can't go wrong with the 'be yourself' advice. They'll love you. My parents did." I wished I could bite the last words back as soon as they slipped out. I didn't mean to bring up the past.

"But your parents were psyched because I was the first guy you'd dated for more than two months."

"So?"

"So what would they think if I was some guy you'd gone out with three times from an Internet reality show?"

I stayed silent.

"This is going to be a train wreck."

"Is it definitely happening tonight?"

"I'm up for it, and Ethan's in, so I guess so."

"Then my advice is don't sweat it. Take PCH and keep your windows down and your radio up the whole time. Think about seeing Cara, and don't worry about the rest of it."

"Thanks." He laughed. "I can't believe this is almost over. It seems like it's gone on forever and in a blink at the same time."

"I hear you." The time with him had passed far too quickly. The time spent watching him date other women had stretched far too long.

"I know this came together in a crazy way, but I'm glad. How come we never reconnected before this?"

"Probably because I was kind of a hag about our breakup."

"Not a hag, exactly."

I laughed. "But close."

"I maybe would have handled it differently. Like not at all," he conceded.

Meaning what? He never would have broken up with me? Or that he would have been nicer if it had been him dumping me? Instead of asking at the risk of looking stupid, I changed the subject. "What time are you meeting Cara? Should you be getting on the road?"

"I'm supposed to be at her parents' place in La Jolla by five, but yeah, I'd better get on the road soon in case there's traffic. My producer hates it when I'm late."

"Ha, ha," I said. *Your producer would rather you didn't go at all.* "Get cracking, dude."

"Okay, dude."

We hung up, and I drooped in my chair. One more date and then the night of the rose ceremony. That's all I had to get through without losing my mind.

* * *

"How bad is it?" I asked.

I'd woken up to the harsh blue glow of my clock informing me I was still a couple of hours from dawn. I shuffled out to get a glass of water only to find Molly hunched at her Mac.

"Depends on whose point of view we're in," she said, pulling out an earbud. "From some people's perspective, tonight couldn't have been better. Make that last night," she said, checking the time.

My stomach lurched. "I don't want to know. I'll watch the video tomorrow." My gaze flickered over the microwave clock. "Today, I mean. Are you almost done?"

"Yeah. Just looping the music in. But you'll be glad to know that Ethan did a more balanced job of filming than Mikey did." She clicked on something and listened for a moment. I downed a tall glass of water and waited. "Done. I'm wrecked, and I'm going to sleep. Don't wake me up for anything. Not the apocalypse. Not Mr. Right. Not even a house fire."

She pushed herself up from the table and trudged toward her bedroom. "Good work!" I called after her.

"You haven't even seen it. But thanks. And now I'm going to die." Her bedroom door closed behind her.

I eyed her computer and debated whether to look or not. I sat down and clicked open the file marked "Cara's Family Date." It wasn't like I'd be able to fall back asleep. I watched five minutes of laughing. Of Cara's younger sister casting adoring glances at Nick. Of Cara casting adoring glances at Nick. Of her parents casting adoring glances at Nick.

So I guess I knew whom the night had gone perfectly for: not me.

I leaned back and considered what to do for the next few days while I rode out the end of this awful downward spiral. Refuse to bathe and then drown myself in Doritos and Dr. Pepper, maybe?

Yeah right. Sometime between now and when the next person asked me how *The Mormon Bachelor* was going, I'd find and affix my perma-grin. "Great," I said, practicing my answer. It sounded like a growl.

At the moment, in the antiseptic light of the computer monitor, I didn't feel like smiling one bit. I'd braced for what I'd seen in the video, but hurt swelled like a heart blister. And the only thing I could do was protect it until it calloused and pray for Monday's finale to come and go faster than a California winter.

I spent another hour reading blogs about viral marketing and new media strategies until my eyes grew so gritty that I shut them to give them a rest. I woke up with the sun streaming through the window and lifted my head off the dining table to see Autumn standing there. She trained clients at a gym near the pier, and she had her uniform on, looking alert and amused. "You have a mushroom-shaped red spot on your cheek."

I rubbed at it. "I think I slept on the table."

"Yeah. It's seven. You want to try to get a couple more hours of sleep? Like, in your bed?"

I lurched to my feet. "Oatmeal. Run. Then function."

An hour later, I sat on a picnic table overlooking the Pacific. It was early yet for the sunbathers but not the surfers. They dotted the waves like seals in their shiny black wet suits. When my phone rang, I knew it was Nick. I didn't even give him a special ring tone. I was just that acutely aware of him.

"Hi," I said, deciding to stave off the multiple voice mails and text messages if I didn't answer.

"Did you watch?" he asked.

"I watched."

"What did you think?"

"Her whole family loved you."

"Yeah. It seems like they're comfortable with her choice." He sounded pleased.

Comfortable with her choice? Fantastic. Nick had the family stamp of approval. My stomach churned. It didn't have room for oatmeal *and* hope-shattering news. I wanted off the phone. Now. "Yep. Glad it went so well. Look, I'm sitting on a bench instead of running, but I better get back at it if I want the two miles I did to count for anything. I've relaxed so much in ten minutes that my heart rate thinks I'm trying to devolve into a sloth."

"Wouldn't that really be evolving?"

"If it allowed me to live on the sand with very little effort and spend all my time soaking up the sun? Yes."

"When you put it like that . . ."

"I've literally got to run. Bye, Nick."

"Bye," he said, but he sounded kind of hurt.

Whatever. I couldn't hand-hold him at the risk of my mental health, for pity's sake. Thanks to sunshine and sea air, I'd barely regained some of the mind I'd steadily lost over the last month. No point in undoing that progress. I hit the asphalt trail next to the sand again, rounding a condo complex with weather-worn blue awnings and passed the volleyball nets scant minutes later.

I'd nearly crossed under the pier when I heard my name.

"Louisa? Is that you?"

I didn't recognize the voice, but I turned then tried not to ogle. I'd seen those washboard abs on display several times in the last Summer Olympics, and the volleyball resting under his arm was a good clue to the voice's owner too. I needed the hint to his identity, actually. No way would I have thought Kade Townsend even knew my name. He stood there smiling, his eyes hidden behind Oakleys.

"You're Louisa, right?"

"Yes. Hi. And you're Nick's friend. Kade?" Also, a world-famous Olympic medalist and all. But let's go with Nick's friend.

"Nice to meet you. I've seen you around. And on the bachelor thing now too."

"Oh. You too. I mean, nice to meet you." I fumbled for something to say. "So are you practicing or playing for fun?"

"Both." His smile widened. "I have a great job."

I returned the smile and wondered what it would take to get him as the next Mormon Bachelor.

"So you're stoked for Monday, right?" he asked.

The finale. "It's a lot of work, but yeah."

He pulled off his sunglasses, and I admired his honey-colored eyes. Seriously, I needed this guy on the show. The single LDS women of Southern California needed this guy on the show.

"Who do you think he'll pick?" he asked.

I lifted an eyebrow at him. "I bet you already know."

"Yeah, I do. It's how I took my rent for him living in my guest room all month. I made him give me the inside scoop."

"Then why are you asking?" I didn't mean to sound peevish, but I'd barely cleared my head of the Cara/Nick funk and now it was back, hanging out like a November pall.

Sunlight glinted in his eye. "Thought it'd be interesting to hear your guess. Has Nick told you yet?"

"He doesn't really need to. Anyone who's been watching the show can figure it out."

"So you say . . . ?"

I fought the urge to roll my eyes. He didn't know how much I loathed this whole topic, but I needed to be nice in case I did decide to try to recruit him as a future bachelor. Assuming I survived this. "I say Cara. Any right-thinking person says Cara."

"Cara's got it going on," he agreed.

She did. "The only hard part in all of this is how to make it seem like more of a surprise when it happens," I said. "I might have to pull my partner in to do some insanely creative editing. Or maybe ask Ethan to help. You know him, right?"

He nodded. "Yes. I think he'll help you pull off a surprise. He's good like that."

I tossed my hair out of my way. "I should finish my run. Go pound sand."

He smiled and slipped his sunglasses on. "Always."

I ran another mile and then circled back, this time up on the sidewalk next to the road. I didn't want to pass Kade and have another conversation about his buddy Nick or the amazing Cara and the whole depressing mess I'd finally managed to push aside until Nick's stomach-wrecking phone call. I'd deal with that reality when I got home and called the Wharton events manager to confirm our filming for Monday. For the next forty minutes on the run back home, I wanted to think about nothing more than the rhythm of my running shoes striking in time to the beat of the classic rock blaring through my earbuds on my Zeppelin-free playlist.

Chapter 18

"Ms. Penske, I promise you that my partner Molly is perfectly capable of managing the filming tonight." I mustered my most reassuring voice to deliver the promise. I *had* to get her buy-in. Had to.

"I'm sorry, Louisa. But the Wharton is taking baby steps into new media strategies for advertising, and we're protective of our brand. I trusted my gut in agreeing to let you do this. I'll be there; I expect you to be there keeping this tasteful and efficient, or I can't agree to filming."

"Of course," I said, my voice full of understanding and none of the bubbling frustration trying to push its way out of me.

"I have your word, then? You'll oversee filming yourself?"

"Definitely. I'm sorry if you had even a moment of worry. We're excited to show off your amazing grounds, and I think you'll be happy with the final cut." I grimaced at my kiss-up tone, but I needed her way more than she needed me.

"You know, I've been watching the series." Her voice dropped. "I'm excited to meet Nick Westman. We're fans in my house."

"He's great," I said, trying not to choke on the words. They felt so stilted, but they appeased her.

"I'm sure he is. We'll see you early this afternoon, then?"

"Yes. Thank you." I pressed end and turned to Molly. "I'll be there. Yay."

"Sorry," she said. "But maybe at the hard parts you can look away."

"I spent this whole weekend trying to get Zen about this, and one conversation undoes it all."

"Well, this one plus every time you've talked to Nick. Or anyone else who wants to talk about it."

"Which is everyone," I said, scowling.

"Despite *that* look," she said, pointing to my face, "I think you've done a killer job of faking like this is the most exciting thing ever."

"You mean I don't look like I'm dying inside? That's something."

"If you're expecting pity from me, you're not going to get it. I've already told you what I think you should do."

"Confess my undying love while he stands with his arm draped around Cara and wonders how he missed my complete inability to read body language and social cues? No thanks."

"I'm done with the pity party. Love you still, but I'm now going to ignore you and get dressed. We need to leave at four."

"I know," I said. "I'll be ready."

Two hours later, she knocked on my door and poked her head in. "No way," she said after one glance at my head to toe black outfit. "You can't wear that."

"Why not? We're trying to blend in."

"You look like a waiter. All the guests are going to stop you and demand canapés or something. Throw some color on. And do *not* argue. We don't have time for that or for you to explain all night to annoyed guests that you don't have any salmon cakes for them."

I tried to stare her down, but she wouldn't budge. "Fine," I said, grabbing a turquoise V-neck sweater. I pulled it over my head. "But I'm only wearing this so I won't be cold when it gets dark."

"Great. Let's go."

Ethan texted as we pulled into the employee parking behind the hotel. *We're here. You?*

Pulling in, I answered. *Meet you at the service entrance.*

I lugged my half of the gear out of the trunk, including the bud vase I'd picked up from the pottery shop. With the glaze fired on it, it looked even prettier than I'd imagined. I hoped Cara would like it because she was about to take ownership. We followed the signs to the service entrance, but I stopped short when I saw both Ethan *and* Mikey waiting for us dressed in button-down shirts and slacks, not their usual T-shirts and board shorts.

"What's up with the fancy threads?" I asked.

"Swanky joint," Mikey answered.

"You didn't have to come," I told him. "Ethan said he'd handle it."

"Right. Like I'm going to miss the wrap-up to all of this. I most definitely needed to come. And just think, for once you won't have a one-camera show. We can do some pretty cool reaction shots with both of us filming."

"Thanks, then. Where's Nick?"

"He'll catch up later when it gets close to filming. He said he's nervous, and he wants to chill before he gets here."

"What about the girls?" I asked Molly.

"I'll call them."

"Let's get footage," I said to the boys. "Keep your cell phones on silent. I think Ms. Penske will flip if we expose her guests to the sound of ringing."

Mikey volunteered to do the hotel exteriors, so I trailed after Ethan while he shot the grounds. When we crossed the lobby and exited into the back courtyard, he stopped and stared. "Whoa."

"I know." I understood the reaction. My parents had brought me here a couple of years ago to celebrate my graduation from USC with a fancy dinner, and I'd fallen in love with the spot. Color burst from every plant and shrub. Something about the barely tamed excess of the tropical flowers and the relentless crashing of the waves against the rocks below had thrilled me then and again today.

"Anything in particular you want me to shoot?" Ethan asked. "Because I've got some ideas."

"Everything in particular. And of course you do. I'd love to hear them."

He nodded and spent the next hour and a half suggesting and capturing different establishing shots. Halfway through, the other two returned from shooting the front and the grand foyer, and Mikey helped Ethan capture the rest of the angles he wanted. We were in the middle of a discussion about how to best shoot the final rose scene when Ethan jumped. "My phone." He pulled it out and checked it. "Nick's here."

I nodded and ignored the sudden pressure in my chest. "Good. We're supposed to be out of here before their dinner rush, so we'll start as soon as everyone shows up. I'll go get him."

"I'll do it," Molly said. "You stay out here and keep an eye on this good-for-nothing crew, or I think Ms. Penske will get antsy. And possibly throw-outy. Pretend you're supervising, and bark orders at Mikey every time Penske looks your way."

Mikey rolled his eyes.

"You sure you can handle all three of them?" I asked. "What if they all see each other? It could be super awkward."

Now Molly's eyes took a quick tour of their sockets. "Relax. And get your game face on. Penske's coming."

I turned to see our elitist hotel overlord hurrying up.

"Hello, Louisa. Our maitre d' informed me that we have a reservation for a party of sixteen coming in within the hour. You're welcome to stay until our originally agreed upon time, but it will get much louder once the dinner party shows up, so you may want to film as soon as possible."

I opened my mouth, but Molly jumped in. "We're good to go. Nick's on the way in from the car."

Mikey waved at someone. I turned to see Nick outside the double doors. Ms. Penske straightened and tugged on the hem of her crisp white blouse.

"You get him set up," I said to Ethan. "Molly, you want to text me when you're ready for the first girl to come out?"

"Sure. See you on the flip side." She strode off toward the hotel.

Nick walked up wearing dressy jeans and a black blazer over a white linen button down. "Hey." He fist-bumped his two friends and held out his arms to me for a hug. I stepped in long enough to give him a quick squeeze and stepped right back out again. Behind me, Mrs. Penske cleared her throat.

I made the introductions. "Mrs. Penske, I'd like you to meet Nick Westman. Nick, Mrs. Penske is the forward-thinking events manager who made it possible for us to shoot here."

"Thank you, Mrs. Penske." He took her outstretched hand between both of his. Her eyes widened.

"You can call me Linda," she said, her voice faint.

"Thank you, Linda. We appreciate it."

"Okay," she said then pulled her hand back and hustled off as fast as she had come.

I stared after her. "Weird."

"Not really," Mikey said. "We see chicks do all kinds of crazy things around Nick."

"We're putting you here, man," Ethan said, pointing to a circle of paving stones six feet in diameter. A discreet bronze sign in the nearby flowerbed of California poppies declared it a picture spot, so Ethan had said we might as well prove it.

My phone vibrated with a text from Molly. *Ready?*

I voiced the question to the boys, who all nodded.

"Most definitely," Ethan said, smiling. "Are *you* ready?"

"Yep." I squatted down and fished the bud vase out of my gear bag. Standing, I handed it to Nick. "I got permission to cut a rose from that bush," I said, pointing to a crimson-covered shrub. "Let's have Ethan shoot you talking about this whole experience and what you've learned from it. Why don't you sit on that bench over there so there's pure ocean behind you for that part and then move to the circle for the final rose?"

"Whatever you say, boss," he said. He wasn't smiling. Sweat shone on his forehead.

"Cool. Who should Molly send out first?" I figured he'd ask for Chelsey since he'd want to get the rejection over with first.

Nick's smile peeked out but wobbled. "Molly and I already talked. I know you got pulled into this last minute, so try not to stress. It's covered."

"But—"

"Don't. Stress." He repeated his order with a tap on my nose for each syllable.

I fished a tissue from my bag and blotted at his forehead. "Same to you." I breathed in the smell of him while I leaned in close to do it. He flinched, and I stepped back. "You're set."

"We need a rose," Ethan prompted me.

I crossed the path to get it, and when I turned around, I nearly bumped into Nick, who reached past me. My stomach flipped at his closeness. I silently cursed Ms. Penske for making me be here.

"I'm going to grab a couple more in case we need back up."

I squinted. "Backup roses?"

"Yeah. Like, what if someone grabs one and rips it to shreds? Or I drop it and step on it? Backup props. I've learned it from watching a zillion prop managers on set."

I pointed to the bench. "Try not to kill them all in the next five minutes. Time to do your interview." I realized my camera guys had set their cameras on tripods right next to each other. "What the—"

"Shh," Ethan said. "Don't worry about it. This is an old camera-guy trick. Trust me. It will make a world of difference in your digital quality."

Nick was standing in the stone circle, not sitting on the bench. "But—"

"And yes, the shot will look better if we do it right here," he said, cutting off my next objection.

Although this made no sense to me, Ethan had started a silent countdown from five on his fingers, so I jumped out of the way before his finger hit one and signaled Nick to start. My heart echoed each finger Ethan ticked down with an extra heavy thump. We were speeding toward the moment where the door between Nick and me would slam shut permanently.

Nick smiled into the camera. "I started this experiment without any expectations. Just hopes. And along the way, I met twenty outstanding women and spent time with another one I already knew. They made me think, and they made me laugh, and this whole experience made me deliriously happy because one of those women stole my heart. Completely." He swallowed and squeezed his eyes shut for a moment.

Pressure behind my own eyes echoed the heavy weight in my chest. I blinked several times to fight off tears.

Nick cleared his throat. "I write. All day long. And when I'm not writing, I'm thinking about writing. And I think about how to tell stories that matter and how to relate pain and happiness to people. Those are the two things I want to explain now, but I don't think I have the words. To have come from a place of hurt so bad that I disappeared into Africa for months to forget myself to be standing now on the edge of a literal and figurative cliff and know how badly I could hurt if I fall . . ."

He ran his fingers through his hair, and a dark thatch stuck up slightly after he dropped his hand. I wanted to smooth it down. I wanted to cry. I wanted to not listen to any of this anymore.

He cleared his throat. "If you're lucky, you get a second chance at love. If you're really lucky, you get it with a person who you blew your chance with the first time. And if you're incredibly lucky, she won't kill you when she figures out how you went about taking that chance."

What? I looked up from the ground. Instead of staring at the camera, Nick stared straight at me. In fact, Ethan's camera had swung around to face me too, and he poked his head to the side to grin at me for a second.

My legs quit working. I sat. Right there on the ground. Ethan's camera followed me down, and Nick's first real smile appeared.

"The whole point of this show was to prove that old-school dating, *really* getting to know someone, deserves a comeback. Louisa Gibson believed it was true and asked me to be the guy who helped her prove it. She lined up almost two dozen girls for the job, and I promised to try. But I never meant to keep that promise. I meant to make a point to her. Instead, I got schooled."

I was flat out stunned. What was going on here? A flash of purple to my right distracted me, and I glanced up to find Molly grinning down at me. Cara and Chelsey were nowhere in sight.

"Here's the true story of how I lost my mind and then my heart," Nick said.

His heart?

"I don't think there's any way I'm not coming out of this looking like a jerk, but there's only one person who I really need to have forgive me, so this is for her." He looked past the camera to smile at me, where I sat on the ground. "For you, Lou."

My mouth went dry.

He looked back into Mikey's camera. "I want all of you to know that from the very first date when I realized the caliber of the women Lou and Molly lined up, I tried. I tried really, really hard to get to know these girls and to find a connection with them. And I did. Everything I said in my blog posts was the absolute truth. These are amazing girls, but each date that passed was ten times harder than the one before it, and I had to do something, or I was going to ruin Lou's whole project. I knew there was no way I could ever pay attention to any of the girls Lou lined up for me if she was around, so I got some friends to help me film. They're two huge reasons this show looked so good, and you'll meet them in a second."

My heart flipped, and I looked up at Molly, but she had her eye trained on Nick and ignored me.

He smiled. "It didn't work. I mean, it helped me pay attention to my dates better, but it didn't solve my Louisa problem. I narrowed it down to the girls that I had the easiest time hanging around, but by time the family dates rolled around, I knew there was no way a relationship could develop with either Chelsey or Cara."

My jaw dropped. I glared at Molly, and her smile slipped. Had she known all of this and not told me?

"They both called me on it," Nick continued. "They'd seen the truth, and they knew that if anything happened between one of them and me, it would be because I had talked myself into it, not because there was something actually there. If you're a single dude watching this show, you're an idiot if you don't jump on a chance to ask either of them out." He frowned. "This whole situation would be so much easier if I could have fallen for one of them, but there just wasn't any real chemistry. I knew it was game over when I went to meet Cara's family. She talked to me before I even went into their house." He took a deep breath. "She told me she'd been watching all the other dates, and she knew that I had fallen for someone besides her, so if I wanted to come in and hang out as friends, she was cool with that, but she didn't see a point in pretending."

My head pounded. I didn't know if it was the start of a migraine or the echo of my racing heart.

"I called Chelsey when I got home from Cara's house and said that I didn't think we were going to work out either. I've never heard a girl sound so relieved. She said that since she was good friends with Molly, one of the geniuses behind this whole concept, she felt obligated to keep trying because she wanted the show to succeed. Then she thanked me for letting her off the hook." He laughed. "This has been the most ego-deflating experience I've had in my life. But enough about me for a minute." He smiled at Ethan's camera. "Ethan, you need to come up here now."

Ethan didn't look surprised, and when Molly hurried over to take his camera, he shook his head at her. "Let Mikey do it."

Ethan took a spot next to Nick. Molly sighed and crouched down beside me.

"You have a lot of expl—"

"Shhh, he's talking," Molly said.

"This is Ethan. He's a talented guy, and we were all lucky to have him making us look good. On these dates, I spend as much time with the crew as I do with the girls. And the crew has to hang out a lot with each other doing riveting stuff like watching us eat. Molly, who has been dragged on pretty much every date through this whole thing, has made everything way more fun behind the scenes. And it turns out, I'm not the only who thinks so."

He handed Ethan a rose and stepped out of Mikey's camera range. Ethan looked nervous for the first time ever. "Molly? Could you come up here?"

Molly had turned a light shade of pink, and she shot me a panicked look.

"Go," I said, finally figuring out what was going on. "You've stuck the camera in everyone else's faces for weeks. Your turn."

"I don't want to."

I glanced over at Ethan, whose expression had gone from nervous to worried. "Unless you hate him, you need to go up there."

Her color deepened. "I don't hate him."

"No kidding. Now go."

She stood and walked to Ethan, stopping in front of him. Nick darted back in, grinning, and took her shoulders to move her so her back wasn't to the camera then darted back out.

Ethan held out the rose to Molly. "So, um, I was wondering if you wanted to maybe go out sometime?" Ethan mumbled. "Be on a date with me, instead of filming it or whatever."

She took the rose and stared up at him for a few seconds, her expression dazed.

"Do it, Molly!" Mikey called.

It snapped her brain cramp. "Yes," she said, and Ethan relaxed. "I think I'd really like that."

Despite the confusion threatening to paralyze my brain, I smiled. I'd been pretty self-absorbed not to see it coming, and Molly still had a ton of explaining to do about why she didn't tell me she was crushing on Ethan, but I liked the idea of them together.

"Cool," Ethan said, smiling. They stood there for a few more seconds, not speaking, and then he pointed to Mikey and the other camera. "I have to help Mikey finish filming."

Which meant . . . it was my turn.

Chapter 19

When Ethan picked his camera up, he pointed it at me again. I stood up, pressed my lips together, thrust my hands out, and let them say, "Well?"

"Maybe now would be a good time for the bench?" Molly suggested, her voice timid.

Nick cleared his throat. Then did it again. Then swallowed and made a choking sound. I stalked to the bench and plunked myself down with my arms crossed tightly over my chest as if they could keep me from falling apart that way.

Nick sat next to me. "Hi."

"What is going on?" I asked, too wound up with nerves to make small talk. I'd spent so much time trying to convince myself that being with Nick was impossible that I couldn't figure out how I felt at the moment. All the reasons why we wouldn't work ran through my mind on a high-speed loop, but they didn't give me the calm sense of reaching the right conclusion that I normally felt when I had worked through a hard decision. Instead, a far scarier feeling had taken up residence in my chest: hope.

He scrubbed his hands through his hair, mussing it worse than before. "When we broke up, it stung. I thought it was because I liked you more than any girl I'd ever dated and that the sting would fade, but a couple of months after you walked out, I felt worse instead of better. I decided I needed to get out of LA to clear my head, so I asked my uncle if I could come stay with them at the mission home in Kenya."

"You went to Africa to get over *me*?" Surprise loosened the grip I had on my arms, and my hands floated to my lap. The tiny flicker of hope grew stronger.

He nodded. "Before we met, I felt unanchored. Adrift." He gestured to the waves below us. "Pick your nautical metaphor. I'm sure it would fit.

You came along, and everything stabilized. And I was happier than I'd ever been. But it all went wrong because I couldn't get the words right. Is that the definition of irony for an aspiring screenwriter?" He gave a small laugh. "Growing up in this business, especially being famous, taught me early on that everybody wants something from me. A shot at the spotlight, mainly. I've been the stepping stone for a few aspiring actresses along the way. I got burned so bad when I was nineteen that I sent in my mission papers. Great motivation, huh? To get away from Hollywood?"

He rubbed his hands on his thighs and thought for a moment. "I did okay when I was with you, but when you left, I bobbed around without a float again, you know? I wanted what you had, your surety about everything."

I sighed. "That's a nice way of saying I'm opinionated, isn't it? Sometimes I wish I could go back in time three years and slap myself around a little."

"No. You're just sure. The only thing I knew for sure then was that my family loved me."

"It's not a small thing."

"It's not. But letting only them in also let me keep everyone and everything else out. And then came you."

"But you let me go." I failed miserably in keeping my tone neutral.

He straightened and leaned toward me, reaching out to touch my knee. "Yeah. I couldn't figure out what you wanted from me, but I knew you weren't getting whatever it was."

I raised my eyebrows. "Do you have it figured out now?"

"Yeah. You wanted me to be better than I was."

"That wasn't it!"

"Yes, it was. You wanted me to be a better communicator, a better partner, or whatever you want to call it. You wanted me to be better at embracing the gospel and to want more for myself than the next acting role."

It was all true. At the time, I thought I was viewing his life with clearer eyes than he did. But in hindsight, all I saw was the impatient perfectionist Molly had reflected back at me. I swallowed. "You're giving me too much credit. I was judging you, and you deserved better than that from someone you were in a relationship with."

"Maybe," he said. "But I couldn't argue that I was coming up short. Then you left, and I knew I didn't deserve to keep you if I couldn't keep my own head on straight."

"But it's straight now," I said. "Why didn't you come after me when you finished soul searching in Africa?"

He winced. "I want us to be an incredibly romantic story because that's what the storyteller in me demands. But more than that, I want the truth between us. So here it is. Your breakup was harsh. I'd already figured out that I didn't want to be with someone who thought that my being a working actor was enough. But dating you taught me that I also couldn't be with someone who might think that nothing I did was enough."

That hurt. It hurt because I hated knowing that I had been that girl to more guys than him over the years, and a wave of self-disgust rolled over me. I was still angry that no one had told me the truth days or even weeks ago, but I couldn't withhold another long overdue apology. "I'm sorry. No one deserves to be made to feel that way."

"It's okay. Your intentions were good, I think. But I came back from Africa with a spiritual renewal that I should have been fighting for every single day of my mission in Guatemala. I've already told you that I was only supposed to be in Kenya for two weeks, but after the first week of me moping, my aunt dragged me down to help out in the office one day. Then my uncle sent me out to tract with the elders. And then suddenly, I was in love with Kenya and loving you hurt a little less. So I stayed until I got the pain down to a dull ache and figured out what I wanted to do with my life. And that's when I sent in my application to USC film school."

"You, um"—I stopped and tried again—"You loved me?" I couldn't take the words in. They were too huge.

"So much," he said, a half smile ghosting over his lips. "But sometimes two people can love each other and still bring out the worst in each other. I had no idea if you loved me back, and I didn't want to undo the five hardest months of soul searching I'd ever done by slipping into messed-up patterns with you."

"But . . . we're here." I pointed at Ethan's camera. "And it involved shenanigans, and I'm more confused than ever about why. Why did you even drive down to surf with me that first day? You're a crazy person, I think."

"I wondered if I was when I suggested it. But I've thought of you constantly for the last three years." He pulled his phone from his pocket and tapped it before turning it to show me an old picture of the two of us on the beach. He'd snapped it after we first started dating to celebrate a perfect morning of surfing. Our cheeks were pressed together to fit us both in the frame, and the two people smiling out at me looked happy together. Really happy. "This was hard to give up," he said. "It's been even harder to forget." He put the phone away. "Kade's kept me up to date on you as much as he can, but he travels so much that the news was pretty sporadic."

Kade had kept him up to date? I thought he barely knew my name, but he'd actually been paying close enough attention to report back to Nick? I don't know if it made me nervous that I hadn't noticed or happy that Nick had cared so much that he'd asked Kade to do it.

"I couldn't resist finding out how life had been treating you," Nick said. "I truly hoped with everything in me that I would find you hardened into a brittle shell of a woman." A small smile peeked out.

"At least I didn't disappoint you there," I said and wished I were joking.

"No, you didn't disappoint me. I knew in the first fifteen minutes on the water that you'd . . . mellowed somehow."

"Mellowed," I repeated, mulling the word. "That's the first time in my life that someone has described me as mellow. What were you going to say first?"

He hesitated.

"Say it," I prodded him.

"Humble. You seemed humble. And saying it sounds condescending."

"Kind of," I said. "But it wasn't humility. It was desperation and borderline defeat."

"It was vulnerability," he corrected me. "And it was the first time I'd ever seen it in you. By the end of breakfast, I had this feeling that now maybe we were both in the places we needed to be for us to have worked three years ago. Suddenly, I wanted to show you what you had missed out on, to make you regret walking away." He shook his head. "Sometimes I can be a giant jerk. So I did my hair all fancy and wore my tightest T-shirts, and you being you eventually called me out on all of it."

"You definitely look better without all the gel." I frowned. "Stop distracting me. I'm still so confused. I've spent weeks feeling miserable while I've watched you date other girls. And fall in love with Cara, I thought. Did you know how I felt?"

"Molly?" he called across the short stretch of lawn to her. "Am I going to be in major trouble if I answer this honestly?"

She straightened. "We both will be. Go ahead and tell her."

"At first I agreed to do this because, like I said, I was being a jerk. But I was curious to see if I was right about how you'd changed based on what I saw from surfing with you that first day. And then the day after the bowling date, I called Molly and told her that I didn't want to date any more girls. I wanted to see if you and I had a shot."

"Molly?" I called this time.

"Yes?"

"How come I never heard a word about this?"

"Maybe I can answer that too," Nick said. "She knew a lot about our history."

I nodded.

"She thought . . ." He trailed off, and I realized he was groping for diplomatic words again.

Molly jumped in to save him. "I thought you'd wreck it if he came at you straight on, so I told him to approach you sideways."

"That's pretty messed up," I said. "You put a lot of girls' romantic hopes in the crosshairs to manipulate me."

She shook her head. "No. Every single girl starting with Merry was warned that even though Nick had agreed to fill in, he was pretty hung up on someone else. We told them they could try getting his attention but that it probably wouldn't work, and I begged them to act like they would on any first date for the sake of the show." She smiled. "After your second date together aired, pretty much everyone had figured out who he was hung up on."

"That's why we tried to keep you off most of the dates, by the way," Nick said. "Ethan said that when you were around, my face was a dead giveaway, but I guess the day at my house gave it away to everyone else."

"Except me." I sat and tried to absorb everything they were telling me, but I couldn't take it in. Instead, everything that had been bubbling inside of me for almost a month now burst out of me, and I jumped to my feet. I wanted to grab him and hug him and shout hallelujah that I wasn't watching him drape himself all over Cara. But I didn't. I yelled at Molly. "How could you let me be miserable? Why didn't you tell me?"

Nick had leaped up as soon as I had. "Because she's a good friend, I swear."

I rounded on him. "How do you figure?"

Molly handed Ethan her rose and hurried over to me. "I talked to your mom and Ashley. I wanted their advice about whether you were heading down a bad road. Your mom suggested I put the brakes on and give you a chance to see Nick clearly." She cleared her throat in an unconscious imitation of Nick's nervous tic. "She said he scrambles your hormones and to keep you guys apart so your brain would keep working."

Heat flooded my cheeks, and Nick grinned.

"What did Ashley say?" I choked out.

"That you needed to build your whole relationship over but to build it on a friendship first. So I told Nick I'd help, but only if we did it my way."

"I wanted to kill her at first," he admitted. "But your mom and Ashley got it right. I know you better now than I ever did in the six months we dated. Don't you feel that?"

I thought over the weeks of phone calls and e-mails and time spent together. "Yes." A reluctant smile escaped me. "Yeah, all right. Sometimes my mom knows stuff."

Nick took a step toward me, but I pivoted to face Molly. "That still doesn't explain why you let me spend the last week in agony. You should have told me."

"I almost did at least a hundred times! But—"

"But I swore her to secrecy," Nick jumped in. "I wanted to give you the happiest ending ever. It's the screenwriter in me." He shot Molly a look that she seemed to understand because she backed away and headed toward Ethan again. He drew an unsteady breath and bent to sweep up the rose that had fallen to the bench. A few petals drifted from the open blossom as it trembled in his left hand. His other hand slipped into his pocket and fumbled for a moment before he pulled it out to reveal a ring box.

I squeaked and looked at Molly, who only smiled.

"I changed my mind about the happy ending," he said. "I want a movie starring us that never ends. It's the narcissist in me." He smiled, and an answering smile of my own almost escaped me.

"I think on the TV *Bachelor*, the story ends with a ring. But that's where I want ours to start." The rose shook harder, and he held up the ring box. "This is exactly what you think it is. I've had it since before we broke up."

I gasped, and he smiled. "I loved you so much then that I couldn't say it. Now I've spent another month falling for you harder every day. I'll wait as long as it takes for you to forgive me and for your feelings to catch up. I want you to marry me, Lou. I'm not asking yet. I know you probably need time to process this all. But I'm here," he said, his voice quiet. He slipped the box inside his jacket pocket and reached over to take my hand, moving slowly like he thought I would dart away if he went any faster. "I am one hundred percent here, and there's nowhere I'd rather be."

I looked down at our connected hands. Slipping mine out of his, I eased the rose from his grip and plucked a petal from it.

"I love you, I love you not," I said, plucking another, and then a few more. "I love you, I love you not, I love you, I love you not." I covered the rest of the bloom with my hand and stared up at him without smiling. I watched his Adam's apple rise and fall twice in quick succession. When I caught the glint of sweat on his forehead again, I crushed the blossom in my hand and yanked, stripping the remaining petals. He blanched, and I uncurled my fingers to let the petals drift to the ground. All except the very last one.

I held it up and studied it curiously. "What do you know? I love you."

A giant whoosh of air escaped him. "You do? And you're not mad at me?"

"Oh, I'm mad at you," I said. "But I'm more happy than mad by a million to one."

"Yes!" Molly shouted.

"I'm still mad at *you*," I told her. "But there's a chance that Nick can kiss me all better."

He reached a hand out, slipped it into my hair, and cupped the back of my head. With the lightest pressure, he pulled me toward him. The familiar feeling of him flooding my senses washed over me. I'd fought it for weeks, but this time I let it come, reveling in every molecule of excitement humming along my nerve ends. It seemed crazy and amazing that I could do this now, that I could draw a deep breath full of the smell of him and smile and not try to hide how happy it made me.

His head bent toward mine, and he moved slowly, so slowly that I wanted to scream until I saw the glint in his eye. This was payback for the trick I'd pulled with the rose, but it worked. I couldn't stand the wait anymore, and I wrapped my arms around his neck. It took only the tiniest tug to convince him to close the distance. In the split second before he kissed me, I closed my eyes, too overwhelmed by everything I saw in his. When his lips brushed mine, their familiar touch erased everything in my mind in a baptism of heat. It was the single-most tender and electric kiss I'd ever experienced, and I'd had plenty of both of those from him in the past. But this one held something new: promise.

I pulled back for a moment. "Ethan?"

"Yeah?"

"Turn the camera off. I don't want to scandalize our viewers."

When Nick bent to kiss me this time, I threaded my fingers through his hair and held him tight. "Nick?" I said a long moment later, after I'd struggled to find enough breath to form words.

"Yeah?" His voice sounded husky, and his eyes had glazed over.

I patted his coat pocket where the ring had disappeared. "You should probably keep that close. Really close."

A smile lit his face, and it was so tender it nearly dissolved me. "I will," he said. "But not nearly as close as I'll keep you. I'm not letting you go again. Ever." His next kiss buckled my knees, and clapping erupted from the diners on the nearby patio, but Nick ignored it.

"Nick?"

"Yeah?"

"We have an audience."

He looked up. "I don't care."

And the words were as sweet as "I love you."

About the Author

Melanie Bennett Jacobson is an avid reader, amateur cook, and champion shopper. She consumes astonishing amounts of chocolate, chick flicks, and books. After meeting her own husband on the Internet, she is now living happily married in Southern California with her growing family and a series of doomed potted herbs. Melanie loves to hear from her readers and can be found through her home page at www.melaniejacobson.net or on Twitter at @writestuff_mel.